THE MAN WHO CAME BACK

THE MAN WHO CAME BACK

Harriet Hudson

This first world edition published 2009
in Great Britain and 2010 in the USA by
SEVERN HOUSE PUBLISHERS LTD of
9–15 High Street, Sutton, Surrey, England, SM1 1DF.
Trade paperback edition published
in Great Britain and the USA 2010 by
SEVERN HOUSE PUBLISHERS LTD

British Library Cataloguing in Publication Data

Hudson, Harriet, 1938-
  The Man Who Came Back.
  1. Romantic suspense novels.
  I. Title
  823.9'14–dc22

ISBN-13: 978-0-7278-6838-1   (cased)
ISBN-13: 978-1-84751-185-0   (trade paper)

All Severn House titles are printed on acid-free paper.

Typeset by Palimpsest Book Production Ltd.,
Grangemouth, Stirlingshire, Scotland.
Printed and bound in Great Britain by
MPG Books Ltd., Bodmin, Cornwall.

Author's Note

Authors can write their scripts to their hearts' content, but it takes a team to turn one into a published novel. In Severn House I've been lucky enough to have struck gold in this respect, and I am most grateful to all members of its team. My thanks are also due to my agent, Dorothy Lumley of the Dorian Literary Agency, to Jean Robinson for local Kentish information and to my husband James Myers for the benefit of his experience with running charities.

One

It had not been the best of days. Why is it that so often when I set off in the morning, humming a song to the joys of life, fate promptly turns round and slaps me in the face? I'd returned home after a monumental slap at work an hour ago. Normally, home is a glorious refuge, especially if Jack is there to greet me, and he had said he'd be home from France by lunchtime. Knowing his unpredictability, however, I wasn't surprised when I put my key in the door of Number Fourteen Edwards Lane, Dulwich, and was hit by the atmosphere of an empty house as soon as the door had opened the merest crack.

Disappointed? Of course, but I still had the delight of his return to look forward to – and return he would, sooner or later.

'I'll always be there, Emma.' That's what he'd told me when I'd taken the plunge a year earlier to move south of the Thames and share his home at Dulwich in south-east London. Few people would trust Jack Scarlet's dancing eyes and quicksilver moods without hesitation, but I did. However ratty I could get over minor issues like forgetting to buy a new loaf, as soon as his tall, lean figure loped in through the door, my heart did a private dance of its own. Details were not important, but Jack never went back on his serious promises. And he'd promised he'd be back on Friday, which was now.

I consoled myself with that knowledge because I needed to talk to him. The magazine I worked for was, my superiors had informed me, moving lock, stock and barrel to Bristol, and since I couldn't, or wouldn't, move with them, I was redundant. I prowled restlessly round the house, which was Jack's, of course, not mine. For once I could find no loving message left on the landline or on my mobile. With my news still burning away inside me, I didn't feel like indulging in any of the hundred or so forms of entertainment that presented themselves for consideration in our living room. Even getting dinner ready wouldn't take long. The spaghetti sauce was soon bubbling away, and I was left twiddling my thumbs.

The phone rang and I flew to it. No Jack. It was my mother, who as usual managed to tie me into another knot of fury when I told her my news. Then it rang again. This time a recorded message informed me that I had won an exciting holiday to somewhere I'd never heard of.

No Jack though, I fumed. More waiting – and there was always the awful possibility he'd say, 'Go for it'. In other words, why not move to Bristol and out of my life?

Minutes ticked by incredibly slowly on the antique French clock Jack loved so much, as I fidgeted over what to do next. I wasn't going to give in and ring Jack's mobile with a plaintive, 'Where are you?'

And then the doorbell rang.

Jack had forgotten his keys again. I leapt up and incautiously rushed to the front door ready to hug him. But the day grew a thousand times worse as the wounds so painfully healed over seven years tore wide open again.

It was a ghost from the past. It was Tom Burdock.

I put flowers on Laura's grave every year on the anniversary of her death. There was no photograph of her on display in my home because I needed none. Every detail of Laura's lovely face was there in my mind, to revisit if I so wished now that the sharp pain had receded – or so I had thought. Laura West, my dearest friend, and the best anyone could wish for. It had been a long friendship, for we had met aged seven at primary school, and the friendship had continued until her death. I had gone away to university, then married Mark Cardale and returned to Kent.

Laura had in the meanwhile become both wife and mother as Laura Burdock. She was still the sweetest, kindest person I had ever met – until she was savagely murdered seven years ago, a few days after her twenty-fifth birthday. Her killer, so most people – including me – believed, was her husband Tom, although he had never been charged.

'May I come in, Emma?'

That voice, so controlled, so familiar, sent a shiver down my spine as I stared at him, holding the door, barring the way back into my life.

'You've grown a beard,' I stammered fatuously. It made him look more self-sufficient, but it aged him. I remembered him as a relatively tall man, but his shoulders were already stooped and he seemed much shorter. He had been the same age as Laura and myself, and so would be thirty-two now, but he seemed older. He had always been an inward rather than an outward person, but now he looked even more closed-in. Tom had been a good friend to me too, and as kind as Laura. I'd always been fond of him – until Laura's death. His unexpected arrival threw me into turmoil. 'And a tan,' I added for the sake of something to say.

He grinned at the stupidity of my reply. What did looks matter? It was still Tom. 'Africa,' he explained.

I remembered then. The charity he'd worked for, Tolling Bells, helped out in emergencies in Africa, and my parents had told me Tom had opted to get the hell out of England after Laura's death. I'd been too busy coping with both grief and the breakdown of my marriage to take much notice.

'Is Jack here?' he asked.

'No.'

'I won't keep you long.'

Invite Tom Burdock in? Nausea rose up inside me, but I suppressed it. This was Tom, I told myself, a man I'd always got on with, whom Laura had adored. I didn't *know* he was a murderer. He'd been a friend, or so I'd thought until Laura's death.

'You'd better come in.' Was that strangled voice mine? Take control, Emma Cardale. Be your usual self. But I was talking to a self who didn't seem to be listening. What *was* my usual self? Then my portcullis of self-defence came down.

'How did you know about Jack?' I asked Tom suspiciously, as I led him into our living room, aware that I was trembling. I'd felt as if I'd known Jack all my life when I first met him eighteen months ago, but I hadn't, and I'd moved in with him only a few months afterwards. 'Been checking up on me?'

'Yes.'

That stopped me in my tracks, but common sense came to my aid. 'Sit down, Tom, and tell me what this is all about. I take it you haven't just come for a chat about old times?'

Tom had been at the same secondary school in Canterbury as Laura and myself, but not the same primary school. I suppose he must have been around, as he lived in the same village as I did, but I was aware of him only in my Canterbury days. Even then he'd been more serious than we were, dedicated to solving the troubles and politics of the world.

'Partly, Emma,' was his reply, and it took me aback. This was the last thing I needed. 'We used to be good friends once.' It was true enough. We had.

'That was before—' I began, but stopped.

He put into words what I could not. 'Before her death. Even you thought I killed her.'

Tom sounded quite matter-of-fact about it, even resigned. I couldn't deny it. I had – and still did – with the reservation that there had not been enough evidence for the police to charge him, and therefore he had to be given the benefit of the doubt. I watched his hands twisting together, as he sat on the sofa, and wondered if he were as calm as he sounded.

'I tried not to,' I said honestly. I could hardly believe that I was sitting with the man who could even conceivably have killed Laura.

'That's what sent me to Africa. I could have borne everything else, Emma, except for the Wests taking Jamie away from me and the blame I saw in *your* eyes.'

That was unfair. There had been enough evidence to suggest Tom could have been involved, and I had never publicly committed myself. Nor even privately. I always talked of it as 'on the one hand' and 'on the other'. Others, including my ex-husband, had been less ambivalent. Tom was the jealous sort, Mark had said. Tom had done it, no question about it. I had to acknowledge that, in my heart of hearts, I believed that too.

'You had the most devoted wife possible, and yet you really believed she was unfaithful to you,' I said flatly. Unwisely, perhaps.

'She was,' Tom came back at me, and I was furious. I knew I shouldn't get drawn into this argument, but I had to defend Laura.

'Laura adored you. She had your three-year-old son to care for, she was busy giving piano lessons—'

'She wanted men too. More than me,' Tom stated coldly.

'In your imagination, Tom. Why on earth should she?'

'Perhaps she wanted to share some of the excitement she saw you getting from life, Emma.'

'*My* life? You're talking nonsense,' I said, aghast. 'My marriage was breaking up.' Even so, I had been faithful to Mark. The trouble had been that he hadn't reciprocated.

'Not sex. You had an interesting life working in Canterbury.'

This, too, was nonsense, although it was true that I had been happy working in a small printing firm there. 'But Laura taught the piano, and she gave concerts here, there and everywhere. She had a full and happy life. I should know. She would have told me, if not. She adored family life too.' I was bewildered at the mere idea of a hidden Laura whom I didn't know, and I couldn't believe that there was one. 'I *knew* her.' Then I realized that the fault was not in me, or in Laura, but in Tom. 'You've changed,' I said.

'Hardly surprising, is it?' he replied bitterly.

'Then after all this time you can't still believe that she had a lover.'

'On the contrary, I'm more certain of it than ever, Emma.' He sat back, and the hands had stopped their twisting. To a fly on the wall, we would have looked like any two former friends catching up on old times, as Tom continued, 'The main reason I've come back is Jamie, and it has a bearing on that. Jamie is ten now – old enough to choose whether he wants to go on living with his blasted grandparents or to live with me. For that I need to clear my name by finding out what really happened, so that I can fight for my parental rights. I don't even have access rights at present.'

'You mean the Wests won't let you see him at all?' It was hardly surprising, I thought, but even so that seemed extreme.

'Not regularly. I've seen him once or twice in their presence. I never fought it. After all, I went to live in Africa. Now it's different. But that's not the reason I've come here this evening. That's on your account, Emma.'

'Mine?' I was instantly wary.

'I wanted you to know I'm working in Canterbury at Tolling Bells' head office.'

'But I'm happy . . .' I started to say, thinking for one appalling moment that he wanted to resume our old easy relationship. That wouldn't be possible because Laura's shadow lay between us.

'You're living with Jack Scarlet. How much do you know about him?'

I froze. 'Is this any business of yours?' What a cliché, but I suppose they are inevitable at the twists and turns of life when shock gets its grip on us.

'Very much so. He was Laura's lover.'

The day of the treasure hunt brought my first clear memory of Laura. It came back to me piece by piece if I thought of her, or it would pop up in my dreams or reach out as I was thinking of something completely different. Like all childhood memories it failed to present itself as a chronological story, but in scraps of images that never properly joined together. Often they seemed on the brink of doing so, but then they'd drift apart again. The one certain element in them all was Laura. The Wests had only just moved to Ducks Green when I met her. Perhaps she was already attending our primary school before that day, or perhaps not, but I was clear that the party was for her seventh birthday. Both her father and mother were solicitors, and they had bought Appley House, which lay on the Cobshaw Road just outside Ducks Green, not far from Canterbury. It was a large, early Victorian red-brick house with a big garden and an apple orchard at the far end, from which the house name was doubtless derived. For some reason I cannot remember, I had been invited to the party. Perhaps I did already know Laura, or perhaps, eager for friends for their daughter, her parents had invited the whole primary-school class. Afterwards, Laura and I never talked about the day of the treasure hunt – not for any particular reason but probably because, as a shared memory, we'd thought we had a lifetime in which to revisit it.

The treasure hunt must have been dreamed up by the Wests, and took place in their orchard beyond the garden. In my memory of it, each child had been allotted a different coloured skein of wool. The skeins had been unwound and twisted round trunks and branches and each child was given one end of their skein. The other was tied, with a small gift, to one large tree near the gate, which led out to open farmland. Laura's birthday was in late May, and so the blossom must have fallen by then, but in my memory the apple trees bloomed on, creating a snowstorm of petals as our eager hands grasped at our threads. They must have been greatly tangled up with one another, and it must have taken much patience to unravel them. We had to do so though, for not only was there the prize at the end of each skein, but Laura's father was standing by the tree with a special prize for the child who reached it first.

Impatient as ever, my fingers soon ran into trouble disentangling my thread from the others, and my clearest memory of Laura is in the sunlight, with her blonde hair tumbling over her gentle face, as she tried to help me: 'Don't worry, Emma, I'll do it. Look, it's easy.' In my store of images I could see her pianist's fingers patiently working away on my behalf because, even though it was her birthday, she could not bear to see me cry. She was my princess, in a magnificent castle, and I adored her ever after. Then the curtain of memory would close on the treasure hunt, and would choose its own time to rise again.

I sat stunned at Tom's accusation, unable to think clearly, in order to separate one tangled thread from another in my maze of a mind.

'Proof,' I hurled at him.

'Did you need proof when you thought I'd murdered Laura?'

'Yes,' I yelled. 'Such proof as there was. But what do you have on Jack?'

The agony was so great that using anger to soothe it was my only way out. Tom must surely be out of his mind, and yet I was driven on to treat his accusation seriously.

'Jack Scarlet was brought up near Lilleybourne, which you'll recall is less than a mile from Ducks Green. He must have told you that.'

'No, and I don't believe it.' My lips were marble – heavy and cold. It was a ridiculous claim. If he had been, I'd have known him as a child. He was only three years older than me. What had Jack said about his past? I couldn't remember clearly. We had better things to talk about: our today, our tomorrow.

'His parents moved to Canterbury and then to France.'

I knew about France at least. We'd visited them there, and no word had been said about Kent, even though I must have mentioned it as my birthplace. Or had I? Because of what had happened to Laura, I had tried to put Kent behind me.

I clutched at certainty like a drowning woman. 'Did you and

Laura know Jack? She never mentioned him. I never met him in Kent.'

'I suppose he must have been around when we were kids, and when Laura and I were married too. Laura knew him well.' Tom's implication was obvious.

'How do you know?' My heart was on hold, and the words shot out like an icicle.

'I saw them in Canterbury together.'

'Hardly proof of an affair.' This was rearguard action on my part because for me the battle was won. This was a fantasy he'd concocted in Africa to cover his own guilt. I began to relax – too soon.

'Of course not. But Jack took piano lessons. Good cover, yes?'

Jack? *Piano* lessons? I was knocked off guard again. 'You're crazy, Tom. That can't possibly be true. Why on earth would he be taking piano lessons in Kent, in his twenties, when he was already living and working in London?' I could hear my voice rising, getting shriller.

'A roving job. Plenty of scope.'

'No way.' I was on strong ground now. This was pure nonsense. 'He'd have been a somewhat unusual pupil, don't you think? Laura would have told me.'

'Would she, if the lessons were a cover?'

His disbelieving cynicism made me furious. 'Yes,' I shouted. 'Is there any proof at all that Jack was her lover? Not much to go on so far. One chance meeting in Canterbury. And why didn't you mention this theory to the police at the time? I seem to recall Mark was your choice for Laura's paramour then.' That, too, had been a daft accusation. Detective Inspector Paul Fritton had told me about it. Mark had denied it, and I believed him, despite our bad relationship at the time.

'Because I didn't know the truth then.' Tom was shaking with rage. 'That's enough, Emma. Don't you think it's been hard enough for me to come here to warn you, without your raking it all up again—'

'Raking it up?' I choked with fury. 'It's you, *you*, doing that by refusing to believe Laura was loyal to you.'

'I did believe it,' he threw viciously back at me. 'But then I found out the real story.'

I'd had time to absorb what he'd said now. 'And what do you mean by *warn*?' I asked quietly.

He shook his head helplessly. 'I don't know. Just be careful, Laura.'

He'd called me *Laura*. He must have realized it, for he rose quickly to his feet, and stammered, 'Think about it, Emma. If you need me, you'll find me at the Canterbury office.'

Warn me of what? He couldn't even tell me.

I couldn't bring myself to switch the light on. I was too numb. This living room represented Jack's and my life together, and now that life could be under threat. To look at it in a bright light would remind me all too vividly of how much it meant to me. Reason had demolished Tom's accusation in seconds, but until Jack returned its aftermath would take longer to deal with. How much *did* I know about Jack's past life? Neither of us had cared what had happened before we met each other. He knew I was divorced; I knew he had lived with a Frenchwoman for some years in his twenties and was single. Precious little more because it hadn't mattered. Did it now?

I looked round the room in the remaining twilight. The DVDs, the books, the pictures – they were all indications of his personality, but there were no photos. So what? I only had one up myself. We both had parents and grandparents who meant a lot to us, we neither of us had siblings, and I'd had the impression he'd been brought up in London. Nothing more. But that was how we both liked it. Going forward, not back.

And yet now 'back' had been forced on me. However long I sat there, not wanting to put the light on, that fact wasn't going to go away. *Jack's Return Home* – wasn't that one of the farcical melodramas that used to be put on in village halls? Fanciful images of stage villains in top hats and black, swirling capes with scarlet linings flashed through my mind. Anything to stop me *thinking*. Anyway, Jack was the hero of the melodrama, and never suddenly turned into the bad guy.

I had told Jack all about Laura and Tom not long after we'd first met, and said I never wanted to talk about it again. He'd understood, and there had been no sign of his having had any prior knowledge of Laura and Tom Burdock, or of Ducks Green.

Or was I wrong? I think he said he'd read about it in the newspapers – as everyone had. We had to move on, Jack had pointed out.

But now Tom had come barging in once more. What should I do? Keep his accusations to myself, since he was clearly raving, or be upfront about it? I could not decide. Those skeins of wool were still tangling themselves in my mind.

At last I heard Jack's key in the lock, and immediately the lights were on and I found myself in the hallway, falling over myself in my haste to open the door for him.

'I said I'd be back tonight. A little late maybe—' Jack gave a rueful shrug, eyes dancing and inviting me to share the joke, as I hurled myself into his arms. That was entirely instinctive, as I still hadn't decided what to do.

'I detect,' he said after a moment, 'that you've been waiting supper for me. Hence the enthusiastic welcome.'

Supper! I must have looked as dismayed as I felt because I'd forgotten I'd even had the sauce on the hob. I'd be lucky if it hadn't burnt away. Unimportant though it was compared with Tom's visit it provided a diversion and I rushed into the kitchen, with Jack sauntering after me. He must have watched me for a minute or two as I struggled to save the sauce and get a pan of spaghetti moving. I could feel his eyes on my back.

'Bad trip?' I asked him, forcing myself to sound casual.

'Ish.'

Jack was an International Economic Analyst – which meant little to me in terms of what he actually did all day. Indeed, I don't think he intended me to know, which pointed to its being some kind of undercover work. I didn't ask questions and so far it hadn't mattered. I wanted to keep it that way, but with Tom's bombshell that could be about to change. I knew a lot of his freelance work was in Paris for the Organisation for Economic Co-operation and Development, OECD as it's known, for whom he used to work full time. I knew he worked for big insurance companies too, but I wasn't sure how this translated into day by day duties. He often talked of difficult cases, of bankruptcies, of economic currents, and torrents of business language would follow before we jointly decided to give the rest a miss. Similarly, if I nattered on about my work problems he listened earnestly and then that, too, was laid to rest after a while. So what did we really share? I've no idea but it was fun every step of the way.

Usually.

Jack has a nose for trouble though. Instead of rushing upstairs and then leaping down in due course for a drink, as he routinely does, he chose to remain in the kitchen. 'Something's wrong, isn't it?' he asked.

'Is it?'

'I can smell it.'

'That's the spaghetti.'

'Don't stonewall.'

I wasn't ready for this yet. I couldn't accuse him of something I didn't believe he was guilty of. 'Let's eat first,' I replied.

'Let's not if the subject is that bad.'

He was looming over me now, the chemistry so strong that it was all I could do not to throw myself on to his manly chest and wail. But I'm not that sort. I'm too tall for a start. If I was five foot four against his six foot something it would make sense, but ladies of five foot six or more stand on their own two feet. As I do – or try to.

'I'm going to be redundant,' I blurted out. It would do as an answer for the moment.

'Not to me,' he said promptly.

Twenty-four hours ago our spaghetti might have been delayed even longer as we would most likely have landed up in bed. But not this time. There was too much that was unsaid going on. Especially by me – I must have been sending out signals galore not to pass Go. And yet I still couldn't speak normally.

'I don't want to go to Bristol,' I finally managed to wail.

'Then, beloved, you shall not do so,' he said, agreeing with my statement even though it must have been nonsensical to him, given that I hadn't yet explained what Bristol involved. He wandered into the living room and I went after him to rescue the situation if I could. A doomed attempt.

I saw his eye fall on the sofa cushions and armchair drawn up by it.

'Have you had a visitor?' he asked mildly.

I'm no coward when the inevitable raises its head. 'Yes. Tom Burdock.'

The atmosphere cooled to minus zero. I saw Jack's hands tighten round the glass he was carrying. The name had registered to an extent that seemed out of proportion, given that we had not talked of Laura's murder since the first occasion. Even when I'd gone to visit her grave the previous year on the anniversary of her death he hadn't questioned me, but had been kind and loving when I'd returned.

'What's he want with you?' Jack's expression was in work mode rather than the home-with-Emma mode I needed.

'He's moving back to Canterbury.'

'That's no answer. How did he know where to find you?'

'I've no idea.' I realized I'd forgotten to pin Tom down on that. 'Easy enough to find out, I suppose.'

'Is it? You told me you'd covered your tracks completely. No one from that time knows where you are except your parents, and they are too sensible to talk.'

'I don't know how he found out,' I said impatiently. 'Does it matter that much?'

No smile. Nothing. 'It depends on what he wanted,' was his reasonable answer.

But I didn't need reason at that moment. I needed reassurance, though I couldn't understand why. Did I really think Jack had been Laura's lover? Of course not. The idea was ridiculous. Did I really think he'd been holding out on me? No, again. Did I need to be *careful*, as Tom had put it? Not in a million years. Not with Jack. And yet there was a distance between us, Jack and me.

'He wanted . . .'

Jack said nothing, watching me. His face was taut, focused on what I might reply; his body, which would in hours be naked next to mine, was remote and tense.

It came out in a rush. 'He said you'd been brought up not far from Ducks Green, and then your parents moved to Canterbury.'

I thought Jack wasn't going to answer, from the look on his face. It wasn't anger, or even surprise; it was as if he was calculating his answer.

'Yes, when I was thirteen. I'd moved on from Lilleybourne primary to Junior King's and then to King's School, both in Canterbury. So?'

That last word wrong-footed me. 'I don't remember you from those days, and I thought you said you were brought up in London.'

'Kent, sweetheart. You must have thought I said Kentish Town.'

'But why didn't you tell me you lived so close?'

He laughed. 'Too much else to talk about. I didn't recognize you from those days. Anyway, I was just a kid. Now, shall we have supper if the interrogation is over? I'm famished.'

Within fifteen minutes, a few mouthfuls of food and a glass of wine we were both joking around as if the spat had never happened. I decided I'd think over the problem the next day. Mornings were always the best time to sort things out.

'Do we have anything going on this weekend?' Jack suddenly asked as we staggered to bed a couple of hours later, replete and mellow.

'Not much,' I replied. 'I said we might call in to Mum and Dad's.' My parents lived in Putney now, having left Kent not long after I did. Laura's murder had affected us all.

'Good. I'm afraid I have to leave on Sunday.'

'Again?' I was dismayed, the ground ripped from under my feet. This occasionally happened, but did it have to be now? 'You'll send the Eurostar profits sky high.'

'Sorry. It's a nuisance, but the case is nearly over.'

'Which case?'

'Same one.'

'How long?'

'Not sure. It could be a week.'

'Oh.'

'Oh what? It's been longer.'

'I thought I'd take a week's leave,' I said, trying to give some excuse for what could not be explained, even by me. 'I'm owed some.' The idea began to grow on me. Make them miss me at work, was part of it; the other part was far more risky. Saturday, the twenty-fourth of May, was the anniversary of Laura's death, and that had set me thinking.

'What will you do?' he asked.

'Go to Tenterden on the Saturday, as planned, but—'

'Not planning to run off with Tom Burdock, are you?'

'You're joking.'

'Never more,' he said ambiguously, reaching out for me.

That night he loved me with a passion that made me forget everything but how much I loved him, a passion that was fully reciprocated.

It was only when he left on the Sunday without another word of enquiry as to what I might do with this week's leave, if I took it, that the sinking feeling of unfinished business returned. I knew it would stay there until I had trampled my fear into the ground so that I could disregard Tom Burdock's visit as the nonsense it was.

I went into work on the Monday morning and announced that I would like to take my due leave before my redundancy kicked in. No one exclaimed in horror; no one cried they couldn't do without me. I was free.

Did that daunt me? On the contrary, it fired me up. I felt I was galloping into battle to defend Jack's and my relationship. For that I needed to face my fears. I needed to know more about Laura's death.

And that meant I had to return to Ducks Green.

Two

In my memory it is always September, as I walked and skipped to school along this footpath through the stubble of corn, forever golden. I hear birds calling from trees already bronzing for autumn; I smell the faint whiff of bonfire smoke; and in the hedges bordering the fields I see spiders' webs, glistening with dew. They proclaim their presence as at no other time of year, as if warning the passer-by that they're looking for winter accommodation in nice, warm houses. I'm told this is a myth, but it's one that lingers with me. September is always spiders' month. I hate it. But then I didn't see them as a threat — only as a curiosity.

Although it was now May, and the trees were full of summer promise, I still thought of September as I set off along the path to Ducks Green after seven years' absence. I'd deliberately chosen to leave my Mini in Cobshaw car park, which was still the same muddy old patch of waste ground that I remembered; this way, I could walk by the familiar route that I once took each day.

If Ducks Green were not so close, Cobshaw would be thought an attractive village, but its rival, much smaller and only a mile away by road, is the hidden jewel when it comes to the picturesque. Sitting so close to the B-road to Canterbury, Cobshaw belongs to the real world, the grown-up sibling. I knew Cobshaw because I'd grown up there, although I lived in Ducks Green until I was six and for the four years of my marriage. I loved Cobshaw because I trusted it, and that night I would be safe in Roxpole House, Kate Terry's home. Dear Kate. Hers was the best bed and breakfast in Kent, but I valued her for much more than her mushrooms on toast.

'Darling,' her voice had boomed down the phone. 'Of course you must come.'

I don't go in for darlings, but in Kate's case it's different. She's Kate, and I hadn't seen her for nearly a year and even that had been a hurried evening in London. I received not a word of blame from her though. Nevertheless, I needed to take this walk to Ducks Green before I checked in. I had decided to strip off the protective coverings of the years and go alone.

Alone – except for the ghosts of the past. Laura's joined me as I climbed over the stile at the end of the grass lane by the side of Cobshaw Vicarage, and skipped along at my side. Although she had lived her entire life in Ducks Green, we spent so much time at each other's homes that she knew the path as well as I did.

The journey was a silent one, save for the occasional twitter of a bird and the hum of passing cars on the Cobshaw Road. Not many because it was a Tuesday lunchtime, when the children were in school. Halfway across the field – still corn – there was a kissing gate for entry into the next field, which for me brought the first wrench of the past: Tom seizing the initiative, not letting Laura or me through until he'd had his kiss. First me, then Laura. How old were we then? Eleven, twelve? Not younger. Because he lived in Cobshaw, Tom had not been at primary school with us, only at our Canterbury secondary school. The kiss at the gate had been a game, but even then it had a quality about it that suggested more. We were on the brink, or was that hindsight insidiously encroaching on what was still more innocent than sexual, despite sex being poured out of every media channel?

Now, however, the face of Tom Burdock the boy transformed itself into the Tom I'd seen on Friday. It was because of him that I was here, but it wouldn't stop at that. I knew I'd have to face him again, but that would be at a time of my choosing, not his.

'I need to clear my name by finding out what really happened,' he had told me.

What really happened . . . I needed to know that too, but I was apprehensive. The worry over Jack's reply to me about his past still persisted, even though it was an irritant: an itch to be ignored rather than a major obstacle. *I must have met him; why didn't I remember him?* And yet there was no way Tom's accusation could have any foundation, even if Laura *had* known Jack. If she had, she would have told me – at least, she would if it had been important. She didn't share her life with me to such an extent that every minute detail of every encounter was passed on to me. I was working in Canterbury while she was based in

Ducks Green, and so as adults we usually only met in the evenings or at weekends.

I racked my memory in vain. I did not, I most definitely did not, remember Jack from my childhood days, although if he had moved to Canterbury as a teenager that was quite possible, I reasoned, especially as he had been at a different primary school. It was mere chance that had led to our meeting in London. He had bounded up to me at a charity do. We had joked afterwards about our eyes meeting across a crowded room, and that's how it had been, surely? I had looked up from a stilted conversation with someone I've forgotten and seen Jack making his way towards me. Instant eye contact, instant tremor.

'Port in a storm,' he'd said casually as he passed, 'Only, I prefer wine. Can I get you another glass?'

Chance, that was all. I was on Jack's route to the bar and we had met. No more than that. Any suggestion that Jack might have recognized me from the past or vice versa was ridiculous. Coincidences happen all the time. But that's the way life is. Once a seed is planted, it grows unless it is firmly rooted out. If you don't check it in its stride, it's mature before you know it. I had tried to root this seed of doubt out, but it was still there as I reached the farm lane that indicated the outskirts of Ducks Green.

Tucked away from the main road, Ducks Green has miraculously escaped the fate of many picturesque villages. It is at the heart of a network of lanes – all single-track, all winding leisurely to their destinations. They are not for faint-hearted drivers. Tall hedges shield them from discovery in summer, and in winter frost, snow and ice make a beeline for them. Not that the village discourages visitors. On the contrary, it does its best to welcome them. The Drummond Arms has rooms to let and menus to make the mouth water – or it did seven years ago. Its bowling green and cricket pitch are on the lane to Lilleybourne, which runs by what used to be a river, the Stonebourne, and is now the stream its name denotes. Taking its time, the lane eventually reaches Elham and far off Folkestone. As for football, Ducks Green condescends to share its fate with Lilleybourne's and the pitch is squarely halfway between the two communities.

Although I lived in Cobshaw as a child, I was at primary school in Ducks Green because my parents had been living there at the time I joined the school. Although we'd then moved, by grace and favour I was allowed to remain there. The old school, a Victorian grey-ragstone building, had been on the Cobshaw Road as one entered the village from that direction, but since I had left it was clear that a new school had been built, for as I approached the village I could see a school and children playing in the yard, which in my day had been farmland. There was another building too, which looked like a new community centre – and, glory be, a car park of its very own.

The footpath had turned into a new access road, and this spurred me on. So far this was not the Ducks Green I remembered, which made my determination to face it with detachment a whole lot easier to achieve. I could see the tower of St Edith's, the Norman church that stood by the side of the old school – if the building still existed, that was. Full of confidence, I marched along the road, which would bring me out by the village green.

'*Is it wise to go back, Emma?*'

I could hear my mother's anxious voice in my head. I had rung her to tell her of my plans, although not the reason for them. I had assured her it was.

Wise? No, it was not. I felt a sickening lurch as I reached the end of the access road and saw Ducks Green spread out before me. I stood at the highest part of the green, which sloped gently down to the main village street. Around the green was an arc of peaceful-looking cottages. They still charmed the eye and ducks still quacked in the pond at the roadside on the far side, oblivious to the fact that they could be considered designer ducks, imported by every self-respecting traditional Kentish village. Mark and I had had the honour of being Guardians of the Ducks for one year. The village shop was still in business and so, it seemed, was the library. St Edith's slumbered on.

To my fascinated, appalled gaze, the village seemed to have raised itself from the depths like the legendary Scottish village that appeared only once every hundred years. Nothing, but bloody nothing, had changed in the heart of Ducks Green. How could it still look so tranquil after what had happened here? How *dare* it? It was as if Laura's death had gone unnoticed.

I steeled myself to be rational. This would get me nowhere. What could one judge from appearances? I decided to stroll down to the Drummond Arms, set on the corner of the green and the Cobshaw Road. Mistake, I realized. First I should walk over to Tom and Laura's cottage where the murder had taken place. I could see it on the far side of the green from where I was standing: red brick, small front garden, lattice windows, *unchanged*. One of the many seventeenth-century cottages in Ducks Green.

I forced myself to walk slowly round to it, not knowing what I feared. Did I think Laura would come running out to meet me, eyes shining, fair curls tumbling over her face? *Emma, guess what? Jamie's reading, he really is. I know he's only three.*

Why had that stuck in my mind? Was it the last time I had seen her? There had been no sign of Tom. I'd just got out of the car on my way home . . .

I shook myself free of memory, telling myself this was just an ordinary cottage now. I managed to walk past it, not stopping, even though every muscle in my body was tense.

'*Tom's bought Number Twelve. Lark Cottage. Well, he and every mortgage company in town,*' I heard again Laura's excited voice telling me not long before their marriage. '*Isn't that marvellous?*'

It *had* been marvellous. The enchanted place, so peaceful and mellow. Roses didn't exactly ramble over the doorway, but they bloomed to their hearts' content in the front garden. As for the rear garden, tended by Laura's green fingers it became one that Monet would have gloried in. Green fingers, slender fingers, musician's fingers. Laura had a gift for welcoming. Her home always seemed to be saying, 'Come in, come in, share this with us.'

No longer. It was, to my relief, just another cottage. The nameplate of a lark rising into the sky, so carefully painted by Laura, had vanished, and had been replaced by a neat figure twelve. Everything looked the same but the soul that had made it special had vanished. Or was that only my imagination? Maybe the reality of seeing it again had blanked out the fantasy I had been nurturing. Whichever, to my eye the cottage now looked commonplace. Mark and I had lived not on the green itself but in Fullers House, a little way along the road to Lilleybourne. Nice enough, but it lacked the special something that Laura gave Lark Cottage. Perhaps the missing ingredient was love, which had slowly evaporated between Mark and myself.

I had known nothing about Laura's murder until I returned

to Ducks Green that night from Canterbury. It had been the twenty-fourth of May, four days after her birthday. I came back to a scene of flashing lights, police cars and a crime-scene tape. I still remember the jolt of the shock I experienced as I realized that Lark Cottage was at its centre. After that it has become a blur of Tom, Mark, neighbours and the Wests, all unable to help one another for the shock was the same for us all. We could not take it in. Not Laura. How could it be?

When Laura had failed to fetch Jamie from the nursery school, and there was no reply to the phone, the school had called her neighbour, who, seeing Laura's car in place, had gone to investigate further by peering in first the front windows and then the rear French windows. Laura had been lying on the floor by her piano. She had been strangled.

The police inspector whom I demanded to see told me she had been attacked from behind. Sometimes memory plays tricks. I wrote earlier that Laura had been savagely murdered and sometimes I still have nightmares of her lying in a pool of blood, not strangled. People talked and talked and rumours flew. Savagely? Of course it was savage; unbelievable that anyone so good, so kind, so young as Laura should have been snatched away by death. I met Detective Inspector Fritton several times and liked him. Did that make it less painful for me? No, although he seemed to understand my grief below his calm, professional, gimlet face, and even to share it. Paul Fritton explained gently to me that there had been no blood, no knife and no gun, as rumour had claimed, but the force of the attack had been brutal.

Motive?

Again rumours flew round the village. Tom was jealous, Laura was having an affair, she was going to leave him and take Jamie, she had secrets in her past, she was a marriage wrecker, even a blackmailer, and she'd done this, done that . . . Only later did it occur to me that perhaps those rumours hinted that my marriage had been wrecked by her – but that was nonsense. Laura had been my shoulder to cry on, to tell me that I was in the right, that Mark was a rotter and that I deserved better.

Before her death, Laura had been the unsung heroine of the village, but gossip makes villains of us all. To me, she was always the princess of that treasure hunt so many years ago. She helped out, she mopped up tears, she loved, she cared, she did what she promised. *Send for Laura* was the obvious solution to any village crisis. Above all, Laura adored Tom. No one suggested otherwise *before* her death, but after it the worthies of Ducks Green apparently saw no conflict in repeating the rumours that a trail of lovers had made their way to her bed.

On the evening of her death, Laura's parents promptly took Jamie into their care, and within a few months they had moved to Tenterden in west Kent. And that's where she is buried. I'd wanted to take care of Jamie myself, and Tom was all for it, but in official eyes blood is thicker than water and I stood no chance. I don't know what went on between Tom and the Wests then, but clearly it had not been pleasant. My parents told me later that Tom had gone through some sort of breakdown. He was arrested for Laura's murder at one point, but released without charge. Nevertheless, it was obvious that the Wests had immediately closed their doors to him, and they were not welcoming even to me. When I visited her grave each year, I was permitted to say a brief hallo to Jamie. I can see Laura in her son. Her eyes look up at me each year, and I go home in tears before I put her memory away for another year.

Whether Tom was guilty of her murder or not, the pressure on him must have been horrendous, but I had been too wrapped up in my own grief to cope successfully with Tom. I left Ducks Green a year after the murder, but by then Tom had already vanished to Africa. The cottage had been sold – to a couple in France, to whom the murder meant nothing save for mild curiosity.

Had there been other suspects? I had no idea. What I did know was that the name of Jack Scarlet had never been mentioned. I knew Laura would not have had a lover, and so at the time it had seemed pointless to worry over what false avenues the police might be treading. Pointless and painful. But now? I knew I must brace myself to rub salt in the wound, grain by painful grain.

I recognized a few faces as I walked back to the Drummond Arms. Heads were down against the May drizzle, and no one took notice of me. Some were walking dogs – perhaps even the same dogs I'd known in my time here; the older generation was clustered round the village shop and post office. Then I realized that there was no post office any longer. The sign had vanished, and another heart of village life had been ripped out. What had happened to Mrs Partridge, whose life and soul the post office had been? Had she retired with no one to take it over, or had it been closed on 'economic grounds' as so many others had been? Uneconomic – how was that decided? Living villages bolster the economy, dead ones drain it, and without a post office Ducks Green must be battling for survival. Laura would have been at the head of every protest march had she still been alive.

Laura . . .

I had to discipline myself to subdue emotion. I needed to walk into the Drummond Arms like a prodigal daughter, at the very least confident that if I was recognized I could handle it.

I was prepared for change, but Ben Barker was still behind the bar. He glanced up at me with his familiar, professional 'welcome' smile – which abruptly disappeared in favour of a genuine grin.

'Good grief,' he said, coming out from behind the bar to give me a kiss. 'Emma Haywood, isn't it?'

'The very same, Ben.' I'm known as Emma Cardale now, so my maiden name should have struck a false note. Oddly, it didn't. It felt entirely right, especially from Ben whom I had known well for years, both before my marriage and during it. He must be getting on for retirement age now, I thought, but he still had the same rubicund face, which belied the speed with which he could move if he chose. He was a short man, and peaceable by nature, and yet I've seen him out from behind the bar in seconds to escort half a dozen bellicose drunks out without a murmur of protest from them.

'Never thought we'd see you again.' Ben isn't one to pull his verbal punches.

'After the divorce I couldn't wait to get away. It's different now.' The name 'Laura' remained unspoken between us, and he clutched at this straw.

'Shame about you and Mark – still think of you together.'

Mark lives in Sturry now, the far side of Canterbury, with his new wife Anna. She's all the things I'm not: gracious hostess, social animal and fashion plate, without even trying. She's also a very nice woman. I like her, although I'm not sure if Mark approves of this. He looks embarrassed when we're together and often laughing our heads off. Perhaps he thinks it diminishes him in some way and would prefer us to be two alley cats spitting at each other. Anyway, we get along just fine, though we rarely see each other. Every so often we have a double date in London. Jack thinks Anna's terrific, but he's only polite about Mark. I look at my former husband with a kind of wonder, trying to puzzle out if I ever felt about him as I do about Jack. I can't believe I did. You don't know the real thing until you get it. And now I have—

Another lurch of my stomach, as I thought of Jack. I forced myself to grin at Ben. 'I was just passing through. Thought I'd see if you still do that terrific cottage pie. I'm a bit late—'

'Not for you, ducky.'

The old silly joke. My nickname when Mark and I were Guardians of the Ducks.

'How's Stella?' I asked. I liked his wife. She was the fiery one of the two, but we got on splendidly. She had signed up as a life member of Laura's fan club when, as a teenager, Laura had rescued her four-year-old daughter from a speeding lorry.

'Still cooking. The kids are off our hands now, though . . .' Ben chatted on, and I tried hard to keep my attention on what he was saying. Then I heard him observe, 'Funny thing you turning up.'

'Why?' I was caught off guard.

'Jane was asking after you.' Misinterpreting my blank expression, he added, 'Jane Magg as was.'

'Oh. Stupid of me.' What else could I say? I would get an old-fashioned look if I said she had slipped my mind. It was hardly likely. Jane had been the friend about whom I felt most guilty when I cut myself off from the past.

Make it a complete break, my mother had urged. Get away from everything and everyone. She is a whizz at suggesting what I secretly want to do anyway. She provides a kind of sanction for it.

Jane Magg had been a loyal friend to Laura and myself. She had been at the same primary school as we had. She had also been at the same secondary school, although in a different class to us. Jane had trained as a teacher, and was teaching at the Lilleybourne school during the years that Mark and I lived in Ducks Green. She'd obviously decided to settle down permanently in the area.

'I must look her up,' I told Ben. 'I'd like to see her again.' It had hurt, cutting myself off at the time, but I had not regretted it – until now.

Ben didn't comment. 'The pie's on its way,' he said.

As I munched my way through the pie, I realized that meeting Jane again was not just something I very much wanted – and indeed ought – to do, but could be the most sensible plan. I would apologize and explain my silence, and hope for forgiveness. If I could talk to anyone about Tom it would be her because, of course, she had also known him well. I wouldn't rush into it though. Step by step, as my mother would say.

Kate Terry is one of my very favourite people. She was one of the few friends whom I still saw from my Kent days because she sometimes came up to London to see my parents, whose friend she also was. But never a word passed between us about Laura.

'Darling.' The door of Roxpole House flew open and I, my shoulder bag and trailing suitcase handle were all swept into her angular embrace. Still the same smell of apple blossom – was it her or the house? I'd never been sure.

I laughed and cried at the same time. How could I have left it so long? The last visit had been a theatre trip, and she'd stayed over at my parents' home.

'Follow me, dearly beloved Emma,' she ordered, and I followed her up the stairs. When Mark and I were at daggers drawn I'd sought refuge there on occasion, so I was no stranger to the house's layout. It was detached and solid with three storeys and an attic. It was red-brick early Victorian, and it was easy to imagine that the famous actors Henry Irving and Ellen Terry (no relation to Kate!) would have been quite at home here.

Kate was no greyer than when I had last seen her. In fact she was darker – all too clearly the results of a bottle. It was too dark for her face but it didn't matter a scrap. Kate was always Kate: lively eyes, brilliant red lipstick that always just missed the lips and adorned her jaw or cheeks, heavily powdered face, startling eyeshadow and mascara. Kate must be sixty-odd now. Once upon a time she had been married, but 'never took to it', as she once explained earnestly to me. 'All that *ironing*. And all that *commiserating*. Tea and sympathy are all very well on stage, my dear, but at home – oh, not for me.'

Kate had been an actress at one time, and a dead ringer for her mother Eileen. Eileen – whom I remembered from my childhood – had also been an actress. 'My mother,' Kate had told me once, 'only married my father because his surname was Terry. Hence the Kate for me. She once met John Gielgud, you see.'

I did. John Gielgud had been born into the famous Terry theatrical family; his grandmother was Kate Terry, Dame Ellen's elder sister, and also an actress. The memoirs of her daughter (also a Kate) were prominently displayed in a bookcase in Kate's home along with every other bit of Terry memorabilia, although as far as I knew her own father bore no relationship at all to the theatrical Terrys.

'And,' Kate's voice had grown even more hushed, 'my mother once met Dame Ellen.'

Kate's mother Eileen had not been as successful as her idol, although she followed in her footsteps with a stormy marital life. Her husband ran off with a chorus girl and left her and her daughter penniless. With Kate to bring up, Eileen turned her back on the stage and her home into a seaside lodging house for touring actors and variety artists. Kate grew up there and went on the stage herself – high drama, naturally – and then both mother and daughter came south to settle in Kent, having fallen in love with Cobshaw, the house and the small cottage at its rear where Eileen lived until age made her move into the main house a necessity. Their B. & B. business had posed a problem in Kent, however, as very few actors passed through Cobshaw, save for some of their old regulars for old times' sake. They therefore decided to extend their range to tourists, and the decor had to compensate for the theatrical links.

'You're in the Irving room, darling. I thought you'd like that.'

It was an honour but I could have done with a more peaceful room that night. The karma was not soothing, even though the Irving room was the grandest in the house. It was full of blown-up photos and theatre bills of Henry Irving depicted in such stirring murder dramas as *The Bells* and *Eugene Aram*. Irving's haunted and tragic face stared earnestly out at the would-be sleeper from every wall. Even his not so successful Hamlet was represented, with Irving musing over Yorick's skull. True, a portrait of Ellen Terry lightened the scene, but this was in her role as Olivia, daughter of the Vicar of Wakefield, who went to the bad. So that brought me little cheer either, as to me she had the look of Laura. No way could Laura have gone to the bad, despite Tom's slanders.

'Why are you really here?' Kate demanded in her usual peremptory manner once I had dumped my luggage and gone down to join her in her kingdom, the kitchen. I found her wrestling alternately with a coq au vin and tarte Tatin.

Partial truth was needed here. 'It's the anniversary of Laura's death on Saturday. I always go to Tenterden, but this time I thought I'd be brave and return here first.'

'Hm. Not quite the whole story, I think.' Kate spun round, poultry scissors poised as though she intended to tackle me next. 'Lady Audley's Secret, is it?' she shot out.

'No way. I've no illegitimate babies to conceal.'

'Something else then. You've had years to remember we still exist here. Mooning after Mark, are you?'

I fell into the trap. 'No way again,' I said indignantly. 'I'm still living happily with Jack Scarlet. You met him when we'd not long become an item. And it's worked out well.'

To my relief, my haunting fear that everyone knew Laura and Jack were friends was calmed. Kate would have had no hesitation in telling me if so.

'I remember. A charmer.'

'And a lot more,' I said stoutly, then seized the nettle. 'He was brought up in Lilleybourne.'

No reaction – but surely there should have been, whether she had known him or not? 'Sure you're happy?' Kate asked.

'Very.'

'So why come back?'

She had me there, and there was only a split second to decide my answer. I could trust Kate. She knew all the gossip but never passed it on unnecessarily.

'Tom Burdock is back from Africa, working in Canterbury.'

'I heard.'

Of course she had. 'How?'

'He's been in touch with Jane.'

Kate knew very well I need not be reminded of who Jane was. My next best friend after Laura. 'And she told you?' I asked.

'Of course not. Her lips were sealed. The postman told me.'

Jane knew Tom as well as I did so it made perfect sense. But she didn't know I was living with Jack so that question still trailed unanswered. It also made perfect sense that I should contact Jane again. She loved Laura as much as I did. As much as everyone did.

'What's she doing now?' I asked. 'Where's she living?'

'Ducks Green.'

'Oh. Where? And who did she marry?'

I was aware that Kate was hesitating – odd. 'She married Paul Fritton.'

'The police inspector?' I was astounded, but I realized they might be a good match. Jane was kind, dependable and a home-maker, and he had seemed the family-man type. I hoped she was happy.

'They've two kids, I think,' Kate told me brightly. Too brightly? She hadn't answered one of my questions yet.

'Where are they living?' I repeated.

'Tom and Laura's old cottage.'

I mentally tried to pick myself up from the floor, unable to believe it. 'Where—'

'Yes.' Kate sighed. 'I had to tell you. You'd find out soon enough. Paul took a fancy to Lark Cottage, and persuaded Jane into it. I think they've changed the name.'

I still found the whole idea incredible. 'Didn't she *mind*?'

'Jane told me she did at first, when Paul suggested it, but then began to think it through. She thought Laura would have approved of her being there with a family; it would take over where Laura had been stopped, bringing it all to life again to wipe out all the bad vibes.'

Kate must have seen the horror still in my face, because she turned on me – for my own good, as usual, I had to admit. 'Think about it, Emma. What did *you* do?'

Only one answer. 'I ran away, but—'

'Jane didn't. She faced it head on. People have different ways of dealing with things. Are you intending to scuttle away again?'

I flushed with anger. 'I don't know – and I didn't scuttle.

I made a new life.' I realized with foreboding it was indeed time to open that closed door.

'All right, I'll face it, Kate.' I had no choice. I wasn't going to be accused of dodging again. Not this time – the old life had banged its head against the new and I couldn't escape it. If for no other reason, I had to discover where Jack fitted in, if at all. This time I had to fight.

Three

I slept badly that night, plagued by nightmares in which I was engulfed in some kind of web, which, no matter how I pushed, refused to allow me any escape. When I finally managed to break out of it I was running desperately, caught between Tom, who was steadily and relentlessly marching after me, and Jack, who was strolling ahead of me. The gap behind me was closing for all my efforts and that in front of me loomed ever wider. No matter how hard I tried to run Jack pulled further and further ahead, unconcerned about my plight.

At last I found myself awake in the real world. The sun was streaming in through the windows, and the last of the dawn chorus, which I never heard in London, seemed to be dying away. Growing up in Cobshaw, I had imagined that with the coming of dawn the birds sang their sweet songs for me alone. At Kate's home, however, the chorus was dominated by the rooks from which her house had gained its name. They nested in the tall trees of Wychley Wood behind the house, which Laura and I had naturally enough thought of as Witch's Wood. The rooks' calls of the day's dawn chorus were loud and coarse – comforting at times, threatening at others.

Downstairs Kate, always an early riser, would be preparing cups of tea and breakfast. I could hear the sounds now. Closeted in a world I knew, I should have felt safe but I didn't. I felt as if I'd been catapulted back like Doctor Who into another age. Outside my private police box my past was waiting to greet me, and within me my future seemed to have shadows over it that a few days ago would have seemed an impossibility. Had Tom really been hinting that there was more connecting Jack and Laura, perhaps even that Jack was Laura's killer?

Wednesday's morning light had its effect, however. Surely I should not pay any attention to a wild allegation from a man obviously still haunted by his past? I loved Jack; I trusted him. I had therefore to accept that he was one of life's warriors – every

shot would be warded off by his shield – and that he would tell
me only what he chose and no more. He had probably been
greatly hurt that I'd even questioned him about his Kentish youth.
He had read the doubt in my eyes and in self-defence closed
himself off until I came to my senses. Perhaps he had even invented
this new trip abroad so that I had time to get over my stupidity.
Far-fetched? Perhaps, but it was possible.

My way ahead now seemed clear. I would do what Kate obviously thought was only right and proper. I would make my peace
with Jane and face the ordeal of Laura's and Tom's cottage.

This time I drove to Ducks Green, rather than walking. I had
taken my courage in both hands and rung Jane. It had been
surprisingly easy. For a start, she'd already heard I was back, if
that was the right description, so the main shock was over. There
was just a startled pause, then her familiar warm voice.

'Come right over, stranger. Second thoughts, make it lunch. I
can whip up something to celebrate and the kids aren't at nursery
school today.'

That could be a bonus, I thought. I'm not used to small children, not having any of my own, yet I enjoy being with them,
and I have enough experience of my friends' kids to know that
they are a splendid conversation point if I ever get stuck for
something to say. With Jane that was unlikely though, if she were
in forgiving mode.

I parked in the old public car park, upgraded since my time
but still behind the former village hall, which had now been
converted to residential use. I decided to take Jane something
anonymous such as flowers or wine, rather than something more
personal as might befit a long-lost friend. Without the post office,
the village shop looked somehow forlorn, and I didn't recognize
the young woman at the till. Or did I? I had a vague feeling
she'd been one of Laura's pupils. She had been a teenager then,
but now looked less pert, although she'd grown up into a sulky
twenty-something with a wedding ring. A look of mild interest
lit up Mrs Sulky's face as she took my money for the chocolates
I'd settled on. Jane had always had a sweet tooth, I'd remembered.

'Mrs Cardale, isn't it?' Mrs Sulky asked.

'It is,' I agreed. 'You've a long memory.' I meant it as a

pleasantry, but I think she took it otherwise as she looked over my shoulder.

'Maybe,' she said.

In a village the size of Ducks Green, with a high-profile murder such as Laura's, she would have good reason to remember me.

For some reason this irritated me. Perhaps I had Kate's words in mind, that I'd somehow evaded my responsibilities. 'I'm off to see Jane Magg – Fritton,' I added. 'She likes chocolates, doesn't she?' Keep the small talk going, I told myself. I didn't want to discuss Laura, but I did want to sound interested in Ducks Green.

'Wouldn't know.' She said it as a statement of fact rather than rudely.

It occurred to me that Jane might not use the village shop very much. I made a last try. 'I heard she's married a policeman. Useful to have in the village, I expect.'

That stirred her. 'You were Mrs Burdock's friend, weren't you?'

'Yes.' I placed her at last. 'And you're Lily. Lily . . . um—'

'Spencer. Dean as was. Yeah.' She looked as if she were about to say something more but if so she changed her mind. Or perhaps I changed it for her by what I said next – goodness knows why, in view of my wish to keep off the subject.

'I left not long after her murder.'

'Oh, that's nice. Have a nice day.' An artificial smile dismissed me – again not rudely, just 'subject closed'.

Assuming my interpretation to be correct, I was puzzled as to why it should be taboo to mention Laura's death after all these years. To anyone but those most closely involved, the edge must surely have been taken off the horror and curiosity with which those less close to it reacted?

I crossed the street and had another look at the duck pond, but none of its inhabitants were interested in their former guardian, and with a vague sense of unease I continued up the gentle slope to Lark Cottage – no, I thought, I must think of it as Number Twelve. I was glad I'd walked past it the previous day, accustoming myself to the sight of it. It was now Jane's cottage, I told myself. Jane and Paul Fritton's. I still had to get used to that idea. I only dimly remembered him from several interviews at the time of Laura's death, but it had struck me even then how quietly effi-cient he was. He had watched me and summed me up, but had

never hassled me, and he had a surprisingly warm smile. He had
made me feel as if he were on my side – a skill that must be an
asset for a policeman.

Now the moment had come I was eager to get the reunion
with Jane over with and knocked on the door, almost, but not
quite, forgetting how many times I'd done this in the past. Luckily,
the colour had changed. It had been deep rust, but it was now
blue. Last-minute nerves flared up inside me, but were quickly
dispersed as the door opened.

'Emma!'

A second later we were hugging each other. It was as easy as
that, and I told Jane so as I stepped into her hallway.

'So I should think,' she told me forthrightly. 'We've known
each other for over a quarter of a century.'

'You haven't changed a bit,' I said.

She pulled a face. 'I don't have braces on my teeth any more,
even if I still have the puppy fat.'

'Nicely rounded,' I joked. I meant it. Jane had never been fat
or even plump, and she looked just as I recalled her. Why is it
that the words dependable, reliable, quiet and loyal seem to carry
such a pejorative undertone that they can't be used to a person's
face?

'Thank heavens,' I added, 'you're still Jane.'

'And you, Emma, still look a hot-rod.'

I laughed. This had been a joke of sorts, Laura's originally.
She'd been searching for some polite way of saying I was impatient and too damned energetic, and hot-rod had come to mind.
I might be laughing now, but I had tears in my eyes too. Were
they for Laura or for the wasted years when I'd turned my back
on Jane?

'Well,' I said, 'you've been busy. A husband and two children,
no less. That's lovely. I wish I had.' That was true – or had been
until last Friday. I'd been beginning to get broody over Jack but
now that might be on hold.

'I'm a part-time teacher at the primary school too.'

'Good grief. Mrs Grenier isn't still there, is she?' The head
teacher of my youth had still reigned there during my Ducks
Green days with Mark, but she had looked ancient by that time.

'Retired with reluctance, full honours and a gold watch.

Or for gold watch read garden tokens loaded enough to equip her for the Chelsea Flower Show. She's still living here, in one of the houses constructed out of the old school. A sad case of Othello's occupation gone, poor old thing. Or maybe I'm wrong. Perhaps she was glad to see the back of us all,' Jane said. 'I see her in the village regularly, though I don't think she's encouraged to pop into the new school. Too much of a disciplinarian.'

'Who's living in Fullers?' I was curious, even though I felt no sentimental attachment to my former marital home.

'New folk. Don't know them yet.'

There was one of those awkward pauses as Jane ushered me into the living room. Involuntarily, my eyes went to the far end overlooking the garden, where Laura's piano had stood, and where Laura had lain dead until the neighbour found her. To my relief the room had completely changed. A standard dining table, chairs and dresser took up the space and two kids hurled themselves in from the garden through the French windows. Laura's garden, I thought before I could check myself, but I didn't have time to brood as Billy (four) and Alice (two) danced around me, clamouring for my attention. Friendly relations were established. I complimented Jane on her offspring (genuinely) and she beamed, explaining that they only attended nursery school three days a week, and so I was in luck.

I'd forgotten what a good cook Jane was, and lunch was highly enjoyable. Plain food, well chosen, well prepared. Conversation flowed easily, and the children provided so much diversion that I had no need to fear Laura's ghost.

'This cottage wasn't large enough for us by the time we had Alice so we bought the two-up two-down cottage next door eighteen months ago. Now there's room for a study for Paul, and a guest room.' Jane hesitated. 'You're very welcome to stay, but I imagine . . .'

'Yes,' I said gratefully. 'Until I get used to –' I quickly amended what I'd been going to say – 'Ducks Green again. I'm only here for a few days anyway.'

Jane grasped the nettle more firmly than I did. 'You must think it odd that Paul and I settled here.'

'I did at first. Not after I thought it through,' I said, reasonably honestly.

'It was either this, or my moving to Canterbury,' Jane said. 'The decision was easier for Paul. He didn't have the emotional connection to Laura that I had, and so he left it entirely to me when the couple that bought it first put it on the market. I thought,' she explained diffidently, 'it was something I could do for Laura. Make her home a happy one again. Was that daft?'

'No. And you have.'

I realized with some surprise that it was true, although I could hardly have said anything else. It seemed no longer Tom and Laura's very special Lark Cottage, but a conventional and friendly family home. Laura's ghost was in my heart, not here.

'Now, tell me why you've come back,' Jane said firmly after the children had retreated for an afternoon nap. Alice in particular had been fighting to keep her eyes open. 'And don't tell me,' she continued, 'that you were just passing. I do realize that it's the anniversary of Laura's death this weekend.'

I'd thought this through. If anyone could help me, it was Jane. Kate was a watchful but detached observer. Jane had been right there throughout our childhood. She knew Tom, she knew Laura. She could understand. I decided to go for it.

'Tom Burdock has come back to Kent. He's working and probably living in Canterbury.'

'I know. He rang me and I've seen him once or twice.'

This didn't deflate me, because I had guessed he must have called on Jane first, even though it couldn't have been Tom who told her I was staying here. That must be down to Ben Barker's powers of news dissemination. I felt mean for having wondered whether she would come clean about Tom. True, it was six years since I last saw her, and she could have changed in the meantime and grown more secretive. She hadn't, of course, bless her. Up front, was Jane.

'It must have been a shock,' I said. 'He came to see me too.'

'Not too much. He knew Paul and I were friendly even when he left, and seemed to take the cottage in his stride.'

'You and Paul got together because of the murder?'

Jane took this on the chin. 'You could say that. I was a witness, as you were. He and I bumped into each other in Canterbury one day not long afterwards and that was that.' Then, with hardly a pause, 'Why did you go, Emma? Or let me put it differently – I understand why you left, but why the long silence? I was away and got back to find you gone, the house on the market, and the estate agents only had Mark's address. He claimed not to know where you were, so did Kate Terry. I rang your parents and they were equally discreet, I presume on your instructions.'

'Oh Jane,' I said helplessly. 'I was a mess, that was why. The divorce coming on top of everything else just broke me up. I just couldn't face anything to do with Ducks Green. I suppose,' I concluded miserably, 'I just tried to blot everything out. A complete failure. I failed in my marriage. I failed Laura. I failed you.'

'Do you think you made the right decision? Do you feel the same now?'

I reached out to take her hand across the table. 'No, no and no. Seeing you again has put it into perspective. I suppose that's what I was hoping for in coming back here. Forgive me?' With a pang I realized it wasn't the whole truth, but how could I explain that I felt I owed a debt to Laura – and, even worse, that I needed to clear that niggle about Jack from my mind?

'Yes, of course,' Jane replied promptly. 'But don't –' she adopted Mrs Grenier's gruff tones – 'do it again.'

'No, miss. Honest.'

We laughed a lot and that was the issue settled. I only wished Tom's problem could be settled as easily.

'Tom seems hell-bent on clearing his name,' I said experimentally.

'Natural enough, I suppose. He's been through a lot, poor man.'

I hesitated, still not feeling entirely on sure ground. I did not want to ask outright whether she still thought Tom was guilty of Laura's murder, and so I compromised. 'Is the police file still open, Jane? Or can't you tell me?'

'It's closed.'

That suggested the police thought they knew who the killer was but couldn't prove it: i.e. Tom, I thought.

'I know that looks bad for Tom,' Jane added, 'and perhaps I shouldn't tell you this, but he wants the case reopened. Paul's looking into it.'

This was good news, surely. 'You don't think that wise?'

'It seems natural enough. Tom wants his son back, and I don't blame him, so he has to be seen to be doing something.'

'He didn't seem exactly rational when he came to see me. Not about Laura. He still thinks –' I managed a light laugh – 'that she had a lover, and even implied there was a string of them.'

There was instant silence, which terrified me until Jane at last replied, 'I thought we dismissed that as rubbish at the time.'

Thank heavens for Jane. 'Of course it was rubbish,' I agreed.

She must have picked up uncertainty in my voice. 'Look at the practicalities, Emma,' she said gently. 'We don't know what happened between Tom and Laura – no one knows what any marriage is really like save for the two involved – but, (a), we know Laura adored Tom and was very happy with him and Jamie. She wanted more children. We, her best friends, never heard a hint that it was otherwise. Even more pertinently, (b), how the hell would she have had the time to fit in a string of lovers, or even one? She had Jamie, she gave piano lessons, she gave concerts, she was on countless committees, she saw her friends—'

'You're right.' I nearly cried with relief. 'You're so right, Jane. That's what I worked out myself, but it's such a relief to hear you say so too. You see, Tom—' I broke off. I'd told her nothing about my private life and with her usual delicacy Jane hadn't enquired, even though I'd rattled on at lunch about my job and being redundant. I should tell her.

'I'm living with someone I love very much,' I explained. 'He's the only person whom I could ever consider marrying again and be sure it wouldn't go wrong as it did with Mark.'

Jane grinned. 'Tom did mention you were living with someone. It won't go wrong, believe me. Mark was a mistake, that's all,' she added staunchly. 'You married too young and he was a wimp compared to you. He couldn't rein you in, my proud beauty.'

I giggled. Wimp? How Mark would love to hear that. Our marriage had broken up over his affair with Anna. Well, that was the apparent reason but of course there's always much more than that. We had grown apart – didn't want to share any more. We'd no interests in common. Increasingly, the path had divided.

'In case Tom forgot to mention it,' I said, 'his name's Jack Scarlet.' I watched for a reaction but there was none. 'He doesn't rein me in either. He lets me stampede all over the place, but not over him.' Even as I spoke, a mutinous thought came into my mind: but where is he, now I need him?

'Tell me about him.'

Encouraged, I did so, as casually as I could. 'He was brought up in Lilleybourne – quite a coincidence.'

'Did he go to our school?'

'No. Lilleybourne, and then Junior King's School, Canterbury.'

'That explains why the name has a familiar ring, but I don't remember Jack himself. Did you?'

'No.' Leave the subject right there, I thought. I didn't like the sound of a 'familiar ring', but Jane had a good memory, and if he'd been one of our crowd she would have remembered.

So I moved on to later time. I told her about my meeting with Jack, about the time we called our 'honeymoon', about my moving into his home, but not, of course, about our first kiss, our first embrace, our relationship – they were between me and him alone. I told her enough though to build up a picture of what our life together was like.

I waxed so enthusiastic that I forgot what Tom had said, and forgot my doubts. But then, with Jane's sympathetic face before me, they came back. 'Did Laura give him piano lessons?' I blurted out.

'Who?' Jane asked blankly.

'Jack.'

She looked at me as if I was raving – justifiably. 'Why should she? How could she?'

'Tom said Jack was Laura's lover. Did he tell you that? *Did* he?'

A moment's horrified pause, then Jane leapt up and came round to me, hugging me close to her. 'No, not to me. But Emma, of course Tom would say something like that to you.'

'Why?' I felt like crying and being strong at the same time.

'Because he must always have been jealous of you and Laura being so close; and, Emma, remember there was also a rumour flying around at the time that he fancied you and that's what made his jealousy even worse. Just rumours,' she added anxiously, 'but you know how they spread.'

Of all the answers, of all the times, this was the fast ball that came out of nowhere. 'He's always been a good friend,' I managed to say.

'Of course, and I never saw much sign of his fancying you, or even of his being jealous of your supposed influence over Laura.

But he knew your marriage with Mark was breaking down at the time he left for Africa, so he probably came back assuming he could pick up his old friendship with you, and then he discovered you're living with someone else. In his fragile state, he's not going to be pleased, is he?'

A thousand 'buts' flew through my mind, as I grappled with this entirely new scenario. 'But you don't believe this, do you, Jane? We all got on so well. How could Tom have been jealous of the time I spent with Laura? And as for fancying me, it was Laura he adored from our schooldays on.' I tried to reason it out. Laura would have mentioned it to me if Tom had been raising objections to the time we spent together. She would have hated to think that she was upsetting Tom. And yet, unwillingly, I had to admit that, tolerant though Tom was, he was the sort of person who would bottle up his emotions, try to conquer them – but if he failed he would blow his top. Laura had told me that sometimes happened over trivial household matters.

'No doubt about that. He did adore her, but you spent so much time with them both that the rumour could easily have sprung up that it was you he was after. I was close enough to you to know it was nonsense, but to the outsider it could have been possible.'

My mind stopped whirling around, and fastened on the salient point. 'Then if village gossip thought he fancied me, why did everyone think he killed Laura in a fit of jealous passion?' Then I saw the terrible pitfall opening up before me. 'Jane,' I said quietly, 'the gossip didn't go so far as to assume that Laura and I were *lovers*, did it? That that was why he killed her, and that that was the reason for Mark's and my divorce?'

The horror of this completely new aspect hit me so badly that I must have gone very white, because Jane reacted immediately.

'Good grief, *no*. No, no, *no*. That's so like you, Emma. Seeing bogeys under every bed. Be sensible, please. Don't you think Mark would have hurled that one at you in an instant if he'd even heard it, let alone believed it? Don't you think Tom would have used that one like a shot, whether he believed it or not? It would have been somewhat easier to have accused you and Laura of a lesbian relationship than to have proved she had a male lover – and that's what he went for.'

The shock had been so great that I began to cry as the tension drained away from me. 'Oh Jane, yes. I'm sorry, I'm going overboard here. I am right, aren't I, in thinking that we all – that's you, me and the police – thought Tom must have killed her because he mistakenly thought her unfaithful to him? And if so, *why* did we think that was feasible?'

'Yes, we did, although I can't answer for the official attitude. But as to why we thought that possible – I don't know the answer, Emma. I really don't. Jealousy, I suppose, whatever the cause. Dog in a manger. Laura's mine. But on the other hand, don't you think it's a good reason for Tom's *not* being guilty of her murder?'

I felt as if I'd wandered into the wrong jigsaw puzzle, clutching my little stray pieces. Jack always tells me I look straight ahead, and that one day I'll get run over by something whizzing round from a side turning. 'I'll think about that,' I said to Jane. Did she mean that if Laura had had nothing to hide – as I was sure she had not – then Tom would have instinctively known that?

'Tom's a good man, Emma,' Jane said anxiously. 'And we may have been misjudging him. Jamie is his main concern. He told me he was going to Tenterden this weekend.'

'To the cemetery? Oh Jane, I was going. Should I?'

'If it's for Laura's sake, go.'

'But what about Tom and Jamie? I don't want to get in his way.'

'Let the Wests worry about that. It's you I'm concerned for. You could be sticking that headstrong noddle of yours into hot water.'

I drove back to Cobshaw feeling considerably better after our heart to heart, once I'd recovered from the shock. For all she'd said, I wondered if there *had* been any general rumour that Laura and I were more than friends. We hadn't been, and therefore what Jane had had to say about Jack was more important to me at the moment. She had been comfortingly supportive over my relationship with him. Firstly, she had said she had no memory of his being around in our childhood or of his parents. The 'familiar ring' could have been from anywhere – even from Scarlett O'Hara.

Secondly, she'd suggested that I ask him to come to Ducks Green. 'I'd love to meet him,' she'd said, 'and it would help you put Tom's accusations in perspective. He's had years to mull it all over, but instead of helping him adjust to reality it's only increased his fantasies.'

Good advice, but just at the moment I was on my own. I couldn't wait for that. I needed to know whether Tom was really going to Tenterden on Saturday or whether Jane had got the wrong end of the stick. It was none of my business if Tom did, of course, as it was his family involved. Nevertheless, I had to face the fact that, sooner or later, I would have to meet Tom again if I was to achieve anything by my visit here. What Jane had told me was opening up so many frightening doubts and questions that I decided the sooner the better, and Saturday would provide a perfect opportunity. On the other hand, I had no wish to risk hindering his talks with the Wests over Jamie, so I needed to clear the situation with him urgently. No time like the present, however daunting the prospect. I had no mobile phone with me and so, as it was only four o'clock, I decided on impulse to try to catch him at his office. I knew the address because I'd checked it in the phone book.

I parked at Canterbury West station and walked through the back streets towards Goose Lane where the Tolling Bells office was. Walking helped calm me down, particularly since my route led past a mixture of medieval, early Victorian and modern buildings. The sense of history seemed to put my problems into some kind of perspective.

As I paused at the last road, however, my eye was caught by a man crossing at a roundabout further along. He was some distance away, but when you love someone you don't need a face to recognize him. You know his walk, the set of his shoulders, and chemistry is not hindered by distance.

It was Jack.

I began to run towards him, but when I reached the roundabout there was no sign of him. Then my doubts set in. I couldn't have seen him. He had been on my mind. I was overwrought. And yet doubt couldn't wipe out that first instinctive reaction: it had been Jack Scarlet.

Four

Still knocked sideways by doubt and disbelief, I forced myself to continue with my plan of calling on Tom. To my surprise the offices of Tolling Bells were rather grand. I suppose I had built up a stereotyped image of a poky garret in a dilapidated building, and of a menacing Tom sitting behind a dusty, makeshift desk with an ancient laptop. It wasn't at all like that. The rooms weren't luxurious, but they looked businesslike and go-ahead: suitable for a charity whose role was to help finance other charities in global disaster areas.

Only Tom and his anxious-looking young assistant seemed in residence, although, as she asked me whether I wanted to see Tom or Lee Hunt-White, there had to be at least three still on the payroll. I remembered Lee. He was the one who called all the shots in the day-to-day running of the charity, and Tom was his executive officer. I'd met Lee once at a do at Laura's house. She'd thought he was the cat's whiskers, but he wasn't my type – he was urbane, silver-haired and aspired to the Greek god image.

I could feel my heart beating with tension as the young girl showed me into Tom's office, but his look of pleasure when he saw me took some of that angst away. It also helped me recover from the shock of seeing Jack's lookalike, as I had now decided that man crossing the road had to be. I began to relax, especially as Tom looked a different person to the haunted man who had turned up on our Dulwich doorstep. He was casually but smartly dressed, even if a world away from pinstripes and tie, and seemed a man with a purpose rather than the lost soul of last week. I wasn't sure whether this would make it easier or harder to talk to him. The beard certainly invested him with a gravitas that helped take him away from my memories of him as Laura's husband. That was good because I was all too aware of what Jane had said. Right or wrong though, the gossip had been about Tom being jealous of my friendship with Laura and, whether or not this was due to his fancying me, it was going to affect the way I thought of him. He represented not the known but the unknown.

'Come in, Emma. It's like old times seeing you bounding in through the door. You were usually waving a tennis racket.'

'Rubbish.' I managed to grin at him, and the relationship promptly returned at least temporarily to the days when his office had been next to the tennis courts that all four of us had used. 'Jack and I still play,' I added, which led me smoothly on to: 'He's away, so I thought it was high time I revisited Ducks Green.'

Tom wasn't going to pull any punches. 'Checking up on him after what I told you?'

That caught me on the raw. 'No way. Just because Jack was brought up in Lilleybourne that hardly means he was involved in . . .' With Tom's well-remembered earnest face before me, I pulled back from the brink of mentioning Laura's murder.

One up to him. He didn't take advantage of my confusion. Why else would I be here, after all? As he must see it, I could have only two reasons for coming back to Kent: either to help clear Tom's name, or to expunge the doubt he had – so carefully? – implanted in my mind about Jack.

'Where are you staying? With Jane?' he asked.

'No. I saw her earlier though.'

'Good. So you know she's living at Lark Cottage.' He seemed unemotional, but I couldn't believe that he was.

'That must have been a shock to you.' I tried to put myself in his shoes when he found out that the house that had so many memories for him, good and bad, was now occupied not by strangers (which might have been more bearable) but by a sympathetic friend and the DI who probably thought he was guilty of murder.

'You could say that. Jane was very good. She told me on the phone beforehand and offered to meet me on neutral ground if I preferred.'

'Did you?'

'I came back to clear my name, Emma. When Lee said he needed more help in the UK office, it was the perfect opportunity. As I couldn't avoid seeing and thinking about Lark Cottage, I decided to take it on the chin and talk to Jane there.'

'Me too, but it must have been very tough for you.'

He brooded for a moment. 'Actually, the reverse, once I was inside. The good times I'd had with Laura there had already been wiped out by the murder and the endless trail of police, scientists and all the world and his wife, so now it doesn't matter whether I go over to Jane's place or vice versa. I can take it.'

'Why didn't you come to stay with Mark and me after Laura's death?' That would have been the obvious solution, and yet I'd no memory of Tom's doing so. 'Didn't we ask you?' I was horrified. Had Mark and I been so wrapped up in our own concerns and grief that we'd never thought of Tom? It was impossible now to put myself back into the mindset of that terrible time. I had only a view through the wrong end of a telescope back through the years and it seemed to be another Emma I was looking at.

'Yes, you did, in fact. Good of you, considering you thought I'd killed Laura. So I turned the invitation down, stayed in the cottage as long as I could bear it and then went to my parents' home.'

There was nothing I could say in my own defence. I *had* thought that he'd killed my friend, but so had Mark, so had Jane and so had the police. I remembered Tom's parents well: their eyes full of sick incomprehension for they, too, had loved Laura, and Tom had been the apple of their eye. Did they, too, believe he'd killed her? I was all too conscious that it was still on the cards that he had. He might even have blotted the truth out of his mind, so that he genuinely believed himself innocent. That might account for his wild allegations against others, such as Jack. I pushed away a fleeting image of that man crossing the road. No, it couldn't possibly have been Jack – he was in France.

'Don't worry, Emma. There's no way I could have come,' Tom finished awkwardly, and I didn't push him further. I was only too glad to leave the subject.

'What are your plans now?' I asked briskly. 'You said you wanted to clear your name. How?'

He hesitated. 'Are we on the same or opposite sides, Emma? I suppose it's the latter, as you're living with Jack Scarlet.'

I froze. I suppose I had been half hoping that I'd been mistaken, and that his accusation about Jack had nothing to do with Laura's murder, only with his relationship with her. Both had to be rebutted.

'I love him, Tom. That's why I have to find out what all this is about. You told me Jack was Laura's lover. Did you really mean that?'

He looked at me as if he was sorry for me, and that really terrified me. 'Yes.'

My self-control, such as it was, snapped. 'But on what evidence?' I yelled at him. 'Do you have any at all? Stop being so bloody mysterious.'

He remained calm. 'I'm not. Look, come back to my flat. We can have dinner in the pub and talk more freely.'

I was too deep in not to agree. If I scuttled back to Dulwich I'd never find out what, if anything, this was all about. But not dinner. That conjured up a far cosier image than I could take at present. I needed to be objective.

'Drink,' I amended. 'Kate is cooking dinner for me.'

'Done. There's a pub near the flat, but I need to pick up something to show you first. I'll drive you there and back to your car.'

'OK.' I decided I'd ring Kate before we left. It suddenly seemed important to let her know I might be a bit late for dinner. At least somebody would know where I was. I realized I was getting jittery with absolutely no reason whatsoever, save that I was stepping into the unknown.

Tom was living in a ground floor flat in a Victorian house on the outskirts of the city. 'Renting,' he explained, 'while I sort myself out.'

I wondered how the 'sorting out' would affect him. Suppose he sorted nothing out over the murder and his plans for Jamie were doomed? Would he disappear again to the wilds of Africa? Not that Johannesburg was exactly the wilds. Would he continue to avoid former friends in case they still looked at him with accusing eyes? Is that how *I* looked at him? I was aware that I was beginning to want this 'sorted out' for his sake as well as for mine. Being with Tom again seemed surprisingly easy, now I had taken the plunge. The monster in my mind was fast giving way to the Tom I used to know, and I didn't want to lose him as a friend this time, if he was innocent – and once I had cleared up this lingering doubt over Jack.

The flat was large, with tall ceilings, and spotlessly clean and tidy, although essentially soulless. Not like Lark Cottage, I thought involuntarily, then put that memory guiltily away. We decided against the drink at the pub as we both still had to drive, and settled for coffee. He was always a dab hand with coffee and it all seemed very familiar – so reminiscent of a hundred such meetings we must have had in the past.

Eventually, I steeled myself to switch the subject away from Africa and Tolling Bells. 'Tell me, Tom.'

He knew what I meant. 'Are you sure you want to know?'

'Want no, but need, yes. How can I help you if I don't know what the evidence is against you or against Jack?'

'All right. You remember what I said in my statement to the police?'

I shook my head, somewhat irritated. 'I don't know what *anyone* said. How could I? Talk got confused with fact, supposition with evidence. Suppose you tell me.'

'Fair enough. I was at the office that day – not the one we have now. We've gone up in the world in the last seven years. But it was in Canterbury. We didn't have much funding then so I was teaching part-time there too. Remember?'

It came back to me. 'Yes, I do.' I began to feel sick as the story came alive once more for me, and I realized that there would be no stopping it now.

'What told against me,' Tom continued, 'is that that day I should have been teaching, but for the one and only time in my life I rang in sick to the school because there was an emergency at Tolling Bells. For the first time ever we thought we had the chance of major funding. So I wasn't at home, although officially I should have been. I was on my own in the office trying to work on this funding application. I was head down over it. No one saw me. With Jamie at nursery school, Laura had been planning to go out in the morning but to return at lunchtime for lessons in the afternoon. Our cleaner had been there until twelve and said I wasn't there, which was quite true.'

'But didn't that support your story?'

'It might have done, but unfortunately I did have to nip back a little later for a file I'd left at home, and the neighbour saw me. Laura came home early, and seeing me there taking French leave, as she thought, she flew into a paddy and told me rumours were going round that I was having an affair. I reciprocated, knowing the boot was on the other foot, and we had a good old set-to before I left to go back to the office. That was about one thirty, roughly an hour before the police thought she was killed, but no one saw me leave.'

'And were you having an affair?' My mouth seemed very dry.

'Of course I bloody wasn't.' He shot an impatient glance at me. 'You should know. She was accusing *you*.'

'Me?' I asked stupidly. My mind just couldn't take this in. *Laura* had been taking this stupid rumour seriously, and had thought I was having an affair with her husband? 'But we weren't lovers.'

'I do know that,' he said patiently. 'Not sure if Mark did.'

Could Mark have thought that too? This just wasn't making sense. It was crazy. So crazy that I felt calmer – Tom really was raving.

'This is getting us nowhere, Tom. Laura can't really have believed there was any truth in it, or she would have accused me to my face.'

Tom wasn't having this. 'If she didn't believe it, then she was saying it to cover up her own little secrets.'

I sighed. 'Proof, Tom, proof. If Mark really suspected us, why didn't he accuse me during all the mud-slinging we had over Anna?'

'Maybe he was afraid his own peccadilloes would be laid open to exposure. You'll remember more clearly than I did, but I thought you didn't know specifically about Anna until after Laura's death.'

I frowned. I just could not be sure. 'Possible, I suppose. But why didn't you warn me what Laura was thinking?'

'Because I didn't know until that day,' Tom said.

I couldn't take any more of this. If Laura had even half believed the rumours, she would have taken it up with one or both of us earlier. *If* she'd just made it up, she could, I had to admit, have been lashing out to hide secrets of her own. But Laura wasn't like that. I knew she wasn't. There was one more possibility: that Tom was lying, perhaps because he was indeed jealous of Laura's and my closeness. At least it seemed no one had been accusing Laura and me of having a sexual relationship. I supposed I should be grateful for that at least, but, whatever the true explanation, I had to make a stand. I knew Laura, and there was no way she could have behaved so normally if she'd been festering inwardly with all those suspicions.

'Evidence, Tom. Evidence, please. False memory is awfully easy to confuse with truth.'

'Not in this case. You don't forget something as stark as being accused by your wife of having an affair with her best friend.'

'I can't believe she really thought that, any more than I can believe that she had a string of lovers herself – or so you implied.'

He had the grace to apologize. 'I take that back. But one lover? Yes, I know she did.'

'How?' I hurled at him. 'Who? What proof?'

'I began to hear rumours and jokes about piano lessons.'

'Imagination,' I said dismissively. 'I'd have heard them too, and I didn't.'

'You were busy fighting with Mark, even if you hadn't winkled out Anna at that point. You were working all day too; you weren't moving in the same circles as Laura.'

'I'd have heard somehow. It's your imagination, Tom.' I tried to keep calm, but my obstinacy made him lose his temper.

'Is this imagination?' he yelled at me. Shaking with anger, he went over to a drawer in the desk, and brought over a bound book, which he flung on the coffee table in front of me. 'Laura's diary. Look at it.'

My heart did a painful skip. I knew about Laura and her diaries. We all did. It was a standard joke amongst her friends. She wasn't a fanatic over writing up the events of every day for posterity. There were no heart to heart confidences. But they were a record, she'd said seriously, of people she'd known – pupils, friends, relations – and the events in her life. She'd intended that by looking at them she could trace her life story step by step. I'd seen some of her childhood ones, and she was right. It was almost as if Laura knew her life would be short, and wanted to relive every single moment of her years. Keeping the diaries was an aide-memoire for her, not for the whole wide world. She didn't use codes, or anything fancy. They were just jottings, including appointments, past and future. The police must have pounced on them, I thought, so the case must indeed be closed if Tom had them back.

Tom sat beside me on the sofa so that he could turn the pages. 'This is the one for the year she died. May—'

'I know when she died,' I cut in. I was edgy and beginning to suspect I was being set up, although that was illogical. This was fact, and I could use my own judgement as to whether it was sufficient proof or not.

'Those circles,' he explained, pointing to ink rings round some dates, 'indicate the days I was teaching. I used to go over that with her. She needed to know because of who was to pick up Jamie.'

The inference was obvious, however. They would also be the days when Laura could have been sure of being alone in the house, for Tom sometimes worked from home for his charity work.

'Is that all?' I asked coldly.

'No. Look.' He turned to her May appointments. I could see that she often used initials. 'Her pupils. See? L.D. is Lily Dean on the nineteenth. M.H. is Mary Haines on the twenty-second. T. is—'

'Toby Martin,' I finished for him. 'Toby was such a regular and pet of Laura's that the T would suffice.' I remembered him well. He had been a tubby little boy who'd so desperately wanted to play the piano like Elton John.

Tom turned the pages to the twenty-fourth. 'He's booked in at three thirty. *After* J.S. at two thirty.'

'Well? Who's that?' I asked in a voice that didn't seem to be my own.

'Jack Scarlet. The afternoon Laura died. The *time* she died.'

I could hardly believe it. 'Are you accusing Jack just because of two initials in a diary and the fact that he was brought up nearby?'

'Of course not. But he appears in her address list of regular contacts at the end of the diary. Look.'

Hardly able to bear it, I did. And there I saw 'Jack Scarlet' with a London address. At first I thought that cleared him, but it was followed by his parents' Canterbury address.

'If that J.S. was her lover—' I managed a last ditch argument.

'There is no other J.S. in the book.'

I forced myself to continue, 'If he was her lover, then she would have put J. in the book, as with Toby, not J.S.'

Tom dismissed this instantly. 'He wasn't a small child like Toby. She needed to make him look like the adult pupil he was.'

'You're not eating,' Kate said crossly. 'That's my best risotto.'

'I'm sorry.' I took a mouthful and registered that it was indeed delicious, but my mind was elsewhere, trying to convince myself that this was more of Tom's craziness and that Laura and Jack were the people I knew and loved, not the two-faced schemers conjured up by Tom.

Another fleeting memory of the treasure hunt. Before or after Laura came to my help? There had been confusion over which colour threads we were given. I liked blue, but Laura had that one and it was her birthday. But she saw me looking at it, and put the blue thread into my hand. 'You have it, Emma. I'll have the red.' Time must have passed because I realized the thread had broken without my noticing. I began to panic but Laura found the loose end on the ground and brought it to me. 'Here it is, Emma.' It was Laura's gentle voice, wasn't it? I had a sudden doubt. It could have been Jane's. I wasn't sure now. Not sure of anything.

'I went to see Tom after I left Jane,' I told Kate.

'No wonder you're not eating. That man's trouble.' Kate had her grim face on.

'I felt sorry for him—'

'That's why he's trouble.'

Tom and Laura had often come to Roxpole House to see Kate with Mark and myself, and in my childhood we had all met regularly at my parents' summer barbecues. They lived in Church Lane, but oddly enough it is Kate's home that comes to mind when I think of Cobshaw now, not the house I was brought up in. I adore my parents and so does Kate, but I took them for granted, I suppose, and that's why Roxpole House sticks out so much in my mind.

'Tom told me his side of the story.' I spilled it all out, including the J.S. and the fact that Jack had spent his childhood years near Ducks Green. 'Did you know the Scarlets?'

'No,' Kate said promptly. 'Remember I didn't move here until you were nine or ten. Now,' she continued briskly, 'about that diary.'

I'd been hoping against hope that Kate might spot a flaw I'd missed in Tom's argument.

She did. 'Did the police interview Jack?'

'I've no idea.'

'So ask him. The police saw the diaries, I expect.'

'If he was here I would, but—'

'—in the meantime it's "he's my man, for better or worse".'

'I'm certain about the better, not sure about the worse,' I said miserably. 'Which is he: a lying Spartan or a truthful Cretan?' I seemed to be caught up in the classical conundrum where someone can assure you he's a truthful Cretan, but might therefore still be a lying Spartan. If push came to shove, I'd go with Jack being the truthful Cretan. Even if by some wild stretch of the imagination the J.S. in the diary did refer to my Jack that still didn't mean he murdered her. Tom could have written those two initials in himself to convince me. If Laura had been having an affair she would have told me, or at the very least she would have indicated unhappiness. And I couldn't believe she'd really thought Tom and I might be an item.

The half-healed wound inside me began to tear apart under the attack from the tenderest of sources. As soon as I could decently leave Kate to her coffee, I ran upstairs. I would ring Jack right now, I decided. I sat on the edge of the bed, fingers quivering, as I checked for messages. None. Usually Jack rang me when he was away, but so far there had been silence. No calls, no messages, no texts, nothing. I needed to hear his voice to restore normality.

I punched the number as desperately as though I was calling 999, and indeed in a way I was. This was my lifeline. The call was answered almost immediately, and hearing his familiar voice made me almost faint with pleasure. How could anything be wrong?

'Emma?' There was anxiety in Jack's voice. Could he have picked up my state of mind without my saying a word? Possibly. I've always believed we have a sixth sense that comes into play even over phone lines before a word has been spoken. 'Where are you?'

'Cobshaw.'

A pause, then a laugh. 'Left me for Tom, have you?'

'No. Where are *you*?' If he said Canterbury, all would be well. But if he said Paris . . .

'Where do you think? Living it up in a Parisian strip club?

Joke,' he added when I did not reply. 'I'll be back at the weekend. Anything I can help with? Are you still going to Tenterden on Saturday? Want company?'

'No, thanks. Kate's looking after me well.'

'I'll be getting back to my lap dancer then.' A click and the line went dead, leaving me sitting bleakly staring at Kate's carpet. I'd made a mistake. I'd used his mobile first, and you can't tell where people are on a mobile. If I'd called the Dulwich landline I'd have known. Too late now. And I hadn't dared to ask over the phone if he'd known Laura. I knew there was something wrong. The Jack I knew wouldn't have rung off so quickly.

'Emma?' A knock at the door, and Kate's worried face greeted me. 'There was a call from Paul Fritton for you. He asked me to tell you that if you want to talk about the murder, you can pop in to see him in Canterbury tomorrow. Eleven thirty would be a good time. He thought that meeting might be easier for you in an objective atmosphere than in Number Twelve.'

Paul looked just the same, although perhaps a little plumper, more contented, when I reached his office the next day at police HQ. Family life obviously suited him. 'Come in, Emma. Jane told me you'd been to see her yesterday.'

'It's good of you to suggest this, Paul,' I began, and then noticed he was looking surprised. 'Or was it Jane's suggestion?'

'I thought it was yours, Emma. That's what Kate said when she rang yesterday evening.'

I groaned. 'I'm sorry, Paul. Kate's been at her tricks again. You remember her?' Bless her, I thought. She could read me like a book and had deduced for herself what the next chapter needed to be. I only hoped she was right.

'Who could forget her?' he answered ruefully. 'In fact I've run into her a couple of times since –' a slight natural hesitation – 'we first met over the case. She's the Miss Marple of Cobshaw.'

'That's a pretty good description,' I agreed. 'See all, put all together, speak nothing until necessary. All the same, I'm still sorry she foisted me on you this way.'

'No problem. Jane told me why you'd come back to Ducks Green. Tom Burdock, I gather.'

'Yes,' I said. 'It's thrown me. He wants to clear his name.'

'Natural enough.'

'True, but I need to know whether he really *is* innocent.'

'Need? Why so suddenly, Emma?' Paul looked awkward. 'Jane was pretty upset the way you disappeared without leaving contact details.'

'I know, and I'm sorry. I hope she's forgiven me now.'

'She's the forgiving sort, as you know. But do stay in contact this time, would you? She needs old friends.'

'Not so much of the old,' I said, to lighten the tone, 'though I'm beginning to feel it. And, yes, I've every intention of keeping in touch. But to answer your question, the need is because Tom came to see me, as I expect Jane told you. He used to be a friend of mine; he declares his innocence but thinks my partner is involved.'

'Jack Scarlet?'

I was full of fear and leapt straight at this. 'Was he a suspect?'

Paul looked at me kindly, but the kindness was cloaked in police mode. 'Jane told me he's your partner. I hope you don't mind. As for his connection with the case, you understand I can't go into the details of that.'

'Yes,' I said desolately. 'You can't answer my question. But is there anything you can tell me about the case?' I decided I'd keep back the diaries for the moment. 'Tom told me about his being seen back at the house about lunchtime and that he and Laura had a row, but no one saw him leave.' I wouldn't tell him what Tom had claimed the subject of the clash was, either.

Paul considered this. 'Jane told you we were thinking over whether to open the case again. We are, because Tom Burdock asked us to. So it's fair to tell you that his car was seen in the pub car park, *not* where he usually parked it outside the house. He's right in saying that no one saw him leave.'

'Or anyone else arrive?' I could wait no longer.

'A child came for a lesson but couldn't get a reply, so he left.'

Toby Martin at three thirty, I thought. 'No one else?'

Another kind look. 'No comment. A step too far to answer.'

'Any comment on this lover Laura is supposed to have had? Neither Jane nor I believe it.'

'Sometimes friends see only what they want to see.' Paul was looking at me sympathetically. 'You'd be amazed how many don't have the ghost of an idea of what their friends get up to. I'm not saying this was true of Laura, but it's something to be borne in mind.'

'Would you personally want to reopen it?' I asked on impulse. I must have hit an unexpected nerve because the answer came very quickly.

'No.'

'Because you think you got the right man, but know you can't prove it?'

'No.' Paul hesitated. 'I sometimes get an instinct that it's best to let sleeping dogs lie. And this is one of those cases.'

'But if Tom is innocent . . .'

'He's not been charged with anything, and so he *is* innocent.'

'Except that there will always be a doubt if no one else is charged.'

'That's no reason to reopen a case. We need new evidence. I'm sorry if that sounds tough, Emma, but it's an area where the law can't reach. Look, I hope you'll come over to dinner before you leave. Jane really enjoyed seeing you again the other day, and the kids have been chatting about you too. You scored a hit with them. Tomorrow?'

Friday: the day before I would leave Ducks Green for Tenterden. 'Fine,' I said. 'Could I ask one last official question?'

'Fire ahead. I might not be able to answer, but try me.'

'Did you read Laura Burdock's diary as part of the evidence?'

'Sorry, Emma. Can't answer. Except –' perhaps he saw my look of desperation – 'it would be pretty odd if we hadn't.'

Five

Kate had been watching me for some time on that Thursday evening after my return from seeing Paul. I don't know why. I'd enjoyed her usual excellent dinner, and we'd chatted away merrily about the state of the modern theatre, about whether Dick Hursey, an old variety artist friend of hers, might be passing through 'town' (as she called Cobshaw), about whether Gielgud or Olivier could lay claim to the Best Actor of the Twentieth Century, and whether (perennial favourite, this) Irving and Ellen Terry were lovers.

'So are you going to Tenterden with Tom on Saturday or not?' she shot at me out of the blue. I'd explained my dilemma to her earlier.

The lemon meringue pie suddenly looked less appealing. '*I'm* still going.' In theory I could make my excuses to the Wests, but I would feel as if I were running away, and after Kate's accusation I wasn't going to risk that.

'Did you talk to Tom about it?'

'No.' I'd been so preoccupied with the diary that I had left that question unasked.

'Ring him.'

'But—' I stopped my instinctive protest. Kate was, as usual, cutting straight through the problem. As I saw it, if I went to see the Wests on Saturday with Tom I'd be seen to be endorsing his case. If I went separately – or not at all – the opposite impression would be made, given that the Wests were expecting me and might not be expecting Tom. As Tom was Jamie's father I could legitimately claim I was leaving the field open for him, but I knew that wouldn't wash with the Wests. So I did as Kate demanded, and telephoned him.

When Tom answered, I knew I'd done the right thing. It was time I stopped concentrating on my personal reaction to Tom, and to what Jane and Paul had told me, and thought of what Tom must be feeling. I put the question to him as tactfully as I could. After all, he might prefer to go to see the Wests alone – but this didn't prove to be the case.

'That's good of you, Emma. I'd like that.'

'Fine.' No sense worrying now over whether I should barge into his Jamie time or not. Tom and I discussed logistics for a few minutes: I would be driving straight home to Dulwich afterwards, so unless he had other ideas we'd have to take two cars. My stomach promptly did a rollover. Dulwich meant Jack. Was I going to tackle him about seeing him in Canterbury, or about Laura's diary? I'd play that by ear, I decided.

'Separate cars would be better anyway,' I pointed out. 'You might like to be alone there for a while.'

A silence so heavy followed that I wondered what was going through his head, but all he said was, 'Yes. Suppose we agree that I'll be in the Vine pub at twelve, having already been to the cemetery. And you can join me after you've been there.'

I rang off and went downstairs to join Kate again. 'All settled,' I said more brightly than I felt. Kate, I realized, had been a refuge, but now I was going to be out there faced once more with the cobwebby, scary mess of Tom versus Jack.

'Good. So what went wrong today?' Kate asked.

Were my feelings so transparent? Apparently yes, so why not tell Kate? She had met Jack once at least, so could understand my situation to some extent. 'I'm still hung up on that diary entry. Paul can't, or won't, tell me anything more except that a child turned up and couldn't get an answer. It must have been Toby Martin who was booked in for three thirty.'

Kate frowned. 'What does Jack say about it?'

'He doesn't know about the diary, only that Tom had told me about his being born locally.' I didn't mention my seeing Jack or his double in Canterbury. Why did I feel I needed to hold this back? Loyalty? Or was it that I needed to sort it out with Jack first?

'Are you going to tell him?'

'I don't know yet,' I said miserably. 'Oh Kate, I can't believe any of this. I can't believe Laura had lovers. I can't believe Tom is a murderer; I can't believe Jack is involved in any way at all. And yet one, at least, of these things is probably true.' Whichever way I looked, a great pit of disbelief opened up.

'Such choices usually depend on who's telling the story,' Kate said briskly. 'Shakespeare had a word for it.' She flung back her head and declaimed, 'If beauty have a soul, this is not she . . . this is, and is not, Cressid.' Then she reverted to being Kate again. 'Act five, scene two, *Troilus and Cressida*. Poor chap, Troilus couldn't believe his eyes that his girl had betrayed him. Myself, I always fancied playing Cassandra, just because of that marvellous stage direction: Enter Cassandra, raving.'

Surely Laura's beauty had a soul, and I had to trust it? Was Kate telling me to look beyond that even at this late stage? There was no point in pressing or even asking her. I doubt if Kate knew herself what she'd meant. She'd once informed me that truth usually emerges in snatches, not all at once in a great flash of revelation.

Perhaps she was right, but that's easier to judge from hindsight. The problem is: as one plods along a path, how can one know which is a snatch of the truth and which is a will o' the wisp leading one into the boggy marshes of misdirection? Ah, that is the question.

I'd come early to Number Twelve (I still instinctively thought of it as Lark Cottage) at Jane's request on the Friday evening, even though Paul wasn't expected home until eight. Billy and Alice had apparently clamoured to see me before they went to bed. A story was then mentioned, Jane warned me, and so I duly perched at the end of Alice's bed while I read both children *The Cat in the Hat* and followed up with – at Jane's special request – A.A. Milne's 'The King's Breakfast'. A traditionalist was Jane, judging by the children's bookshelf, and I think she got as much enjoyment out of listening as the kids did.

'Do you plan to have children, Emma?' she asked me outright, when we returned downstairs to wait for Paul.

'Plan? Too soon,' I replied lightly. 'Want? Yes. Jack likes children.' It tore at me to think of that, with the worm of suspicion still eating away inside me. And yet, what was that suspicion based on? A name in a diary and a mistake, probably of mine, over where he had been brought up. Not much to set against eighteen months of pure happiness.

'Good, so I hope –' she gave me an anxious look – 'that it works out.'

to my relief that there was no one else at the grave. Tom had been as good as his word. When I reached it, flowers were piled high – not just one bunch but several – including a posy, which I guessed was from Jamie. I'd told him two or three years earlier that Laura had loved forget-me-nots, and since then he had insisted, so the Wests told me last year, on putting his own posy on the grave. He was only three when Laura died and could hardly have vivid memories of her, nor had he yet reached the age when the loss of his mother would be expected to translate itself into such actions.

I wondered what the Wests had told him about her death, how they referred to Tom, and I shuddered at the possibilities. But Laura had an elder brother, who had children of his own, so Jamie's family life was not restricted to his grandparents, and the Wests themselves were reasonable people. They would think through the effects of their attitudes on Jamie. I liked them and had always done so – grateful, I suppose, for that treasure hunt at which I had been given the gift of Laura's friendship.

'And gift it was, Laura.' I laid my flowers on the grave. It had a simple, polished granite stone, with just 'Laura, beloved daughter of Anthony and Celia West, mother of Jamie' and the dates carved on it. No mention of Tom, nor even of Laura's married name. It was as though the name of Burdock had to be blotted out, although as far as I knew Jamie still bore Tom's name, not West. If Tom was innocent, however, that was an unnecessary blow. I realized I was increasingly beginning to feel he was innocent, although there was no logical reason for me to believe it now, any more than there had been at the time. But where that led me was a step too far to contemplate.

Tom was waiting for me in the Vine as promised. He wasn't looking in my direction as I entered, and when he did notice, a smile lit up his face with a comfortable familiarity. 'Let me get you a drink.' He was already halfway to the bar.

'Thanks. I'll have a half of shandy.' I felt like dulling the sharper edges of the turmoil inside me with alcohol, albeit weak.

'I'm glad you're here, Emma,' he said as he returned to the table, drinks in hand. 'It makes it a lot easier.'

'Perhaps harder,' I pointed out. 'It depends on how the Wests react.'

'They can react any way they please. I told them we were coming together. We've nothing to hide.'

I was uneasy about it though. Quite apart from the question of my being seen to be on Tom's side over Jamie, there was also a risk that to the outsider our camaraderie might be mistaken for something warmer and deeper. Friendship turning to love is a well-worn theme in romances, and the Wests did not know about my private life with Jack. So far as I was concerned, what I felt for Jack was no contest with my feelings for Tom. It wasn't a matter of degree, but of quality. The sharp edge of love itself has disadvantages. It is more vulnerable than platonic love, more open to fear of loss, of hurt, of rejection and even of misconception. Not in the case of mine for Jack though. I'd got over the worst of that, I told myself. When I reached Dulwich this evening Jack would be there, sweeping me into his arms with a kiss full of promise. Even at the thought of it, my body began to tingle.

'Is going together the best plan?' I asked Tom after we had ordered lunch. It was still worrying me that it was making a statement I didn't want to put my name to. 'You'll need to talk to them alone, and be alone with Jamie. Perhaps we should compromise. I can talk with Jamie while you're having your heart to heart with the Wests. Then I'll get going on my journey home while you take Jamie out.'

He agreed, and the lunch was enjoyable, even though we were both tense for our separate reasons and it was a relief when it was time to leave. 'Forward the Buffs,' I said, with a light-heartedness I was far from feeling.

'More like the Buffeted.' Tom grimaced. Nevertheless, he had talked a lot about Jamie over lunch and must have been excited at the thought of meeting him again.

The Wests lived some way along the Appledore Road, too far to walk, and so we took both cars. It was a large house, much like their old Ducks Green home, Appley House, although it was a great deal newer. This one, too, was red-brick, solid and attractive to look at, and had the same shady trees in its front garden. Each time I went there I had a jolt of false recognition, as though I could walk round the side of the house into a spacious rear garden, down the path and into the orchard, where once again a treasure hunt would be in progress.

The door was opened by Anthony West. He was looking apprehensive, and his usual hearty welcome (although genuine or false, I could never tell) was missing, even though he tried his best. 'Emma, good to see you.' Then he forced himself to nod briefly to Tom. 'Didn't recognize you under the beard, Tom. Come in, both of you.'

I had expected he would lead us through into the conservatory or garden as the day was dry and warm. Instead he took us into his study. Time for serious words, I thought with sinking heart. I was right.

'In view of what you said on the phone, Tom, we thought we should have our solicitor present. Hope you don't mind.'

Tom obviously did, but I thought he dealt with it well. 'Of course not. I can understand why you feel it's necessary, but I hope it won't be at this stage. All I want to do is talk it through reasonably with you, and to see what Jamie thinks of the idea.'

'That might be difficult,' came the quick reply. 'He's still a child, remember, with childish ideas about long-lost fathers. We don't know if you're in a position to bring him up alone, or even if you plan to stay in this country.' Anthony was getting too far ahead of himself. He must have recognized that because he switched tack. 'Hope you don't mind my asking, Emma, but does your arrival together mean you're personally concerned in Tom's ideas for Jamie?'

Just as I had feared. 'No,' I said firmly. 'I'm here with Tom because we both loved Laura and I was staying in Cobshaw, that's all.'

Anthony still looked uneasy and I had a sudden fear that Laura had indeed thought Tom and I were having an affair and had passed her doubts on to her parents. Surely they could not have behaved so normally to me, both before and since Laura's murder, if they thought I had betrayed her?

Tom was more annoyed than upset. 'No, we're not a couple,' he said shortly. 'Emma's living in London with her partner. I live alone, but that doesn't stop me being able to offer Jamie a home if it's in his interests. I'm in a rented flat at the moment, but I'm planning to buy a house in Kent – just where, I'll decide when we have talked about Jamie's future.'

Anthony relaxed a little. 'You'd better come through, and we'll get it over with. We don't want to stop you seeing Jamie while you're here, so we'll make it as quick as possible. Emma –' he turned to me – 'you'll find Celia and Jamie in the garden.'

Feeling like a schoolgirl again, being ordered around by Laura's parents, I hurried through the conservatory into the garden. I could see Celia weeding in one of the borders, and Jamie was kicking a football around. On seeing me he came up to greet me – rather reluctantly. After all, I thought, he only saw me once a year, which was hardly going to build up much rapport.

'You've grown taller,' I said fatuously.

'Everyone says that,' he muttered scornfully, with the bravado of a ten-year-old. Celia came up to welcome me and to prompt us all into temporary communication. Jamie gradually relaxed, chatting about school football teams.

Celia must be in her late fifties by now, I realized, and was growing older as gracefully as I would have expected of her. Her hair was much greyer than I remembered it, but there were fair lights in it, which gave it a fashionable edge. I had wondered what her reaction would be to seeing me this year in view of Tom's intentions, but I need not have worried. She had always greeted me warmly, which suggested that she and Anthony had not heard any ill of me from Laura. I could put that fear at least to one side.

'Are you still working, Celia?' I asked. She and Anthony had a joint partnership in Tenterden.

'Of course. We can't afford to buy each other out,' she joked. 'The conveyancing market is down, but other sides are compensating . . .' All the while we were talking, I was conscious of Jamie, who had resorted to his football in preference to adults' talk. As always, I was struck by his eyes, so much like Laura's. Celia must have noticed my looking at him.

'He grows more like her every day,' she observed.

'Is that harder for you or easier?' I asked.

'Easier, I think. Much. It reminds me that something of her is still with us. And you, Emma? You're with Tom—?'

I stamped the hesitation out immediately. 'Not romantically. Here, just because I always come, and I knew he was coming too.'

Celia was obviously relieved. 'It was a great shock to know

he's back in England for good now. You can imagine how we're feeling.'

'I can. And I'm so sorry, but Tom's a reasonable man.' Our eyes met, and I realized that the Wests still believed him their daughter's murderer. And I? What did I feel, torn between the comparative easiness of being with Tom now and the image I, too, had nurtured for seven years? Answer: I couldn't reconcile the two. My only hope lay in moving forward towards the truth − and there lay an even greater black hole of uncertainty.

Celia grimaced. 'As a solicitor, I of all people ought to know about innocence and guilt, the law and justice. But when it's your own daughter . . .'

'I can understand that. I felt the same as you. But now he's back I'm beginning to wonder. It's not that he protests his innocence, but that he's determined to clear his name.'

'By fixing the guilt on someone else,' Celia said wryly.

Like Jack, I instantly thought.

'I know the facts,' Celia continued, 'but we've heard from the police that they won't reopen the case. We translate that as meaning they still think Tom killed Laura, but that there's no new evidence to prove it. So how could we let Jamie go to him without a fight? Legally, he is innocent, but that doesn't make us feel we want to surrender Jamie to him.'

I plucked up my courage. 'He still seems set on the idea that Laura had a lover. I can't believe it though. Did anything ever suggest that to you? Or −' I might as well go one step further − 'that Laura thought that Tom and I were having an affair? He said she threw that accusation at him on the day she was killed. Did she suspect that . . . I'm sorry, but it's tormenting me. It was absolutely not true, if so.'

Celia looked horrified, leaned forward and took my hands in hers. 'Dear Emma. I think suspected is too strong. Laura told me there was a rumour going round to that effect, but that she didn't believe it. Nor did we. She thought it was Mark making mischief, and that seemed quite possible to us.'

Mark? My antennae were immediately raised. 'But it's still in your minds, and so when I came with Tom today you assumed—'

'I'm afraid so.'

'I can understand that, but there's someone else in my life now. The first since Mark and I were divorced.'

'I'm so glad.' Celia paused. 'Do you remember that treasure hunt we had for Laura's birthday once?'

My heart did a sudden skip, but whether with pleasure or apprehension I could not tell. 'I've never forgotten it. I met Laura there.'

'I know. Do you know what she said afterwards?'

'No. I don't think we ever talked of it.'

'She was a little scared of something, probably because she couldn't see what was happening. She knew Daddy was giving everyone a prize, but that he had an extra special prize for the one who got to the end first. She had to hang back because Anthony quite rightly said she shouldn't win the special prize because it was her birthday. So everyone was hurrying and rushing past her – except for you, who stopped for her.'

'*Me?*' I was shaken. 'No, it was the other way round. She helped me.'

'Not the way she told it. Something frightened her, and you helped. I remember that clearly because I was chatting to Liz Scarlet—'

'*Who?*' Dear heaven, what was this coming?

Celia looked surprised. 'One of the other parents. The Scarlets lived in Lilleybourne. There was a son—'

'Jack,' I said through stiff lips. 'His name is Jack.'

Six

The drive home was a nightmare. I wasn't even sure that it was *home* any more. Home is a refuge from the world, a place where one can draw breath and be certain that 'this, at least, is mine'. Granted, the house was legally Jack's, but houses and homes are two different concepts. If you're lucky they're the same place; if you're not, then the ground is cut away beneath your feet. And here I was driving towards a place I was no longer sure was home to meet a man I was no longer sure I knew. There were so many questions to be answered that to say my emotions were mixed would be an understatement. I felt they'd been put in a food processor and ground into a smoothie that I didn't fancy drinking.

I conceded that I could have been mistaken over what Jack had originally told me about his childhood when we first met – easily done, since it hardly seems an important factor when one is beginning a relationship. But there's no way I could have been mistaken over whether he had ever mentioned Laura or not. It was I who had brought her name up, her whole story tumbling out a month or two after I had first met Jack. But *was* that the first time we'd met? If his parents were friends of the Wests, I could easily have bumped into a much younger Jack. And yet surely I would have remembered the name? I had talked a lot about my childhood and youth during our partnership, so logically he should at least have remarked that he had lived not far away. But he had not done so. Not even when I had spoken of Laura's murder. He had listened, he had made pertinent comments, he had comforted and he had, or so I had thought, understood. Since then the subject had only cropped up once, not long after I first moved in, when I had told him awkwardly that I was taking a day off work to go to Tenterden in west Kent – and why. Again, he'd made no mention that he had even heard of Celia and Anthony West, although if his parents were their friends he would not only have heard of them, but also have told his parents about my connection with the past.

And, of course, there was something worse. If his mother had been at that treasure hunt, then it followed that Jack had been there too. And yet, amongst that mob of children – perhaps fifteen or more of us – did I remember a young Jack? I did not. When one tries to force such memories to return, danger lurks. Up might come an image of something that is of today's making, or that never happened at all. So I tried to force nothing; as gently as possible I raked through my images to see if anything represented a ten-year-old boy who resembled the Jack Scarlet I now knew.

Logic pointed out that if Jack's life had impinged on Laura's to any great extent she would have mentioned it. I remembered a couple of casual boyfriends she had had before she settled down with Tom. Neither of them was Jack, I was sure of that. Jane would have remembered too, and yet she had treated Tom's accusation as rubbish, put it down to jealousy. Or – horrible thought – had she been keeping something from me? Had she been scared to tell me because I had talked so much of being happy with Jack?

When I drew up outside Number Fourteen Edwards Lane, I could see the house was in darkness. Jack had gone by train to Paris (or so he had informed me) and clearly was not yet home. Usually, the disappointment would have dampened me quicker than a candle-snuffer. There's a joy about coming home to a house where the lights are burning, but a house in darkness feeds depression. It requires effort to enter it and reclaim it as one's own. Where Jack was concerned the difference between the two was usually multiplied tenfold, but not on this occasion. The silence and the darkness were almost a relief, and the routine of switching on lights, hot water and even central heating, since the day was not warm, helped me to calm down. When Jack did return I would be the one in control, in temporary ownership of 'home'.

I tried to examine my feelings logically as I made myself a mug of tea. Wonderful, strong, comforting tea. What exactly did I think Jack was guilty of? Just keeping me in the dark about Laura? There seemed no doubt of that. But what of the grey area that lay beyond? *Why* had he done so? Surely if he knew the

Wests, he must to some extent have shared their grief at Laura's loss. His address was in her diary, his initials there at the very time that she died, implying that he had been taking piano lessons; was that a cover as Tom had claimed, or could there be another J.S.? When Paul had investigated those initials, as he must have done, he would have followed Jack's movements up, and so that must be why Paul hadn't wanted to tell me any more of the story. But the corollary of that was that if he knew Jack was innocent, Paul *could* have told me so.

And then Jack arrived home. All six foot of him. In the flesh. The *real* Jack Scarlet, not the semi-monster haunting my suspicions. Doubts fled as he hugged me, then crept back, and I felt myself becoming tense again.

'Sorry, train was late,' he explained as he freed me and went to pour himself a drink.

'Train from where?' I called out before I could stop myself. I'd intended to leave awkward questions until later.

His head popped round the corner of the living room door, and he looked surprised. 'Train home,' he said, not very helpfully.

'From Canterbury?' It was out before I could stop it.

There was silence from the living room. It went on so long I hoped he hadn't heard me, but he had. I went to join him. He appeared to be busy fishing out the daily newspaper, and glanced up at me. 'That sounded loaded, Emma.'

'I saw you there.'

Heavy sigh. 'Ah.'

At least he wasn't denying it. 'Let's talk, Jack. Like now.'

'Tomorrow?'

'No. Now.'

'Not a good time for heart to hearts.'

'Now.'

'Before supper?'

'There is no supper – yet.' I caught a glimpse of his face, and had to bite back a laugh that bubbled up from nowhere. Stupid, stupid, but Jack had that way of catching me off balance.

He saw that too. 'That's better.'

I reclaimed the high ground. 'Not much.'

'You win,' he said agreeably. 'What does your heart want to tell my heart?'

I wasn't having that. 'It's the other way round, Jack, and you know it.'

'I don't.'

'Stop fencing.' I sounded angry, and I was, although with every word the urgency seemed to recede. Was his crime so very bad? There must be some innocent explanation, so there was no need to attack him so vehemently.

'I'm unarmed.'

'You're always armed, Jack.'

He went very still. 'I have to be, Emma. I wouldn't be able to do my job if I wasn't. You must have realized that.' He sounded really hurt, but I steeled myself from penitence until I knew where I was.

'Yes. On matters of work. So were you in Canterbury on a job?'

'Very temporarily. The job's actually elsewhere.'

Reasonable. I knew he couldn't talk about his work – many people can't for one reason or another, but in Jack's case, where crime was often involved, he had to keep his mouth very firmly shut if he was to retain his role of roving economic analyst. He was called in on cases where the figures didn't add up, or were suspected of not doing so.

But Jack was a long way from off the hook yet. 'Why didn't you tell me your parents were friends of Anthony and Celia West?' I asked. 'They were Laura's parents.'

He hesitated a fraction too long. 'I knew the name but not whether they were close friends or not. How well do you know your parents' acquaintances?'

Good point, but this was different. 'You must have known Laura too.'

'*Must* have? Where's this going, Emma?' He sounded quite amiable, but I could tell I should choose my words carefully now. Especially as that's what he was doing.

'I need to know the reason you didn't tell me.'

This time the answer was prompt. 'Are you going to believe me if I do?'

'I hope so.' It came out as a miserable squeak, and I was furious with myself for letting my feelings overwhelm me.

'Look.' Jack sat down beside me on the sofa, and put his arm round me to cheer me up. 'This is the case for the defence. You told me about Laura and her death about a month after we first met. Right?'

'Yes. You'd got tickets for *Othello*.' I put on a brave face. It was hard, since the instant image of Othello strangling Desdemona all too easily translated itself into a picture of Laura's body lying dead on the floor by her beloved piano.

'The story of you, Laura and her death came pouring out as though you'd never told it before to anyone. Do you agree?'

'Yes. I'd been trying to put it behind me, and hadn't intended to tell you – until it happened.'

'That's what I thought. Your words were tumbling over one another. You weren't speaking to me: you were speaking to yourself, as though you were determined to clear it out of your mind now that it had risen up again. You needed help.'

'I wouldn't put it quite that way.' But Jack was right. I saw that now. I *had* been speaking to myself. All the pent-up anger and grief that I'd been consciously suppressing for years after I left Ducks Green had spilled out. I hadn't been able to talk to Mark about it properly because we were hardly on speaking terms that final year. He moved out a few months after Laura's death and I had been on my own. No, I corrected myself, there had been Jane and there had been Kate and there had been my parents. I could speak to them all and receive tea, sympathy and advice, but that wasn't what I needed then. I needed to tell someone *everything* and with someone involved even on the periphery, like my parents, that wasn't possible. My parents were so fiercely protective of me that they would say what I wanted to hear. The more time passed the more I had repressed the story – until I'd met Jack, and could speak freely to someone who wasn't involved at the time, but who was 'on my side'.

'All right, I agree,' I said to him awkwardly. 'I needed help.'

'So, what would have been the point of my putting in useless words such as, "I know her parents. I knew about it"? I couldn't add anything, so I thought it was better to let you get it all off that lovely chest of yours so you could leave it behind you. Otherwise you would go on thinking we were sharing the same experience, and that you could go on talking about Laura, supposing this, supposing that. I was in the same position when you announced that you were going down to see the Wests for last year's anniversary. I decided to gamble that my name wouldn't crop up, and if it did I'd explain afterwards. Reasonable?'

Damn him. He was right. 'But today they did mention your name,' I told him. 'You were at the party where I first met Laura. Appley House on the Cobshaw Road. There was a game in the orchard – you'd have been about ten.'

He looked taken aback. 'I don't remember that.'

'It doesn't matter.' I could cope with that. What I couldn't cope with was that diary, and it took all the courage I had to raise the subject. But I had to or it would be niggling away inside me. So, being me, I raised it.

'Tom Burdock showed me Laura's diary. Your name and address were at the back.'

I couldn't read Jack's expression, but I felt his arm stiffen around me. 'Anything else you'd like to mention?'

'Your initials were in the diary for two thirty on the afternoon she died.'

I couldn't look at him. It was out; it was done, for better or for worse. His arm was withdrawn, and he sat hunched up, not looking at me. 'Not guilty, my lord,' he said with obvious effort.

'So you must have known Laura.'

'Must I?' He looked at me with an odd expression on his face. 'If you say so. Very well, I knew her slightly. Why didn't I tell you? Same reason as I gave just now. We'd have spent our love life discussing Laura and how wonderful she was.'

'She *was* wonderful.'

'Of course. Everyone says so, and in fact I think I believe it. But that doesn't mean I want to live with her ghost.'

That was a blow in the face. 'That's unfair,' I said angrily. 'It's only since Tom came back—'

'Ah. The man who came back,' Jack said mock-sadly. 'Tell me, Emma, do you love me?'

'You know I do.'

'I don't. If I rolled out the old romantic cliché "do you trust me?" you'd have to say no, wouldn't you?'

'No – yes – I don't know.' So much for discipline. With Jack looking at me with such apparent detachment and the atmosphere so charged between us, heaven help me but whether I trusted him or not, I loved him. Or was it I was so caught up with desire that it was blinding me?

He was watching me with what I interpreted as amusement. 'So, what are you planning to do about this situation, Emma? Stay on here, despite the fact you seem to be considering me in the role of Laura's murderer? Or would you prefer to leave me to wallow in my guilt?'

'Do you want me to leave?' I was sick with horror at the way this was racing ahead.

'I want to live with the Emma I love, not with this one.'

'So do I,' I said stupidly, and he laughed. *Laughed?* How could he? 'I mean the Jack I . . .' Then, as he still watched me, I knew without doubt what I had to do. 'I'll go back to Ducks Green,' I said dully. 'As soon as I've finished my last two weeks at work.'

'To enquire into my past?' Jack was furious now, and his eyes glittered in a way I'd never seen before. 'Is the idea to ensure I'm well and truly guilty before you guillotine our relationship for good and all?'

'No,' I shouted. '*Not* that. I'm going to find out what happened to Laura. I'm going to find out whether she really did have a lover—'

'And in the process you'll no doubt be trying to eliminate me.' A pause. 'I mean, of course, from your enquiries, not from this earth.'

'You're being ridiculous,' I said. He was, he *was*. 'I need to know whether Tom was lying when he said Laura was having an affair. She—'

'I don't want to know,' he cut in wearily. 'It's you I care about, not Laura.'

I tried to explain. 'Then you *do* need to understand how I feel about her. If she wasn't the person I remember, if she had another life, I have to deal with it.' Then I told Jack about the rumours that had been flying around: that Laura had been told Tom and I were lovers, that Tom was jealous of Laura's relationship with me and even my own nightmare that Tom might have thought us lesbian lovers. Fortunately, he laughed at that one.

'So you see,' I concluded, 'there's unfinished business, to say the least, and you seem to be part of it.'

It was impossible to tell what he was thinking. With Jack it often was, but never had it been more important for me to know.

'Very well,' he said at last. 'I'll set your mind at rest. I had an alibi for the day of her murder. It's true I was in Kent, but I was helping my parents with their move to France.'

'Did the police ask you for an alibi?'

He looked astounded. 'Good grief, no. Why should they have? Ah, I see, the initials in the diary. Of course. Not me.' A pause. 'Where will you stay? At Kate's again?'

I hadn't got that far, so I snatched at the obvious. I wanted to be at the heart of the case, to seize it with both hands. 'Probably at Jane and Paul's. He was the inspector on the case, and Jane was a good friend to both Laura and me. It makes sense to stay there, if I can. Also, they're living in Lark Cottage, where Tom and Laura used to live.'

'Right.' Jack was brisk again, now that it was settled. 'Shall we have something to eat? I told you we should have waited till afterwards for all these questions.'

That night we lay apart. We kissed goodnight, but that was all. There was a division between us as marked as the sword they used to put in a bed after a proxy marriage.

In the morning I was listless and heavy-eyed as though I had a hangover from alcohol, rather than from an overdose of emotion. Jack, however, was leaping around as though nothing had happened at all. There were things to do, he said, on a Bank Holiday Sunday. Walks in Dulwich Park, tennis to play and he'd like to nip in to see the latest exhibition in the Picture Gallery. 'Interested?' he asked. 'We could eat at the cafe there.'

'Good idea.' I forced myself into jollity. When Tuesday came and work loomed it would be easier, but jollity right now would be tough, I thought. In fact, after breakfast had been dealt with, it was easier than I had feared. Perhaps I'd been overreacting; Jack was right. We should have left the 'discussion' until the cool light of day. Here, on a bright Sunday afternoon, life resumed a normality that it had lacked last night. Children played, parents strolled, lovers embraced. I took Jack's hand tentatively in mine and our fingers intertwined reassuringly, as though to convince both of us that we would come through this glitch. For a moment I wished I'd just shut my eyes and mind to Laura's story, but the feeling soon passed. I couldn't leave it here. It had gone too far for both of us, and the only solution lay in Kent.

It was Jack who raised the subject first. 'Are you still going to Ducks Green?'

'Yes.' I longed to add something such as, 'But don't worry. I love you, I trust you,' but somehow I couldn't. Not because they might not be true, but because I might not get the words out with the commitment Jack seemed to be demanding.

'In that case, it's not such a bright idea to stay with Jane and Paul. Why don't you distance yourself mentally by giving yourself your own turf?'

He had a point. 'Stay with Kate, you mean?'

'Not even that. You might need *real* space. Somewhere you can cater for yourself, maybe, and not in Ducks Green. Cobshaw would be all right.'

'I can try. Kate would be upset—'

'*I'm* upset, but I can still see your point of view. So will she.'

I had an inspiration. 'Kate's got that self-catering cottage she lets out occasionally. Don't you remember? She was talking about it when we had that dinner on the South Bank with her. Her mother lived there for a time.' As with the wood itself, Laura and I had misunderstood its name, Wychley Cottage, and thought of it as the Witch's Cottage. From what I had glimpsed of it last week, however, all witches seemed to have vanished.

Jack brightened up immediately. 'Sounds good, if it would work. You'd have company if you needed it, and someone else there just in case.'

'In case of what?'

'Darling Emma, don't forget there's a murderer around. True, it might be me, if you're still thinking along that line, but just in case you've got that wrong, be careful.'

Be careful – but of what, of whom? It could be a cliché like 'take care', but Jack seldom used clichés. If he said it, he meant it. In any case, how could one 'take care'? Look both ways three times before one crosses the road? Never leave a key in the door? Never leave a ground-floor window open? Simple enough rules to obey, but an unpinpointed anxiety for someone merely creates fear in them, rather than helping to solve the cause of it. And Jack would know that more than anyone, so he must have said it with due thought behind it. He could even have meant 'be careful what you pry into regarding me'. If he had known the Wests, including Laura, there could still be some connection I did not know about. After what he'd said about Laura's ghost, however, I didn't want to go there. Not now.

I telephoned Kate about Wychley Cottage, and it was amazingly easy to fix. 'Of course,' she agreed. 'I'll just air it out and make sure you've got loo paper, then you'll be tickety-boo.'

It occurred to me that with her advancing years cooking dinner every night for an unspecified period, even with my help, would not have been an enjoyable prospect, irrespective of our friendship. Kate, too, needed her space.

Jane had been far more difficult to handle, both delighted that I was returning, but disappointed that I wasn't going to be staying with her. I pleaded that I was intending to stay some weeks. 'Where else better to spend a summer?' I added lightly. I also told her that Jack might be joining me – a white lie, but it gave weight to my argument. From the sound of her voice she was slightly miffed, but she agreed it was sensible. Provided, of course, that I came over to see her often. We could have great trips out. I would, I assured her, and added that I expected to see them all at the cottage. We could all go to the seaside one day. That pleased her. A picnic, she said jubilantly, and I remembered she was a dab hand at them. Nothing pleased her more than to take a picnic into the woods – sometimes just her and me, sometimes Laura too, and in later years Tom and Mark had gone as well, not to mention Jamie.

Then for two and a half weeks I concentrated on work: wrapping up outstanding matters, saying goodbye to colleagues (very few of whom were migrating to Bristol with the magazine) and parting without too much sorrow from my employers. For the moment I could plan no further than the Kent visit, but when I returned – and when would that be? – I would have to think about another job. A small ache in my heart reminded me that not so long ago I had been dreaming wistfully of nappies, perambulators and the patter of tiny feet – but that depended on Jack, and so the dream had taken a step backwards and maybe vanished forever. Optimistic as usual, I consoled myself that something would turn up, but then I was forced to remind myself that unless one did a bit of the turning oneself, one was unlikely to reach a satisfactory conclusion.

When Jack was around, which wasn't often now, he seemed on a plane I could not reach; he was friendly enough, even loving, but I was aware that the X factor had disappeared. I hadn't the strength to cope with wondering whether this was purely my imagination, whether it was stemming from me, rather than Jack, or whether it had really vanished for good. Had I blown it? But then he was the one who had held back on me, and, I had to remind myself, still could be.

Now May had passed into June, Kent was looking its prettiest, flaunting its summer greenery at its best. Long stretches of motorway and A-roads reminded me that Kent was now divided by heavy transport lines and railways from the coast to London, but on either side of them still lay riches beyond compare. In my Ducks Green days I had taken them for granted, assuming they would never vanish, but returning now into a glorious summer of roses, cottage gardens and mellow red-brick cottages nestling into the landscape made me see Kent with a fresh eye. Three weeks earlier I had been preoccupied; now I was sure of where I was going on a glorious Friday afternoon.

I turned off the main road into the lanes I knew so well; they looked just the same as I had always known them. No wider, thank heavens, and the hedges overlapped them protectively as if to hide them from strangers. The hedgerows were rich with wild flowers, the hawthorn was flowering, and herb Robert and red campion dotted the greenery on both sides of the lanes with pink. As I drove along the ridge of the downs, I could almost smell Ducks Green in my nostrils, and the car seemed to pick up my eagerness. That was a strange word in the circumstances but it was true. I *was* eager. Eager to meet my battle head-on, to solve the puzzle for Jack's and my sake, and eager to see Tom again, convinced that I could sort the problem out to clear his name.

Kate had told me she would be out when I arrived, but she would leave the key amongst the gillyflowers. This was a test, of course, to see if I had become so townified that I'd forgotten what gillyflowers were. I had, actually, and I'd had to look them up after our conversation had ended. I'd thought they were wallflowers but the dictionary informed me sternly that gillyflower was a name for several fragrant flowers, of which wallflowers and stocks were only two.

I scrabbled for the key amidst decaying wallflowers in the rear garden. It was no great problem to find it, as a large, cardboard plaque with Kate's handwriting on it was propped up, reading: *key hidden here.* I laughed. Kate is good at jokes, and no one other than me was going to find their way down this path.

I continued to the gate at the far end of her garden. Kate was as good a gardener as she was cook, which was surprising given her upbringing in a seaside lodging house. Wychley Cottage faced the garden across an unmade-up track called Love Lane, which rambled for about half a mile around from Cobshaw High Street. Only the first hundred yards were tarmacked, Kate had warned me, and so, none too certain of where I could park, I'd left my car temporarily outside Kate's house. The seventeenth-century cottage lay in a little garden of its own, entered through a wicket gate. It was a surprising dwelling to find behind a nineteenth-century house, as if the centuries had marched on, leaving it forgotten in the woods.

And so I entered the witch's cottage once more. Kate's mother Eileen had once seen Laura and me peering cautiously at it from behind some bushes. Although we must have been nine or ten at the time, we had frightened ourselves silly with fearful witch stories and half believed her to be one. Eileen had explained there were good witches and bad witches, and fortunately she was the good kind. After that, I took Eileen in my stride, especially as she was a dab hand with home-made cakes and buns.

I could hear bees in the flowers, and the sun was warm. I felt like that child again as I let myself into the Marzipan House, as Laura once called it after we had got over the witch connection. I've no idea where that name came from, but I happily accepted it. There was no smell of baking buns in the oven, but on the table there was a cake provided by Kate. I'd said I would cook for her this evening, and full of enthusiasm I unpacked my clothes and possessions, then reacquainted myself with the cottage.

It was compact with two bedrooms, bathroom, kitchen and a

tiny parlour and even tinier dining room. By the time I had unpacked and arranged the few books I'd brought with me, I felt I was claiming ownership nicely. I need not have worried about bringing books. I'd forgotten that Kate's and her mother's collection would keep me going nicely for the next twenty years or so. It seemed everybody who had ever stayed with Eileen in her seaside lodging house must have written an autobiography, judging by the number of signed copies I picked out of the shelves. It was a testament to a life largely vanished, but it remained in this small cottage. A few posters on the walls and, to my delight, an old Punch and Judy booth on the landing. I wondered how on earth that had got there and why.

'That's the way to do it,' I squeaked out. As a child, I hadn't been too sure about Punch and Judy, but now I could appreciate it. A tale of murder, for children. Odd, really. Unlike me, Laura had loved it. *Go on, go on*, she would say, watching Punch whack his wife. Then, with equal glee, she would applaud the policeman giving Punch his comeuppance, together with Jack Ketch dispatching him from this world. That brought me down to earth with a thud, and I was back with Laura. Had she really thought at the treasure hunt that I had been kind to her, rather than the other way around? And what was it that had frightened her? Did I really know the true Laura? With childhood friends one doesn't ask questions: it's like falling in love – one doesn't ask the questions first, one just does it. So does a child with friends. Once accepted as a friend, no questions need to be raised: a friend is just that. As Laura and Jane were to me.

And, in due course, Tom.

'Remember me?' he'd said, leaping down from the gate he'd been perching on. He was clearly waiting for Laura – or perhaps I was wrong about that. Both Laura and I did remember him. When we went to secondary school, he was in another class, but we must have met him early on. I suppose I must have known him by sight before that because he lived in Cobshaw, but I couldn't recall him playing any part in our lives before secondary school. We would have been eleven or twelve or so when we saw him in the woods that day, and despite the fact he was obviously waiting for us, he seemed quite shy.

Laura picked up on this immediately. 'We're going to the

cinema,' she said. There was a small one in Cobshaw. 'Come along if you like.'

Tom had shrugged, but the rest of his body language, even to unsophisticated twelve-year-olds, suggested he was only too keen. Somehow he had then become part of our gang – at least during the summer months, when we would roam round Canterbury and our two villages, and later further afield on joint trips out. There were school dances too, and games. Both Tom and I had an interest in drama and joined the dramatic club. Laura wasn't interested, but valiantly helped with lighting and props.

Surely it had always been Laura whom Tom liked, not me. I thought back but nothing suggested otherwise. I used to tease her: 'What's he kiss like? Go on, Laura, you fancy him rotten, don't you?' Big talk. I was still a virgin then, and remained so until I met Mark at university. And what about Laura? Had Tom been her first choice? I was sure he had been. It was true I had once accepted a date from Tom in my last year at school. It was also true that the reason I did so was that I'd just been dumped by someone else and only my bruised feelings had caused me to accept. It could well have been the same for Tom. Fortunately I got chicken pox, so far as I recalled, and Laura had stepped in.

Stop, I told myself. There's no proof he was ever interested in me. But what, I thought uneasily, was happening now? There was no sex in the air that I could sense, and yet something was surely around. As Kate's mum would have said, I could feel it in my bones.

Seven

My bones weren't calling out quite so loudly the next morning. I'd had a good evening with Kate, and to my relief there had not been a mention of our mutual 'old days'. With Kate the present and future days were far more important. Did this sit comfortably with her love of theatre, old and new? Oh yes. She treated each book and item of memorabilia as old friends whom she could pop round the corner to visit whenever she liked. As I grew up, I was so used to hearing her talk of David (Garrick), Edmund (Kean), and Henry and Ellen (Irving and Terry respectively) that I really thought they were living in Cobshaw. So they are, in Kate's mind.

After subduing a craven impulse to go to a Canterbury supermarket, I decided to drive into Ducks Green again so that I could pick up some more provisions. Jane had told me the butcher was still in business – chiefly, I suspect, because the one in Cobshaw had closed down. By going to Ducks Green I could fulfil a promise I'd made to Jane on the phone to 'come and see her immediately', and I could make a date for her and Paul to come over to Wychley cottage. They could bring Billy and Alice – so perhaps lunch would be better? My mind raced ahead as the sun gave it more the feel of, if not a holiday, at least a break. It gave me a breathing space to think over the problem I'd left behind in Dulwich: Jack. From what he'd told me, I could put him on hold.

No, that was dangerous. People don't stay on hold. They march on, and one could never be sure which direction they would take. But that, I realized, was true of myself as well. Which direction would *I* take?

On a Saturday morning, Ducks Green acquired a different persona from its weekday self. Those who counted themselves amongst the supporters of the village shops were out and about. During the week the clientele to be seen on the green and in the shops and pub was different; on Saturdays males of all age groups appeared, not just the retired and young. There was a sense of family and a sense of community. Several people looked up and half smiled as I walked across the green to the narrow lane that led off what was proudly called 'The Street', i.e. the part of the Cobshaw to Lilleybourne road that ran through the village itself.

News must have gone round the village that I was 'back' again because I was greeted the moment I walked into Mr Cherry's – no addressing him as Harry while he was working in the shop. Always *Mr* Cherry. His tiny shop was little more than the front parlour of a country cottage inhabited by succeeding generations of Cherrys. His larders and working area were at the rear, converted from what must once have been an abattoir in times when butchers did their own slaughtering. I doubted whether there would be another Mr Cherry when Harry came to retire. His son, so keen to take over when he was a child, was now a lawyer in a smart London firm.

Mr Cherry was so much the friendly village butcher, complete with apron and roly-poly figure and even sporting a hat on occasions, that not only he but everyone in Ducks Green knew he was hamming it up – but so what? It didn't mean he wasn't genuinely pleased to see me.

'Young Miss Haywood. Well, I never.'

'Little Em, you used to call me,' I joked.

He chuckled, and an amiable conversation ensued over chickens, organic meat and hearty stews. Then Jane came panting into the shop behind me. 'Saw you on the green, so I rushed across to say you must stay on for lunch.'

'Thanks. That would be great.'

The world resumed a normality as further discussions took place on pies and eggs. Everything was just as I remembered from my life here. Whatever happens, food goes on. Sometimes it fades away in importance and hides its true value in times of trouble, but it's always with us as comforter, basic supplier of needs, distractor, soother – and, I reflected as I paid my bill, gobbler of money.

'I need vegetables,' I told Jane, feeling marvellously 'normal'. Everyday life can be a good panacea. 'Is the farm shop still going?' There had been one along the lane to Barham. Even in my time it had had its ups and downs, but it was often the best place for fresh produce.

'Thriving. Better take the car though.'

Jane elected to come with me, as Paul was at home with the children, and I found myself slipping back into my old shoes very comfortably – except for one thing. There was no Laura now.

The farm shop was better than I remembered it, although the same couple was running it, and was busy with weekend shoppers. If the Pearsons remembered me, as they claimed, it can have been with no great affection, however, for their welcomes of return seemed muted. I was puzzled, as I had always got on well with them, but then I remembered that Mark had been a favourite with Mrs Pearson, at that time a buxom forty-year-old. That must have been why I didn't seem to be their Number One Prodigal Daughter.

There was someone else in the shop whom I recognized: Mrs Grenier, the former head teacher at the primary school.

'You remember Emma, don't you, Mrs G.?' Jane said, giving her a hug. What temerity. I was amused, as Mrs Grenier hadn't been the hugging sort or the kind to welcome contractions of her name. She still wasn't, judging by her pursed lips and sharp look of assessment as she looked me up and down.

'I do. Are you back for long this time?' I almost felt she'd be disapproving if I said yes.

'I'm not sure,' I answered casually. 'I'm between jobs so it all depends what happens.'

'It's sometimes a mistake to come back.' Her tone of voice intimated that I'd made one this time.

'I'm enjoying it.' I was determined not to be riled. 'It's good to see old friends again and know that they're still friends.' I put an arm round Jane, who looked pleased, but I had an uncomfortable feeling that Mrs Grenier still retained the power that used to terrify me in my schooldays: as if she were looking right through any mask I might be wearing and reading my mind. In short, that Mrs Grenier knew that I must be visiting for more than a summer break with old friends. And she did not approve.

'Grim,' I said lightly to Jane, after we left.

She laughed. 'She only does it to annoy. She's a sweet old thing really.'

'You'd think Lucrezia Borgia was a sweet old thing,' I said affectionately.

'No. I wouldn't,' she replied indignantly. 'I'm very careful over my friends.'

My turn to laugh. It was good to be back.

Indeed it was – at least on one level. 'I could get used to this,' I said happily after a terrific 'spur of the moment' lunch put on by Jane. She must surely have planned this home-made soup, and a fantastic warm salad of new potatoes, chicken and broad beans in a mild curry mayonnaise. Billy and Alice wolfed it down, so she had her children well trained food-wise. The salad was followed by a delicious lemon tart.

'By which you mean having children?' Paul joked, in answer to my comment.

'Being around them anyway. It's fun.'

'Try having fun when they're having tantrums in the middle of the night,' he said with feeling.

Not a word was said about Tom Burdock, and the only mention of Laura was a passing reference to her love of birds. I left Number Twelve feeling envious. Families could indeed be fun. But where was mine?

As I turned into Love Lane, drove along the bumpy track to Wychley Cottage and parked the car, I was still feeling the after-glow of a happy meeting. I had to unload the goodies, otherwise I might have been tempted to park outside Kate's house and nip in for a cuppa, instead of coming this way. It was fairly dry, thank-fully, otherwise the car would have sunk into the boggy mire that Kate had warned me about. The tarmac ran out several hundred yards from the cottage and after that I was at the mercy of ruts and bogs, stones and weeds.

As I climbed out the trees overhead seemed a friendly shelter, but by the time I had taken everything inside I was very aware of how lonely this spot seemed. It wasn't, of course, because it would take two minutes at the most to walk through the cottage gate, across the track, into Kate's garden and up to her door, and yet the silence struck home to me. It was mid-afternoon, not time yet for the birds to be making their suppertime food rounds, and there was no other noise at all. This, I told myself, was what I had wanted. Peace and quiet. I was there to make plans, not wonder whether I had done the right thing.

Jane had diffidently slipped me a photo of Laura as I left. I hadn't seen it before, and it was taken during our schooldays. Laura, standing on the tennis court, racket in hand, smiling shyly at the photographer. It was a reminder that I was in Cobshaw for a purpose – two in fact: so that my life could move on, and so that I could repay my debt to Laura for her friendship. Or, I recalled with a painful jab, to find out if the Laura I knew had ever existed.

I forced myself to study the photo more closely. Once I would have looked at it superficially and thought how lovely Laura was, and a rush of warmth would have consumed me. The face looked just as gentle, just as kind, and yet now I tried to look beyond that. Was there something more that I had missed? I had been her friend, not an inquisitor. I had never dissected my view of her in order to make judgements. There had been no need. Now there was, or I could get no further. This was the girl who might have been wondering whether I was indeed having an affair with her husband, and also the girl about whom that husband was wildly jealous because he believed she was unfaithful to him. The two didn't add up. It was true that one could have been the result of a childish reaction: if he's having an affair, why shouldn't I? But Laura wasn't childish, and nor was Tom.

Could I be a judge of that, however? Sexual jealousy makes children of us all, reason vanishes. I should know. Assuming that these were genuine beliefs, not defensive fantasies of either Laura's or Tom's imaginations, where did that leave me? And, I reasoned, Tom's fantasy – I longed, and hoped, that it was – about Laura couldn't have been instantaneous, it must have festered and grown, so what was it based on? On more, surely, than two initials in a diary. He must have watched her, secretly followed her and sensed something wrong from her behaviour. He would have found nothing, I thought at first. I remembered nothing unusual in their behaviour to each other, and I had had plenty of opportunities to observe that.

And then I remembered my own experience. Friends and family had been stunned when Mark and I broke the news that we were separating. They couldn't believe it; they told us it was the result of Laura's death, and that it would pass, but it wasn't and didn't. That had been a factor, but the true reason lay between us. Mark had been having an affair – no doubt about that, as he never denied it. But why? Our personalities provided the obvious answer. We married too young, we were developing in different directions, and, I was forced to consider, I spent too much time with Laura. I had had no idea at all about Anna's existence, and nor, it transpired, had any of our friends.

Or was I wrong about that? I had a sudden, unwelcome memory of Laura's face one day. We'd been at Kate's, I think. Yes, that was it. We'd been talking about *Romeo and Juliet*. It was not a literary discussion, but idle talk on how their love would have developed if they'd married and had children, or if Abelard and Héloïse had done so. It had been fun. Kate had said they'd be divorced within years. I had stoutly maintained they would all have been faithful unto death – but then I had seen Laura looking at me oddly.

'Oh no, Emma. Be careful. You're wrong.'

Had she been talking about herself and Tom or about Mark and me? When had that conversation taken place? Did it matter? I couldn't judge; I was building too much into it. But the unease stayed with me.

Kate had invited me to dinner on the following evening, but had tactfully decided to leave me on my own this evening to get used to the cottage. It had been strange going to sleep the previous evening, alone and in such a deep, deep darkness. I hadn't slept well, but I hoped it would get better. I made myself some pasta, put on the television and had just settled down when I heard the click of the gate.

Kate? It could only be her. The security lights came on as instinctive panic gave way to common sense. No burglar in his right mind would walk, or even drive, along this mile-long lane just to rob a casual guest.

I went to the front door, put the chain on and opened it. But it wasn't Kate. It was Tom.

I tried to be welcoming. I wasn't scared of him, far from it. But this wasn't something I had expected to cope with yet.

'Don't tell me,' he said. 'You're making a soufflé.'

It was something Laura had often said, picked up from our schooldays when a soufflé had seemed an impossibly pretentious dish. I laughed and removed the chain. 'Come in,' I said. 'And tell me what you're doing so far from home.'

'House-warming present,' he said, handing over a bunch of roses. Not shop-bought, but garden-picked, I realized. One up to him – but roses?

'Great. I was just wondering who I could share this Chardonnay with.'

'One glass.'

I made necessary small-talk while I mentally prowled around him, trying to guess why he'd come and to decide whether I was glad or sorry.

'How did you find me out?' I asked, remembering his unexpected appearance at Dulwich.

'I wanted to tell you what happened after you left Tenterden that day. You disappeared so quickly, and it didn't seem right to tell you over the phone. I hoped you'd ring me –' he shrugged – 'but you didn't, so here I am.'

'Sorry,' I said guiltily. 'I was bent on finishing my last two weeks at work.'

'Last two?'

'I'm redundant.'

'Temporary or permanent?'

'Temporary,' I said firmly.

'How long – sorry, I've a reason for asking, Emma. A week, a month?'

'No idea, but probably nearer the latter.'

'Want a temporary job?'

'What as? Gardener, cook, chief executive,' I joked, 'or local pub barmaid?'

'No, at the charity. We could do with some temporary help.'

My first instinct was to decline the offer very firmly, but then I reconsidered. Why not think about it? It would put me on the 'inside' of Laura's story, rather than the outside. I wouldn't just be a temporary visitor but someone with a part to play.

Tom grinned. It was just a friendly sort of grin, not a 'come into my parlour, said the spider to the fly' type. 'You wouldn't need to chain yourself to the office chair,' he said. 'We're putting on a big event on the twelfth of July. It's a Saturday, and Petra, that's Lee's wife, needs help, but only until then.'

'What sort of event?'

'How much do you know about Tolling Bells?'

'Not a lot,' I confessed. Tom had joined the new charity not long before Laura's death, and Lee had told him they might be looking for someone to help expand the charity with the idea of opening a Johannesburg branch. I had had other things on my mind, and so the details had passed me by. 'I know the general idea is to help out where needed in Africa.' It sounded a broad remit.

'Right. In fact, Africa, China, wherever, but chiefly Third World, hence the Joburg branch. There are thousands of charities all beavering away to help their own special cause, but there aren't many that have an overall view of what's needed where when disaster strikes.'

'Unless you go up to the United Nations, I presume.'

'Quite, but we're a small, flexible charity and grant-making foundation. We can tap in to particular needs and give grants to other charities, as needed, for them to carry out the work. Often, with the best will in the world, a charity coming in from outside can't just take over a situation and begin work. They need local help and often political advice, as well as money. That's where we come in. We're the link.'

'Sounds good, but who funds you?'

'Ask Lee. He's the fund-raiser. I'm the organizer. And one thing I have to organize right here is a few big dos a year for potential and present donors.'

'I've no experience—' I began doubtfully. This sounded interesting though.

'Not necessary. The one coming up in July is a huge, posh barbecue in the garden of the chair of our trustees, the Manor House at Holt Capel. And before you ask, we're hiring a huge marquee. Petra is organizing it, but there's more than she can handle. Invitations, diets, hog roasts – you name it, it needs to be done. Why don't you come along to the office on Monday morning? Petra's coming in, and so you could meet her to have a chat about it. We might even be able to pay you something, but don't bank on it. Grateful thanks are more in our line.'

'Sounds familiar.'

'Good.' Tom glanced round the room – and of course his eye fell on the photo of Laura, which I'd propped up on a bookshelf.

'Jane gave it to me. Sorry, but I only just got it.'

'I ought to be able to face it, but it still gives me a knee-jerk reaction.' A pause, then, 'Why did you come back, Emma? I thought you'd abandoned us again.'

'How could I?' I was annoyed. 'You made sure of that when you brought Jack's name into it.'

He flushed. 'I'd no choice. I was horrified when I heard you were living with him.'

'How did you hear?'

'Someone at a party told me you were living with Jack Scarlet. Easy after that.'

This sounded far too general an explanation for me to swallow, but it was clear I would get no further, so I switched tack. 'Give me more evidence about Jack's involvement with Laura,' I demanded. 'There must be more to it than two initials in a diary. Did you know Jack in your Ducks Green days? Did you meet him at Tenterden? Did Laura talk about him?'

'Hardly.'

'Then why are you so sure he was her lover?' I meant to get to the bottom of this puzzle at least. 'The initials could stand for any John Smith. A new pupil.'

'The only person who came was young Toby Martin, an hour later.'

'All right. You said you'd met Jack yourself. Where? In Canterbury? Ducks Green?'

No reply.

'Tell me, Tom. I have to know if I'm to give your accusation any consideration at all.'

'My parents knew him in his Canterbury days.'

'So did the Wests. They haven't accused Jack of murder though.' I tried to be objective, but there was a taut note in my voice that I couldn't keep out.

'Laura mentioned his name and said I'd met him at her parents' house. I recognized him when I saw them together in Canterbury.'

Here we go again, I thought. 'You told me that already. Not enough.'

'They were kissing. And not like friends.'

'Not enough.' I felt close to tears. 'Kissing doesn't mean—'

'He admitted it,' Tom shouted.

Dead silence. 'When?' I managed to say.

'I met him in Africa.' He saw my stunned face. 'I'm sorry, Emma.'

'When?' I whispered.

'A few months back.'

I'd heard enough. I suppose I should have badgered Tom for details of all these parties, but I couldn't. I'd ask Jack . . . but first I needed to sleep. To curl myself up into a ball and ask myself where my world had gone. And then tomorrow I would rise again, and face what to do. Tom could be mistaken or lying, so should I return to Dulwich and tackle Jack? Or stay where I was and struggle through the story of Laura Burdock?

Tom was still looking at me anxiously. Go, I wanted to say. Just go. But he still sat there.

'Tell me about Jamie,' I said with an effort. 'That's what you said you'd come for.'

'Sure you're up to it?'

'Yes.'

'The Wests were quite reasonable in the circumstances,' he told me. 'The answer was basically sod off, but with their solicitor present they could hardly express it so bluntly. I *am* the boy's father. There seems no doubt of that. They didn't ask for a DNA test.'

'You're pretty bitter, Tom.'

'Wouldn't you be?'

'Yes. But from their point of view they must still believe you killed Laura.' I remembered Celia's words, but they were for me, not for Tom. 'I'm sure their logical minds dismiss it, but that doesn't help when it comes to Jamie. Did you get on with them all right during your marriage?'

'No. They never thought anyone good enough for their precious daughter. I was so imbued with that idea that *I* didn't even think myself good enough for her. Did *you* think I was?' he shot at me.

'How on earth can I answer that? You were a friend. I didn't judge you.'

'Did *you* ever look twice at me? A lot of girls did, but you didn't.'

I swallowed. I needed to head this one off quickly. 'I had my mind set on going to university at eighteen.' That was when

Tom had seriously begun courting Laura. I had no need to say there had been no chemistry between us, so far as I was concerned.

Tom calmed down. 'I'm sorry, Emma. You don't deserve all this.'

'Perhaps I do,' I said wearily. If I'd looked harder, I wouldn't have hurt Tom's feelings all those years ago. I would have seen the tension between him and the Wests. 'Anyway, what about Jamie?'

'It's been agreed that he should get to know me better. If he's willing, I can have him for one weekend a month, situation to be reviewed yearly.'

'That's good, isn't it?'

'No, it's not good, but it's fair, at least until I get myself settled. Then I'll rethink the situation.'

I'd thought the sky had remained blue for the whole afternoon of the treasure hunt, but last night I dreamed of it again. There'd been a cloud that came up so suddenly that I glanced up, wondering why I was chilly. It was May, so that was understandable, but Laura was shivering too. 'I don't think I like it here any more,' she said, and then ran over to speak to someone else. We were both clutching our threads of wool, so of course mine and hers were torn apart and I was left holding my blue thread upset and alone until someone, Jane I think, came to join me.

Eight

'Just thought I'd pop in and see how you're doing. You can tell me to pop right back out again if you like,' Kate greeted me, when I opened the door to her next morning. I'd seen her coming through the gate and had been there like a shot. I could do with company, I thought, if only to stop the roundabout whirling in my head. Morning brings clarity, but sometimes too much all at one time.

'Come right in and share some breakfast,' I said gratefully.

'Never touch the stuff.'

'You cook full English for me.'

'That's different. Maybe coffee would be an idea.'

'Then you'll have to watch me plough through my muesli. I don't operate without it.'

'What's your operational plan?' Kate enquired, following me into the kitchen.

'Going to Canterbury tomorrow morning.' As I made her a mug of coffee I told her about Tom's suggestion, which interested her. 'Holt Capel Manor, eh? Very nice too. I think Noël used to nip over there every now and then. Long before its current resident, of course.'

Noël Coward died a long time ago, but I was prepared to believe her. Eileen, Kate's mother, had known him, and so it was possible that he had also nipped into her seaside boarding house.

'The Manor has a twenties, anyone-for-tennis sort of garden, so far as I remember,' Kate continued. 'Or it used to. It's probably completely changed now. A crime if it has, but that's progress for you.' With hardly a pause, she continued, 'Is it wise to take this job, do you think?'

No mistaking what she meant. Was I wise to stick my head into a possible lions' den in this volunteer capacity – even though that assumed that Tom had something to hide? 'I don't know,' I replied frankly. 'If I'm to find out what happened to Laura and why, I need to be inside what's going on, not outside. Anyway, you're the one who accused me of running away before.'

'Touché.' Kate pulled a face. 'But there's a difference between standing your ground and taking the offensive before you've reconnoitred the battlefield.'

'That's why I'm probably going to do this job.'

'You don't fancy Tom, do you?'

'Kate!'

'Why the surprised face?'

'Because I'm living with Jack.'

'Hardly an answer. Good coffee this.'

'Thank you,' I snapped. 'And the answer's no, I don't fancy Tom. I *like* him. And the more I like him the more I feel I need to—' I stopped; I could see where this was leading, but it was too late to call a halt.

'Find out whether he's innocent,' she finished for me. 'Fair enough. But where does that leave you with Jack? You said Tom claims Jack was having it off with Laura.'

My glaring Achilles heel, of course. 'That's a separate issue.'

Silence. Kate wasn't even bothering to take up the cudgels on that one. Of course they weren't separate. Yet I couldn't tell her that Jack was most certainly involved to some extent, and the only question was how much. 'Do you remember a Liz Scarlet?'

'No. Should I?'

'She was around when I was a child, as Jack was.'

Kate lifted an eyebrow – deservedly. Then I remembered that she had only moved to Cobshaw when I was about nine or ten, well after the treasure hunt at which Liz Scarlet had been present, and Jack's family could easily have left by then.

'So?' she enquired politely.

'She must have been Jack's mother.' I broke off. 'You think I'm mad, don't you, Kate?'

I received a prompt reply. 'I think you're in danger.'

'Physical danger?' I asked uneasily.

'Let's hope not. But danger all the same, Emma. You were a happy person when I met you and Jack in London. Are you now?'

'No, but—'

'And who put that "but" there?'

'Tom, but—'

'He spread doubt – and meant to.'

'Isn't that fair enough if he's innocent?'

'Doubt's like a bad flu virus. It affects every aspect of life, and takes a mighty long time to clear up. And worse, you're never sure quite where you got it from.'

I stared at her. 'I do in this case. From Tom.'

'Maybe, but he's still the Tom of seven years ago. Doubt lies latent. That's why it's so dangerous. For seven years he hadn't had to face the problem. Now he's back, in the same area where it all happened. Perhaps he's not seeing things straight, or even remembering them straight – and that could apply to Jack.'

I clutched at this hope, but in vain. 'But there was the J.S. in Laura's diary. Facts are facts.'

'Not always. They depend on the source.'

'And if that's Laura?' I was so intent on fighting my corner that I hadn't seen the heffalump pit yawning before me – and I'd fallen right into it.

Kate was looking at me pityingly. 'Question *any* source.'

How many times had I seen *Othello* and wondered why he never questioned what Iago told him? How many stories had I read in which the hero or heroine never questioned the character who was most obviously lying? But it's always so easy when it's someone else's situation. Always so impossible when it's your own.

'*Look behind you!*'

The audience is yelling out to the hero/heroine to beware. Can't they see what's creeping up on them? Only when the audience yells loudly enough . . . But what if there's no audience, and only a Kate to suggest that I looked behind me? A thousand objections. Even though she'd met him once, Kate didn't *know* Jack as I did, she didn't *know* Tom as I did and she didn't know Laura – not as I knew her, anyway.

I rang Jack that evening. We had one of those conversations that only partially satisfies. It establishes a communication but the real issues remain unspoken, although just to hear his voice was reassuring. There had to be some good reason he hadn't mentioned Africa.

'How are you?' I asked.

'Fine, and you?'

'Doing well. Wychley Cottage is lovely.'

'Good. The gas bill's in, by the way. I've paid it.'

'Oh. The window cleaner's due . . .' I could hear the tension in my voice, and ended the call as quickly as I could. My heart was beating as I clicked off. Where on earth was I going with this? Canterbury, yes, but I was pushing blindly through bushes, hoping to reach open land on the other side. The job, I thought. That would give me a firm base from which I could reach out towards the truth.

When I reached the office on Monday morning the hum of activity, compared with the air of desertion on my last visit, was reassuring. Tom came out to welcome me, and ushered me into his office, where Lee and Petra were waiting. Lee was a different type to Tom. He was older for a start, maybe mid-forties, and still looked the social animal I remembered. Perhaps one had to look the part to be a fund-raiser, I thought. Though he was casually dressed, that, together with the silver hair, gave the effect of being stage-managed. Perhaps that was why he and Tom made good partners. Tom really was casual. Petra also looked a social animal. Younger than Lee, perhaps forty, she was elegant and blonde, with a lively face, and I decided I could work with her – depending, of course, on what she required of me.

Unfortunately, it didn't seem to work out the other way. It went well enough at first. The men went into Tom's office to let us 'chat in peace' while Petra spelled out my 'duties' (liaising with caterers, guest lists, travel arrangements, press presence and so on). Then she gave me what Kate would have called 'an old-fashioned look'.

'Tom said you were a friend of Laura's.' She did not look as though this was a recommendation.

'Yes. School friends. Did you know her?' It seemed unlikely as Laura and I hadn't cared much for socialites.

'I did. Not well, but I don't think we two met, did we, Emma?'

'Not that I can recall.' I'd have remembered.

'Tom seems to have recovered pretty well, considering,' Petra said.

'Considering what?' I decided I'd nail this cool blonde. 'That a lot of people thought he murdered her?'

'Quite.' She gave me an unamused glance. 'Did you think so?'

'It was one of the rumours flying around at the time. The husband dunnit, the parents dunnit . . . Knee-jerk reactions, rarely true.'

She didn't press me after this evasive answer. 'The lovely Laura rather asked for it.'

'Didn't you like her?' A stupid question, but her reply had shaken me.

She gave me a smile – a genuine one, I thought – which gave me a glimpse of a human being. 'Let's not go there, shall we?' And we got down to more details of who should do what, when. Much safer ground.

I'd arranged to meet Jane for lunch in Canterbury, after I'd finished my grilling at Tolling Bells. She had some shopping to do and it seemed a nice idea. We found a friendly family Italian restaurant and Jane sank down exhausted by her morning shop, still surrounded by bags.

'I've left the car by the station,' she told me. When one lives in a village like Ducks Green, one doesn't get much choice of transport, only a trip of several miles to the railway station or a bus every few hours. 'Now, Emma, tell me *all*.'

I began with Petra – not exactly Jane's sort so plenty of scope for dissection there. I duly dissected, and Jane frowned. 'I think I remember her. We used to belong to the same tennis club, I think. I do remember she was a member of Tom's fan club.'

'She didn't seem inclined to be one of mine.'

'She wouldn't be, not if she knew you as Laura's friend.'

'That's a bit unfair. A lot of water has passed under the River Stour's bridge since then.'

Jane laughed. 'If it's any comfort, she doesn't much like me either.'

'Why not?'

'Same reason. We're all tarred with the same brush. We belonged to Laura's circle.'

'But she's still in it in a way – her husband's working with Tom. Did she believe Tom murdered Laura, at the time?'

'Don't know. So far as I recall, she, and maybe the whole club, thought he was either innocent or driven to it.'

'Driven by what?' I was beginning to get exasperated – not with Jane, but with this continued use of Laura as a dartboard for accusations to be hurled at her. 'Not more stories of lovers? You don't believe that, and nor do I.'

'No, but . . .' Jane hesitated. 'If, just *if* there was something to it, Lee might have been right on Laura's radar screen. His and Petra's daughter, Clare, was in her teens then, and I'm pretty sure Laura gave piano lessons to her at their home in Whitstable, not in Ducks Green. She did go to clients' homes sometimes, if she could leave Jamie at nursery.'

'And?' I asked stonily.

Jane flushed. 'You did ask me, Emma.'

'Sorry.'

'I don't know the logistics, but rumour did say Laura and Lee were together for much longer than the piano lessons took.'

'Claptrap,' I said defiantly. 'Just as with Jack. All gossip, no fact.'

Jane said nothing, and I reached a penitent hand out. 'Sorry. You're right. I did ask.' And, I realized miserably, I'd had to ask. I'd said I wanted to find out the truth and so every avenue had to be followed, blind or not, unpleasant or pleasant.

My grandfather, a Londoner, remembers the bad old days of London particulars, the thick black fogs and smogs of pollution before the clean air acts came in. He says of any crisis in life, that when caught in a particular you should inch yourself forward, not back. I had no choice now but to inch forward, and yet I wondered where this fog was going to bring me out, as I drove up the lane towards Wychley Cottage. The required destination or some unknown land I did not recognize? As I passed the row of cottages lining the last made-up part of the track, the path ahead looked unfriendly to say the least. The sun had vanished and a light drizzle had taken its place. It began to seem as if I'd entered the witch's wood of my childhood. No Eileen to greet me with hot buns, however. Then I braked hard, as I saw a familiar car on the patch of ground designated as the parking area. It wasn't Kate's. It was Jack's.

A mixture of emotions gobbled greedily at me. Chief of them

was instinctive pleasure, but in its trail came bewilderment, amazement and, somewhere on their fringes, fear. Fear not of Jack himself – or was it? – but that his arrival somehow portended an unknown territory that I didn't want to venture into.

I had no choice, so I parked and went inside the cottage, calling out Jack's name. A bag indicated that he had come to stay. Why? A dozen answers presented themselves, none of which convinced me. If Jack was in Cobshaw during a working week, there had to be some reason for it. Even as I wrestled with the problem I heard his voice outside and then Kate's. I hurried to the door.

'What's wrong?' I blurted out, convinced there was something so terrible that they both felt they should be there when I discovered the truth. My parents? My sister?

Jack's face changed from laughter to shock and so did Kate's. 'Nothing,' he told me, as he kissed me, 'nothing at all.'

And at that moment I believed him.

As reunions go, this one was rating minus ten, I thought on the Tuesday morning. Yesterday evening Jack and I had been polite strangers, this morning we might have been married for years, and now he had set off on his job – to Folkestone, he said – and would be absent for the entire day. I had been too full of Tom and Laura to be able to see Jack objectively as the man I loved, and Jack was still withdrawn behind his mask. Ever since we had first met, I'd teased him about the series of masks he possessed: the worker, the joker, the host and so on. Only the lover wore no mask. Usually. At breakfast this morning, however, one mask was firmly in place. I diagnosed it as 'reasonable man'.

'What's wrong, Emma?' he asked, when my silence obviously got too much for him. It wasn't a deliberate silence, just one that I couldn't think of anything to fill. 'You're doing great. Including a new job, so Kate tells me.'

'Very temporary volunteer.'

'With Tom Burdock's gang.'

'Yes.' I couldn't stop. 'He said he met you at a party in Johannesburg.'

'Did he? Maybe he did. I was there not long ago.'

There was always an explanation, I thought, and I baulked at asking my most burning question: had he really admitted to having an affair with Laura, as Tom claimed? Why had he sought Kate out to chat with? They must have been instantaneously chummy as she'd divulged the information about my job to him. It made me wonder if he had been in touch with her by phone before his arrival here. And, as my mind leapt into gear, could he even have implanted the idea of the cottage in my mind? It was he who had suggested Cobshaw, and he had been present at the original dinner where, I remembered, she had chatted about it. If so, why? It was unusual for Jack to act so surreptitiously, but perhaps not where Tom Burdock was involved. Perhaps, a thud inside me suggested, that was *why* he might have decided to take a hand.

Stop, I told myself. That way, as King Lear pointed out, madness lies.

'Is that why you're here?' I continued carefully.

'Yes,' he answered frankly – or was that the mask talking? 'Or at least partly. I was worried about you, and as the job is still on, it seemed practical to commute. Folkestone isn't that far away. Two birds with one stone – great, particularly as my favourite bird is you.'

He sounded so reasonable that I tried not to sound ungracious. I did my best to atone, but the situation between us still lay undigested at breakfast. Was Jack really there because he was worried about me – and if so was that physically or mentally? If the latter, he wasn't helping by his presence, and if the former surely it was unnecessary. He was right in one way. To have company was good, but his arrival had the air of something more than he had told me. Was he there just as a companion or as a warder? Kate would have seen through that, surely, and warned me.

In vain I told myself I was being ridiculous. Insufficiently proven accusations had brought me to this point, something I could not have believed of myself a month ago – before Tom had come back into my life. And now, if I wasn't careful, I would see threat everywhere: in Jack, in Tom, in the dark trees surrounding the cottage, in the long and lonely lanes and in the crowded, anonymous city streets.

Get moving, I told myself briskly. That's the best cure for wild imagination. Jack had already left for Folkestone, but it was not

until my Mini was bumping along the lane towards Cobshaw
High Street that I felt free again.

And how ironic that was, I thought bitterly. Here I was 'feeling
free' from the man I loved and lived with, when I was on my
way to see my former husband. 'Come to dinner,' Mark had said
cordially when I'd telephoned the day before.

'Not good in the circumstances,' I had briefly explained. 'I'd
love to see Anna again, but I need to talk to you about our time
together.'

'Ah.' Mark had slowly absorbed this at the end of the phone
line, and for a moment I'd thought he'd refuse. He was never
good at chatting on emotional matters. I'd misjudged him,
however. 'Do I suspect you've heard that Tom Burdock's back in
town?'

Did the whole world know why I was here? 'Afraid so.'

'So it's a business meeting at the pub then.' Mark laughed, but
it sounded artificial even at the other end of a phone.

'I hope you and Anna will come to dinner with me at Wychley
Cottage while I'm here. You remember; it's at the back of Kate's
house. I'd love to catch up with Anna.' Even as I spoke, I thought
of Jack. How good a grouping would that be at the moment?
With so much tension around, it could be tricky. Perhaps Jack
would have left before then . . .

How insidious thoughts can be. Jack leaving? When I'd spent
so long in the times we'd been together in London wishing he
was not dashing off to Paris? I fought to subdue panic. I had to
go on now, otherwise there would be no going back to happier
days at Dulwich. No more evenings of laughter, wine, jokes and
anticipation of sex. No more walks in the countryside. No this,
no that, no person to share life with, no person to love. There
would be awkward silences, which we would both try to bridge
– silences caused by Tom Burdock. No, I realized, that was unfair.
The silences would be caused by my reactions to what Tom had
thrown at me. If I fought my way to the end of this nightmare
tunnel, I might find a bridge to cross back to Jack. If I didn't, I
couldn't bear the thought that Jack would walk out of my life,
all because of a man who came back.

I tried to convince myself that Jack had contributed to this
situation himself. Why hadn't he told me about his Kentish past?

There were questions to be answered, and answered they would be. All the same, it was ironical to think that they might be answered by my former husband.

Mark is a high-powered accountant. When we were at university he was an idealist, full of what he could do to save the economies of the world, and quite rightly so. I had listened breathlessly to long descriptions of how this measure or that might be the answer to global problems. As time had passed, however, idealism had given way to the practicalities of business life – and, worse, internal politics. He came home talking not of whether such and such could save a global disaster, but of whether so-and-so's work would advance so-and-so further than Mark. Anna seems more placid than I am, and more accepting of the ways of the world. Anyway, they are obviously happy and that's what matters. I hadn't seen either of them for nearly a year, and I genuinely looked forward to seeing Mark, irrespective of the reason.

Mark had suggested we met at a pub in the village of Chartham Hatch, which produced wonderful food, served in a huge garden. It was its glorious best in mid-June, and was a perfect spot for us to discuss 'business' at our leisure. He grinned as he said this, and for a moment I glimpsed the old Mark, the one I'd fallen for, amazing though it now seemed. He was just as good-looking as when we had first met, but that didn't stir me any more, and nor did Mark. He just seemed a pleasant man. Nevertheless, there was a special rapport between us that subtly reminded me (and I suspect Mark too) that once we had been passionately in love.

We chatted idly for a while, and I thought Mark seemed uneasy. One of the advantages of having lived with someone is that you know their moods and expressions inside out. Right now I put this down to his being anxious about what I might say, but it turned out to be something completely different. Something he was clearly longing to get off his chest.

'Anna wanted me to tell you – so you don't get a jolt when you meet her – that . . .' From his look of worry, I thought for one awful moment that he was going to say she was mortally ill, but it was nothing like that. 'She's pregnant,' he finished.

I was delighted. It really was good news. 'I'm so pleased, Mark,'

I said warmly, and saw the anxiety leave his face. 'When's the baby due?'

'September,' he said, and proceeded to give me all the details of the birth arrangements.

I realized that he'd been worried about telling me because he and I had tried for a baby and had not been lucky. It brought back my pangs over having a baby with Jack, and I ached for my former relationship with him to be restored.

'So,' Mark said, now all cheery, 'what did you want to talk about? As if I didn't know: Laura and Tom.'

That obvious? 'Do you mind?'

'It depends. If it helps clear the matter up – though I don't see how it could – no, I don't mind at all. But you know me, I hate pure nostalgia trips.'

'It could help. I do need to talk it over with you, Mark.'

'Then fire away.'

This was a different, more confident Mark than the one I had last seen, even though that was only a year ago. Perhaps it was the thought of the coming baby anchoring him down, giving him a future identity as a family man. And that, I thought, was good.

'Tom wants to clear his name,' I began, telling him about the Dulwich visit.

'How's he going to do that?'

I was taken aback. I had been so intent on how I was going to do it that I hadn't given much thought to Tom's plans, but Mark's analytical mind had got there in one. 'I don't know.' The good thing about past lovers is, when there is too much at stake to risk speaking the truth in current relationships, one can often talk more freely to them.

'Sure he isn't planning to do it by upsetting those involved? Like you, Emma?'

Was he? That was a new thought, and an unwelcome one. Could Tom consciously or unconsciously be trying to clear himself by incriminating others? I needed to think this one through, uneasily aware that if this were the case it would make me a pawn in Tom's game, whereas I needed to be a queen protecting my king. King Jack. So far I had done precious little in the way of protection. Rather the opposite.

'Again, I don't know,' I said, 'but I've got to the point where

I need to know your side of what was going on in Ducks Green at the time of Laura's murder.'

He looked rather grim, but at least he replied. 'Why not? Water under the bridge now.'

I clutched gratefully at this. 'Tom thought, and still does, that Laura was having an affair.'

'Not with me, she wasn't,' Mark whipped back.

'No.' I grinned at him, and he managed a smile. There was no need to voice what we were both thinking: that he had met Anna by the time of Laura's death. I was surprised to find the hurt had entirely vanished now. When I thought back to the termagant I must have been then, she seemed a different person. And yet the passions that the discovery of his affair had aroused must still be within me. Even though that cause had gone, another might have the same effect. I should remember that.

'What was your take on this possible affair of Laura's?' I continued. 'I suppose we must have talked about it, if only at the time of her murder, but I can't remember.'

'Truth excused?' he asked, and when I nodded, continued, 'I thought it quite likely.'

That really staggered me. 'I thought you were a Laura admirer.'

'I was, but no one's perfect. The trouble is you believed she was.'

Had I? Reluctantly, I realized that he was right. 'But what made you think she was unfaithful to Tom?' I longed to add 'perhaps with Jack', but I couldn't. For a start, pride would not let me.

'No idea. Just the impression one gets after a while.'

'Very helpful.'

'You asked.' He looked reproachful, and I quickly backtracked.

'Sorry.'

'That's OK. It's natural. There's an old Chinese poem about old habits being hard to overcome.'

Mark? Chinese poems? I must have looked astonished, for he added, 'Anna got me into reading them.'

Anna was a magician then, I thought, although I murmured something appreciative.

'Any idea who this lover, if he existed, was?' I held my breath, scanning his face for any sign of embarrassment that I could interpret as his thinking it was Jack.

'Not really. You're the one who would have known. You or Jane.'

'Neither of us do. Do you think it could have been Lee, for instance, Tom's partner, or –' I managed a laugh – 'even my partner, Jack?'

That did rouse him. 'Lee's a possibility, but how does Jack come into it? Was he around then? I thought you'd only recently met him.'

I could have fallen at his feet and blessed him in my gratitude. 'I have, and I don't remember any Scarlets around while we lived in the area. They were living in Canterbury and were friends of Laura's parents, although they were in the midst of moving to France at the time of Laura's death.'

'I could have met them, I suppose, but I've no memory of it. You were the one who brought this up though, so why ask me?'

I decided to be upfront. 'Because my memory might be blotting out unpleasant thoughts, such as whether Jack could have been involved.'

Mark shot a keen glance at me. 'Is that what Tom suggested?'

'Yes, and there's evidence in Laura's diary that she did know him.'

'Sorry I can't help. Except –' Mark looked awkward – 'don't you think you're still hung up on Laura the goddess?'

I'd asked for it. 'In what way?'

'You thought she made the sun shine. I got fed up with it sometimes. She was nice enough, but she had her own agenda.'

'Explain, please.' I had to face this here and now.

'Sure you can take it?'

'No, but I have to.'

'I began to feel that Laura was a stirrer. Nothing you could pin down, but everything around her – and very much including you, Emma – somehow got muddied up.'

I wanted to shout and yell to say that it wasn't so. That what had passed hadn't been like that. But how could I? I didn't know what the past was like now. It seemed a place I had never lived in, and yet I had walked, talked, reasoned, functioned, laughed, cried and *lived* there.

'There was a rumour going round that Tom and I were lovers and Laura picked up on it,' I blurted out. 'Did you hear it?'

He stared at me, and for once I could not read his expression. '*Were* you an item?'

'Will you believe me?'

'Yes. You've nothing to lose by telling me now, and I know you well enough to be sure you won't lie just for the sake of getting back at me.'

I felt like crying. 'Thanks, Mark. The answer's no. Tom and I weren't lovers, and never even came close. Nor will.'

'So point proved. Laura was involved with false rumours. And so I might as well admit that I did hear it. Made me feel pretty good at first because I'd met Anna. But I watched you all the same, and I couldn't believe it was the truth. I told Laura that, and she did a good job of pretending to be grateful.'

'How do you know she was pretending?'

'Because after her murder, Tom told me that she had still been repeating the rumour on the day of her death. They'd had a major row in which she'd accused him of sleeping with you, and he'd retaliated. And before you ask, he didn't name names. Looking back, he could have thought Laura was having it off with someone, but didn't know who, and so he was trying me out to see how I'd react. I didn't give him a hard time because I was sorry for him. He was in a real mess.'

I tried to think this through, but I still felt the instinctive need to defend Laura. 'That doesn't make her sound like a stirrer, only a jealous wife.' I was aware that my lips were trembling even as I spoke.

'I'll say one thing for you, Emma, you never give up, do you? Not where Laura's concerned. She was a *stirrer*,' Mark insisted, 'and I can prove it. I won't go so far as to say she had a hand in destroying our marriage but she contributed. For one thing – how did you find out about Anna?'

Of all the hits, this was the most unexpected, and I grappled with the memory. 'I think I just suspected something was wrong, but I couldn't grasp what.' It had come and gone in little pieces, as the treasure hunt story still did.

'And what or who first planted that suspicion?' Mark shot back. 'Lipstick on the collar? Love letters in the pocket? All that old stuff?'

'No. Nothing like that.' I tried hard to remember. And then I did.

'Emma, I thought you said Mark was going to London, but he wasn't. He was in Canterbury with a tall, willowy girl. Her name's Anna. I'm sure it was quite innocent . . .'

'Laura,' I said dully. 'It was Laura.'

Nine

On that far-off summer's day, I could see Laura with another girl who might have been Jane, but the cloud had passed, and whatever had upset Laura seemed to have been forgotten. They were giggling, but not at me, and I hurried to wind up my thread so that I could catch up with them. As I did so, they turned to smile at me in welcome. Even such summer days have their dark side, however, and this snatch into the past ended without explanation. I don't know whether the discordant note I sensed had really been present or whether the Emma of today was transposing some underlying fear back into what had been a harmless child's game. The treasure hunt had remained in my memory as untouched by trouble; if there had been some darker element, I had obviously been powerless to help, for one can only help when the enemy shows its face. Help what? Save whom? From what?

I was glad that I did not have to drive through Ducks Green that evening. After my lunch with Mark, I wanted to be home in Cobshaw, not to have to be reminded of Lark Cottage or Appley House. I desperately wanted to stay in the present, and not be jolted yet further into the past. That was a quicksand, which would drag me down. Tomorrow I'd have to face it again, however, because that is where the answers must lie.

As I turned off the main road into the street that ran through Cobshaw village, the pub, the shops, the school, the houses and even the small supermarket that had largely replaced the independent shops of my youth, all looked comfortably re-assuring. We are the *now*, they seemed to say. The TV would be blaring in the pub; the village noticeboard would be displaying all those vital messages about drama, football and gardening clubs, the Mothers' union, the WI and the parish council, etcetera. The board seemed to be proud of its role, as if silently boasting that there were no questions that could not be answered there. We are as we are, Cobshaw was claiming, and I was glad that I was a tiny, temporary cog in its machinery:

a tenant of Wychley Cottage, a volunteer in a Canterbury charity.

It was only when I turned into Love Lane that the reassurance vanished. Instead of the refuge the cottage had at first represented, it now seemed the very opposite. There was Jack to face – but that was not what was troubling me as the car bounced along the ruts. I told myself it was the overhanging trees, blotting out the light. That must surely explain it, plus the fact that I had Mark's comments about Laura still to deal with. Nevertheless, there was a third factor, which was making this seem once again a witch's wood, and the cottage a trap, not a refuge. I could see Judy Garland in my mind, as she journeyed towards the Wizard of Oz, unaware that the Wicked Witch of the East, in her pointy black hat, was cackling her socks off as her crystal revealed her prey taking the bait.

Enough. I was brought down to earth with a bang when I saw Jack's car outside the cottage, back from Folkestone already. Forget about wicked witches and concentrate on Jack, I told myself. There was something about this whole situation that I wasn't yet grasping. Fact: Jack must surely be involved in it somehow, but I still found it impossible to think of him as public enemy number one. That was fiction, not fact.

He wasn't watching TV or glued to his laptop; he was reading a book, lounging in an armchair in the tiny conservatory Kate had built on the rear of the cottage for her mother to sit in. I felt the usual stab of pleasure as I saw him, and this time, thankfully, it didn't disappear.

'What are you reading?' I peered over his shoulder and kissed him on the cheek. He jumped, as I don't think he'd heard me come in.

'This. Found it on Kate's shelves.' He seemed rather embarrassed.

'*Little Women?*' I asked incredulously. 'Bit off your normal route, isn't it?' Louisa May Alcott's story of four girls brought up in hardship in small-town America just after their Civil War might have had my parents and Kate glued to it, and thanks to the remake of the film I'd read it myself, but it hardly seemed up Jack's street. He was normally a thriller a day man. 'Is this a side of you I don't know?'

'Perhaps.' He tossed it to one side, and devoted his attention to me. 'Good day?'

'So-so,' I said carefully. 'And you?'

'So-so. Cup of tea?'

'Terrific.' What was all this about? Cups of tea? Jack didn't mind tea, but it wasn't like him to suggest it, and certainly not to make it, yet there he was heading straight for the kitchen. My antennae waved furiously, but I'd deal with it cautiously.

When a mug came back, and Jack had re-established himself, he seemed to have had much the same thoughts. Small talk – or was it? 'Who did you meet today? Petra again?'

'Mark. My ex.'

'I do remember who he is,' he said mildly. 'May I ask why?'

Two can play at nonchalance. 'Yes. I wanted to ask Anna and Mark over to dinner, but thought I'd catch up with him first.'

'Did he remember me as Laura's lover, plus possible murderer?'

So there it was, out on the table between us, as certain as my mug of tea. 'We were discussing Laura herself, not you.'

'Plus, I'm sure, your new boss, Tom.'

'Only as regards Laura. If she did have a lover –' I saw the warning signs – 'and no, don't interrupt, then she wasn't the girl I had grown up with. Something must have happened.' I'd keep quiet about the 'stirrer' aspect for the moment, I decided.

'Unless Tom had lied.' Jack's expression had retreated into mask mode. 'That occur to you?'

'Of course,' I said, determined to stay calm. 'Especially as he claims you admitted being Laura's lover when he met you in Johannesburg.'

Jack groaned, and came to sit beside me on the small cane sofa. It creaked its usual protest, but it reminded me that he and I were still one. 'Did it also occur to you, Emma, that your new boss might be out of his tiny mind?'

'Yes, well . . . no.' It hadn't, I realized. I'd been too involved to see him objectively, and I rapidly considered the idea. 'Obsessed yes, but not paranoid.'

'Really?' An ironic eyebrow was raised. 'Sweetheart, I have news for you. Or rather advice. Take care. And before you squeak "why?" ask yourself whether evidence can be faked. And then ask yourself why he's so keen to get you involved in his life again.'

'I saw Laura's diary, and so did the police.' Calmness left me, and I could feel my temperature rising rapidly. I'd taken a false step. The police had clearly attached no importance to it. But was I fuzzy about that? Paul hadn't specifically said he'd seen it. The diary had been in Tom's possession . . . I swallowed, as I bore Jack's 'faked evidence' in mind. I tried a different tack. 'Why should Tom come back to clear his name, if he was guilty?'

Jack hesitated. 'Jamie, for one reason.'

'You're right,' I grudgingly agreed. 'But—'

'Give over on the buts, Emma. Just watch your back.'

I managed a laugh. 'I'm helping Petra arrange a do, not going on a six month vacation with Tom Burdock.'

'I'm glad of that.' Something in his voice made me turn to him and in a moment I was in his arms, and all was right with the world. His mouth was muffled in my hair as he continued, 'Emma, I don't know what Tom's like as a person; all I'm saying is that you should watch out for yourself, because you don't either. From the way he's behaving he seems a haunted man. You think of him as the boy you knew in your schooldays and who then married your best friend. But people evolve and sometimes change in unexpected ways.'

'Like Laura,' I said. Laura the stirrer. I had defended Laura vigorously, but I was beginning to accept that it was possible Laura had not been the person I'd believed her to be. As for Jack . . . logic said he could be fooling me, he could be sweet-talking me, but instinct – or was it love? – called me in the other direction. And at the moment love was winning hands down.

I'd arranged to meet Petra at the Tolling Bells office on the Friday morning, and she would then take me to Holt Capel Manor, where the event was to take place. July the twelfth was only three weeks away now. When I reached the office, however, plans had changed. 'I'll take you over,' Tom told me. 'Petra's been delayed. She'll meet us there.'

I had a few qualms after last night's talk with Jack, but I put them out of my mind. Tom was Tom; he wouldn't suddenly turn into a murderous monster.

Nevertheless, the journey didn't start well. 'Jane told me Jack's back,' he said casually. 'Planned, was it?'

'No. He just arrived. He's working in Folkestone and it seemed a good idea.' I tried not to sound defensive. Any normal day this would be a perfectly standard exchange.

'Folkestone?' Tom queried.

'It's a bit of a drive, but not impossible.'

'I thought I'd seen him in Canterbury, that's all.'

'Maybe,' I said shortly. I didn't want to get drawn on this. If Tom imagined Jack was snooping around because of my involvement with him, or even, it occurred to me, looking into Laura's murder, I didn't want to know. It could also be in self-defence, if he had known Laura better than he was admitting to me. With Jack at the cottage, and my volunteer work for Tolling Bells, I had no intention of being the punchbag in the middle. Not good – I needed to have a free hand, not to be tugged between my old friendship with Tom and my love for Jack. It would be the last straw if Jack thought there was something romantic going on between Tom and me, and decided to weigh in.

'How's the Jamie situation?' I asked brightly.

He warmed to this, and told me all about the weekend he and his son had spent together. 'I think he enjoyed it.' There was enough hesitation in Tom's voice to convince me that he was still worried about the future, however, even though I didn't doubt that the weekend had been a success.

'We did laddish things.' Tom laughed. 'Football, thrillers on DVD, computer games. He likes being outside though. Like Laura—' His voice broke.

I couldn't help responding, even though it brought me right into the area I'd hoped to avoid. 'Are you getting any further with clearing your name?'

A grimace. 'It's a lot harder than I expected. Everyone seems glad to see me back, and yet there's a distance there that I can't cover. It's like pushing my head against a cushion. It gives, but no breakthrough.'

I felt like that with Tom. If Laura was a stirrer, that meant she could well have stirred up the rumour of a mutual attraction between Tom and me – especially if it hid her own doings. Yet I could hardly ask Tom outright if he did fancy me. Sitting beside him in his car, I could swear there was no chemistry between us, but then I amended this. Not a sexual chemistry perhaps, but certainly an empathy that suggested a tie between us that was more than a shared past. Was that what Jack sensed too, just from my behaviour and what I said about him? Could that be why Jack was here? No, I dismissed the idea. Jack wasn't that sort.

And yet, I was uneasily reminded, I hadn't thought that Laura was *that sort* either.

'Could the cushion be only in your mind?' I asked Tom. I had enough cobwebs, veils and thorny hedges of my own to tackle, so I could sympathize with him.

'Probably.' He hesitated. 'No, *possibly*. Look, there's the Manor House.'

Holt Capel was a tiny village tucked away near Goodnestone, some way off the Sandwich road. It was new to me, which may seem surprising as I grew up not that far away as the crow flies. But Kent's network of lanes easily ensures that such places can escape notice from the twenty-first century. Not that the Manor appeared to be aiming at that. It was a large, turreted mid-Victorian house, which even at this distance seemed to be flourishing with twenty-first century money. It was certainly impressive, and ideal, I imagined, for fund-raising purposes, especially as it belonged to the chair of the trustees, Sir Neville Wilson.

'Is he an enthusiastic chair?' I asked.

'Yes. He barks, they woof and the staff howl.'

I laughed. 'Can't wait to meet him.'

'You'll have to, I'm afraid. He and his wife are in London during the week and won't be back until this evening. His secretary's come to take us round today.'

I recognized Petra's car on the forecourt, and Tom and I walked over the gravel to the front door. By the size and splendour of the lawn in front of the house, the rear promised to be quite something. Statues were tastefully adorning the shrubbery bordering the lawns, and a huge cedar tree in the middle of the grass looked as if King Solomon might have planted it.

I suppose I expected a flashy, trophy secretary, and so was surprised when the door opened. Tom obviously knew her from the affable greetings.

'Morning, Christine.'

Christine looked much more interesting than my stereotype blonde. She was well into her fifties and had a no-nonsense look about her smartly trouser-suited self.

'Has Petra given you an up-to-date figure for the guest list yet?'
I asked her as she led us through the house to the rear gardens.

'A hundred and sixty and counting.'

I whistled. 'All donors to the charity?'

Tom answered for her. 'Quite a few potentials. That's the point. We want to make them feel part of the gang.'

Since Petra and Tom were there and spearheading this operation from the logistics angle, I'd thought there would be little for me to do except to observe. In fact there was a lot. The caterers' representative was there, and I discovered to my surprise that I had definite views over the drinks and buffet arrangements, and where people should sit. When I'd finished that lot, Petra took me inside to show me the invitation list, which she said that either Christine or she would 'whizz' over to my laptop. Then there were names, addresses, things to sign, data protection acts and gift-aided contributions, etcetera. All in all, my head was whirling by the time we'd finished and Tom had driven me back to Canterbury.

'What do you think?' he asked me.

'About the job? Fine by me.'

'You and Petra getting along OK?'

'Yes, though I doubt if it will be a friendship for life,' I said frankly.

Tom laughed. 'She's all right when she lets her guard down and becomes a person.'

'Does that happen often?' I asked politely. Petra had been definitely in hostess work mode, and any glimpses I'd had of the real woman had been quickly dispelled by another dose of name-dropping and orders.

'Nope. Not with me, anyway. Christine's a different kettle of fish.'

'Yes, I liked her.'

'Did you recognize her?'

'No. Should I have done?'

'Christine Martin and husband Ken are Toby's parents, Laura's pupil. They bought Appley House a year or two ago. Where the Wests used to live.'

And where the treasure hunt had taken place.

*　　*　　*

At last I could see the tree where my blue thread was going to end.
Around me excitement was growing; we were jostling as we hurried
towards the finish. Laura was at my side and someone with dark hair,
Jane probably. And another face too, framed with fair hair, almost as fair
as Laura's, but the memory slipped away even as I clutched at it. There
was a strange sense of terror still. Could I see Jack's face there? I thought
perhaps I could. But maybe that was today again, putting its stamp on
the past, determined that the true picture couldn't be seen.

I'd been looking forward to entertaining Paul and Jane at the
cottage and I'd invited them over on the Monday evening, the
twenty-third of June, partly, I admitted to myself, as a bulwark
between Jack and myself. I'd invited Kate too, probably for the
same reason. Jack's great buddy, it now seemed. Jack had been to
see Kate several times, I discovered. I told myself it was of no
importance, but the uneasiness remained. Nevertheless, the evening
boded to be a peaceful one; we had friends to dinner in Dulwich
often enough, and this gathering wasn't going to be that different.

Or so I had thought. It began naturally enough. Paul was late
and coming straight from work – normal enough for a police
inspector – and Jane and Kate were chatting away and drinks
were flowing, while I was in the kitchen getting the meal ready.
Before Kate arrived (dramatically dressed in red and looking suspiciously like Sarah Siddons as Lady Macbeth) Jane had wanted to
help me out. She'd changed her mind as soon she'd seen my
haphazard approach to the noble art of cookery.

'You haven't changed,' she laughed. 'I came out to suggest we
went on a picnic tomorrow. I know a magical place. The children will be at school and so it will just be us, like the old days.'

But in the old days Laura had been there, I thought before I
could stop myself. I agreed though. 'Great idea. The forecast is
good – sun from late morning.' I'd enjoy it, and it would be a
welcome break.

Jane returned to the living room and through the serving hatch
I could hear her and Kate chatting happily about the subject
dearest to Jane's heart.

'How's your brood, Jane?' Kate enquired. 'Getting on all right
at nursery school?'

'Oh yes.' Billy and Alice's antics were described with enthusiasm, although, to be fair, not overdone, and they were indeed delightful children.

'I wanted to have a baby once,' Kate observed.

I popped my head through the hatch. 'You never told me about that. What happened?'

'The fifty per cent essential ingredient decided it was too much too soon. We put it off and then I got put off.'

'Were you married?' Jane was clearly grappling with why on earth someone would change their mind so radically.

'Briefly,' Kate answered cheerfully. 'Luckily, I have a brother who'd done his duty by the family and so my mother was quite happy to let me get divorced.'

'Ah, but you can't imagine what you've missed.'

'I can,' Kate said briskly. 'Nappies and screaming.'

'But that's not the point,' Jane said, distressed. 'It's the creation of continuing life.'

'You've certainly got two lovely children.' I popped my head through again to be a dutiful friend. It was news to me that Kate had ever yearned for motherhood and I was beginning to feel I didn't know anybody properly any more.

'But suppose they grow up into monsters?' Kate asked.

'They won't,' Jane replied blithely, and then to me as I came into the room with a bowl of salad, 'What about you, Emma?' And at that moment Jack came in from the garden.

He probably saw I was trapped because he came over and put his arm round my shoulders. 'We're going to produce a brood of our own soon, aren't we, Emma?'

Were we? I was stunned at how easily this vexed question seemed to have been solved. 'Sure,' I joked happily, 'I've got their names down for Alleyn's School and Dulwich College already. You have to start early.'

'That's great,' Jane said enthusiastically.

Kate gave me a quizzical look, and I winked back at her, as if to imply this was just one of Jack's jokes. As well it might be, I reflected. Fortunately, Jane wasn't looking at that moment. She would have been shocked. For her there was no choice about it. Children followed marriage (or partnership, if pushed) as the night the day, and if they didn't, it was the greatest tragedy for all concerned. I saw her point, but I also saw no point in the tragedy

aspect either. Good Queen Bess had had no children, but she
hadn't done too badly in life.

Then Kate chimed in. 'Emma says you've become a *Little
Women* fan, Jack. Planning to read *Good Wives* next, are you? You
could follow it up with *Little Men* and *Emma's Boys.*'

'Sounds good to me,' Jack threw back at her, laughing as though
he hadn't a care in the world, Perhaps, I hoped, he hadn't.

Jane looked puzzled, although I'd have thought she would have
known Louisa May Alcott's quartet of books, with her love of
traditional literature, but at that moment Paul arrived, looking
stressed out.

'Bad day?' Jane asked sympathetically, getting up to give him
a welcome kiss.

'Very,' he answered briefly.

'I walked here, so I'll drive you home tonight,' she offered.
'You have a drink or two.'

Theirs was a partnership that seemed to work well, I thought,
and certainly Paul was eager to accept her offer, and gradually
began to relax.

I had been basking in the happy glow of Jack's words. No
matter if he meant it or not, he'd *said* it, and that was surely the
most important indication. Perhaps because Paul was still carrying
the weight of work, the light atmosphere seemed to trickle away,
however, and although we ploughed on manfully the evening
failed to take off.

'We've met, haven't we?' Paul asked, as he shook hands with
Jack. He was eyeing him closely, more than social intercourse
would warrant.

'Possibly,' Jack replied. 'I used to live around these parts for a
time years ago.'

'Where was that?'

Still a little more to this than straight chit-chat, I thought
uneasily. Or was that hostess nerves at the fact that the conversation hadn't exactly been scintillating yet?

'Lilleybourne as a child, then Canterbury.' Jack's voice indicated
that the conversation was at an end.

'Maybe that's where we met,' Paul murmured hastily, but I
noticed throughout the evening the occasional puzzled look in
Jack's direction.

Jack has a distinctive face, not the kind you would forget, and Paul seemed preoccupied, as though still mulling it over. Laura came into my mind, but I pushed the memory out again. It hurt too much, although grief was no longer the only reason for that. After a quick glance at me, Kate must have decided to take the mantle of the evening on herself. She regaled us first with stories of the love affairs of the stars, past and present, and then tales of her mother's seaside boarding house lodgers, until at last Jack, and then the rest of us, joined in.

After we had shut the door behind Kate, the last lingerer, I looked at Jack. 'Was that just merry banter?' I asked bluntly. We both knew to what I was referring.

'If that's the answer you want.'

I longed to say no, that I desired nothing more than to be part of a new Scarlet family. But I couldn't. Not yet, with so much on my mind. I loved him, of course I did. So what to say . . .

'After,' I choked out.

'After what?' he persisted, although again he must have known what I meant.

'After it's sorted.'

'And what is *it* exactly?'

I did not answer immediately because *it* seemed to me indefinable. It wasn't a question of trust; it wasn't a question of love or murder. It was just a blanket of fog that had to be worked through inch by inch. But Jack was waiting for an answer.

'The treasure hunt,' I blurted out. 'Your mother was there, so you were there too.'

'What was this treasure hunt, and why is it so important?' He spoke quite gently, as though he really wanted to know.

I hesitated, torn between a desire to share and the nameless fear hanging over me. I compromised. 'It was when Laura was seven and her parents gave a party at Appley House; it's near the old school and church in Ducks Green. There was a treasure hunt in their orchard; we all had strands of wool to unwind and the first one would get the big prize.' It sounded crazy put into words.

'And did you win?' he prompted me when I came to a stop, unable to define what was so special about it.

'No.'

'Did Laura?'

'I don't think so.'

'And you remember me there?'

'No. Your mother was there though, and there were several older children there so it was quite possible.'

'But why is it important?' he asked me very gently, taking me into his arms, as though he could tease memory from me.

'I don't know, Jack. I don't know.'

Ten

'This picnic of yours . . .' Jack said at breakfast the next morning. He hadn't been there when Jane had proposed it, but I'd mentioned it to him when we woke up. He hadn't commented then, and so I was surprised that he raised it now. 'Where are you going?'

He was frowning, which immediately put me on the defensive. What was so wrong about a picnic? Nothing, I decided. It wasn't as if Tom were coming.

'I don't know where exactly, but I have faith in the Kentish weather – and in Jane,' I replied. 'It might look a bit murky outside, but it's going to clear up.'

Jack didn't look impressed. 'Where are you going? Off to the seaside?'

'Locally, I expect. It's somewhere Jane knows. Having to get back to pick up the children would make it too tight to go far afield.'

The subject of children backtracked me immediately to the evening before, and Jack's plan for us to live happily ever after with children of our own. Why is it that with Paradise in sight, we fallible human beings think it might be too good to be true and start picking holes in it? I wanted to hear Jack repeat the offer, or reassure me that he didn't regret it, but that was a doomed hope at breakfast-time, I reasoned. Should I raise it? No, the time wasn't right and I risked a rebuff. Anyway, I still had a sneaking qualm to wrestle with. Somewhere deep inside me a serpent was stirring, reminding me that Laura's murder still lay between us and our Garden of Eden, or, to be specific, Jack's odd attitude to the whole question of Laura. I told the serpent that I had to move forward, not duck the issue, but it still wriggled its protest.

Jack had moved to the kitchen sink to wash the dishes and, as I picked up the tea towel, I heard myself say, 'Mark believes it was Laura who first alerted me to his affair with Anna.' As there was no reply from Jack, I pushed on with, 'And what's more, he told me Laura did this all the time.'

I sensed Jack freeze – or was that my imagination? 'And what do you think?'

'It's shaken me. I'd never thought of Laura in that light.' I'd only thought of what she had meant to me. But the question was: what had I meant to her?

Instead of saying something helpful, he came out with, 'And now?'

'I can't get that far yet.'

'You have to.'

Jack was right. I'd chosen of my own free will – albeit prodded by Tom's visit – to revisit the past, and the downside was that I was stuck with examining whatever it revealed, whether I liked it or not. I couldn't just wrap it up again and put it away. The difficulty was that it might be history, but history is never set in stone, however much one might like to think so. It's being viewed through the lenses of today's perspective, and however much one struggles one can never be sure that some other aspect is not obscuring the view. I said this to Jack, concluding, 'Somehow I have to get today's glasses off.'

'Only you can do that.'

True, but not helpful. 'Tell me one thing, Jack,' I pressed him, aware I was treading in dangerous waters. 'You knew Laura, even if not well. Could you believe it of her that she was a stirrer, that she stirred once too often and that someone killed her for it?'

I saw him swallow, but it can't have been me he was thinking about. He was staring out through the window into the garden beyond, but not looking at it. He was far away in some other place, where I could not follow him. He shook his head, but not to deny the truth of what I'd said.

'My turn to say I don't know,' he said, and for a moment I thought there were tears in his eyes.

I must have imagined it, for Jack had then briskly turned to ask whether I had any shopping requirements that he could get in Folkestone, and the moment had passed. Even so, it lingered in my mind, perhaps because I'd never heard Jack say 'I don't know' before on any important issue, and I'd never seen him look so vulnerable. Perhaps that was because I had been seeing him through my own lenses of self doubt at that moment. He'd left for Folkestone shortly after that, seemingly as normal, and I had

would fester. Once out, it might get resolved, especially if I had help along the way. I needed that, and this was surely the best possible place.

I was there now with Jane, but when had I been there before and with whom? Not with Mark. Not with my parents. Perhaps it had been with Laura and Jane herself. Perhaps Tom too. We could have come in a sort of gang, those of us who lived in or near Cobshaw or Ducks Green.

I plunged right into it. 'I thought everyone loved Laura as much as we did, but I've discovered they didn't.'

'That often happens,' Jane observed. 'Everyone has to be disliked by someone.'

'Even someone as kind as we believed her?'

'Even she. She was too beautiful not to be disliked,' Jane said practically. 'Isn't there a famous whodunit about a beautiful woman whom everyone thinks is the manipulator, but who turns out to be the victim?'

'Laura wasn't a manipulator,' was my immediate reaction. Then I remembered Mark's words: *she was a stirrer.* That meant manipulation.

'Not in the usual sense,' Jane replied. 'But she was so good to look at that it put her in control in a way; we deferred to her because we loved her. That was fine for you and me, but for women who didn't know her so well, it must have been galling to see their husbands falling over themselves to gain her attention. It wasn't Laura's fault – and she did end up the victim.'

I thought of Lee Hunt-White. I thought of Jack, and pushed him out again. 'Tom's partner, Lee,' I began. 'How well do you know him?'

'As much as I do his designer-clad blonde bombshell wife, but that doesn't add up to a lot.'

· 'Remember we talked about his possibly having had an affair with Laura?'

A pause. 'Yes, and do you want to know what I've been wondering about?'

'I'd like to.' It was more of a 'had to'. I couldn't go back now.

'That it was possible, but Laura might have been one of those ice-queen beauties. She attracted all those men because she was a stunner compared to us, but she didn't do anything about it, and perhaps didn't even intend to attract them. But how could the wives know that?'

I clutched at this life-saver, which could well be the answer. 'And so how could Tom know that?' I began to see how Tom's jealousy could have arisen without cause. The more he saw that look in men's eyes when they were with Laura, the more a jealous man might have imagined it was mutual desire. Then I saw where this might lead me. 'That brings me back to Tom again as the most likely suspect.'

'I know,' Jane said, 'but at least it wouldn't be Jack.'

I didn't fully understand at first. Not Jack? And then I realized what Jane hadn't dared to spell out. That a man maddened by a woman he desired, who deliberately teased and then drew back from the brink, might be capable of anything. And that, theoretically, could apply to Lee or Jack. I was back in the quagmire, which meant I would have to struggle out of it again. No doubt about that, I had to.

'Laura was the victim.' I felt disloyal to Laura by even discussing her with Jane, but I had no choice. 'Mark told me she stirred up trouble, and since then I've thought of a couple of occasions when she had talked about other people in a way that might come under that category. Now you're adding that she could have been a deliberate tease?'

Jane looked horrified. 'Oh no. I can't really believe it. She might just have been trying to warn you to keep your eyes open about Mark, just as I might over Jack. I don't believe that Laura was malicious. Full stop.'

She was so agitated that I put my arm round her, and she calmed down. 'No,' I agreed, 'let's think of her as the victim she became.'

I would try. Oh, how I would try.

I poured Jane another glass of wine and, as she sipped it, she said, 'I'm sorry, Emma. It's you who ought to be getting hysterical, not me. You must feel trapped.'

'By Ducks Green?' I hoped that was what she meant.

She didn't. 'I meant between Tom and Jack. Being so fond of Tom and so in love with Jack, and they must be at daggers drawn, each believing the other a murderer.'

I shivered. 'That's what Tom is implying, and Jack hasn't

pronounced on what he feels, although it's pretty obvious.' I wondered how I could even be sitting there discussing it. 'There's no love lost between them, but I'm not certain the dislike is anything to do with Laura. They're so different, it could be instinctive dislike. Tom's steady, reliable and family orientated; Jack's a rover, a mixer and has every appearance of unreliability except on important matters.'

'Is Laura an important matter?'

'Oh Jane.' She had struck to the heart of it. Whichever way I came at it, I felt distanced from Jack over Laura. 'Something is coming between us, and it must be Laura. Yet he won't talk about it. He wants me to trust him.'

'And do you? It's important, as you and he both want to start a family.'

'I know. I can't imagine parting from him and so I have to get over this hurdle first.'

'Is he jealous about your working with Tom?' Jane looked really worried now.

'He's no need to be.' I felt almost apologetic. 'I like Tom, and can't believe he murdered Laura, whatever the row they had was about. I feel that we're friends and on the same side. Everything going for us, but the magic has never been there between us.'

The minute I'd said this, I felt I had said something significant, almost scarily so, and yet I couldn't see what. Tom was Tom.

'Perhaps that's because Tom could still be guilty of strangling Laura.'

'Probably.' I began to feel sick, but it was nothing to do with Jane's glorious picnic or with the wine. I'd realized what had been significant. Not Tom, but the word magic. But what was significant about it? I stood up giddily, hoping the movement would clear my head, but the view of Canterbury began to swim before my eyes, dissolving into yesterday's memory . . .

'What did you get, Emma?' Laura was sharing the excitement of my unwrapping the parcel tied at the end of my blue thread. I can't remember now what was in it, only the look on Laura's face: kind, curious, involved. Behind her was someone else, but I still could not grasp who. There seemed no face to linger on in memory, only a blur. How could I be sure that these memories came in their original sequence? It seemed to me there was something missing.

In this particular memory I could even smell the grass, hear the bees on the last traces of the apple blossom and the hum and cries of the other guests, distanced as in a film with only the main players audible. But mostly I remember Laura's yellow hair tumbling over her face, and the expression in her eyes. Eager, affectionate and not jealous of what I had received. Jane was with us – or was it another girl? I could no longer be sure. Laura – and this time I'm certain it was her – put out her hand to touch my arm. 'I know somewhere lovely,' she said. 'I found it when I was out walking with Daddy and Mummy. I ran on by myself and found a sort of magic place. Shall we go, Emma? You could come too.' She turned to the other girl – but there the memory faded.

'It was here,' I cried. 'No, not here, but *near* here.'

'What was?' Jane asked blankly.

'Laura's magic place. Did you come?'

'Emma, you're raving,' Jane told me kindly.

'I'm not. Laura and I used to go there.'

Her lips pursed together. 'Where?' Jane wasn't one for the fantastic.

'The magic place,' I repeated, still not knowing what I meant by that.

'But where was it?' Jane was growing impatient, which was hardly surprising. I wasn't making much sense, except to myself.

I stared out around the field. Nothing, except for the wood behind us. What lay within it? I glanced back along the path, and remembered my involuntary turn to the right. Could that have been instinct kicking in?

I hurried back, only vaguely conscious that Jane was following me. She must have thought I was crazy – as perhaps I was.

I turned at the same point as earlier, and was shortly faced by a barbed-wire fence and overgrown hedges. Behind the barbed wire was rotting wood fencing, overgrown with ivy, bracken and nettles. How did I know that? I was torn between trepidation at my certainty and an odd excitement. This was not a public foot-path or presumably the barbed wire would not be barring it, but that, too, was rusty and decaying, and it was no great matter to cross it.

'Where are you going?' Jane called out behind me, as she saw me going into the wood.

'I don't know,' I yelled back, 'but I'll find it.'

Once inside the wood I knew exactly where I was going. To the magic place – wherever and whatever it was. The path was not too overgrown by ferns and weeds, owing to the cover of overhanging trees, but even so I had no conscious idea of what to look for. I would only know when I arrived.

And twenty yards in, I did.

'Bluebells,' I said out loud. There should be bluebells here. There were *always* bluebells.

Jane heard me. 'They're over,' she called plaintively. 'It's June now. Come back, Emma. Please.'

I looked round and she was white-faced, having just climbed over the fence herself. I wished I could stop, but there was no way.

'You stay here, Jane.' I turned into what must have seemed to Jane an impenetrable mass of ferns and undergrowth; in fact they were hiding a wall, an ancient stone one, overgrown with ivy so thick that it must be holding the wall up by itself.

'I'm coming,' Jane panted from somewhere behind me, and I stopped.

'We climbed this, Laura and I,' I told her when she joined me.

To children that would have seemed perfectly normal, and so I climbed right over it now, with Jane bewailing my actions behind me. Once over, I knew where to go. 'Down to the stream,' I cried in triumph.

What to a child is a glorious stream, full of potential, can be a dried-up ditch to an adult. This was one now, anyway. Perhaps after heavy rain it might be full of water again, for water-loving plants and indeed mud at the bottom indicated that. There had been bluebells there too, bordering the stream under the trees, and I could hear the trickle of that stream from long ago. But this wasn't the magic place. That was further along. I knew that now. I couldn't remember what was there, but I knew this was the way to it. I began to stumble along the bank through the marsh marigolds and lords and ladies, until the way forward was blocked by a thicket hedge so solid that there was no opening.

'It's like Sleeping Beauty, isn't it?' Laura whispered in my ear. 'Oh, the poor prince, trying to force his way through.'

'Suppose there's nothing on the other side?' I whispered back.

'There is, there is. We have to paddle along further.'

And so I did so now, scrambling down into the ditch, trying to avoid the worst of the boggy places. There was no other way.

And so I came once more to the magic place.

I knew it immediately. The ditch had turned suddenly and beyond the wall it opened out into what had once been a pond, surrounded by banks of grass, and cut off from the rest of the grounds by a tall thicket hedge running round the rest of the arc. Within it the pond and its small surrounding garden were still sleeping there alone. The pond was now only marked by reeds, irises and ferns, and an overhanging straggly willow. I could see no water down there, only mud.

Someone, sometime, had decided to make this place impenetrable, with the stream as its only entrance. Now, even in June, it looked a sad place, but then – how can I describe it? Slowly, it crept back into my mind and took life again. It must have been neglected even when we found it as children but there were roses and water lilies there in my memory; there was Laura leaning over to see her reflection from the bank on which we sat. There was even a stone loving seat. I went over to see if it was still there, and clearing away the ivy I could see it was. Laura had told me that she'd got lost one day, and found this place by chance. Her parents, not finding her, had called out, and she'd scrambled back, not telling them of her discovery.

Over it was what had been some kind of arbour, now broken by the weight of dead branches. No roses last forever, but a stray bush gone wild could be seen on the far hedge, where I remembered them in profusion.

We did not question then who this place belonged to. We did not need to. It was ours.

'What is it?' Jane had clambered along the stream and had climbed up behind me.

'Laura's magic place.' I could hardly get the words out, not sure I was able to share this memory yet. 'We used to come here. Did you come too?'

The answer was obvious and Jane looked even more overcome than I was. 'Yes,' she said, staring around her, looking bewildered. 'Yes, I'm sure I did. Not often though.'

'Laura told me about it at the treasure hunt. You were there too. You were the other girl, weren't you?'

'What treasure hunt?' Jane asked, but when I explained she still looked puzzled. 'Yes, I think I was there. What of it?'

She seemed to be appealing for me to remember for her, but I couldn't. We were both at the point when unsummoned memories give way to those we are actively trying to grasp.

'It all seems linked, that's all.' The words sounded daft, even to me.

'I don't like it,' Jane declared, and I could see her shivering.

'How old were we?' I asked abruptly. 'We were only seven when we first came here, but when did we stop?'

Jane shrugged. 'Goodness knows. We just grew out of it, I suppose. Probably when we went to secondary school. The boys didn't go in for magic.'

'Tom. Was he around then?'

'Earlier than that, I think. He wasn't at Ducks Green Primary with us, but he lived in Cobshaw and used to join in with the sort of gang we'd formed with some others. I suppose we forgot this place because in time we all felt we'd outgrown magic.' She gave a puzzled look around. 'It doesn't look very magic now, does it?'

'No, but I remember how I felt that first time Laura brought us here.' Us or me? Whichever, I remembered the sense of privilege when Laura showed me her secret place and with what wonder I had explored every corner, feeling like the child in Frances Hodgson Burnett's *The Secret Garden*. This was Laura's secret garden and she had shared it with me.

There was a difference between then and now, however. As I stood there with Jane I was no longer a child, and I knew there were different forms of magic: white and black. I knew that black witches can dwell in woodland cottages as well as white ones, and I wondered whether in this secret place the black witch, too, had been present, and if that was why the magic had been lost, and thus our memories of it.

'We used to walk further up the stream,' I said out of the blue, surprising myself. Without waiting for Jane, I scrambled down into the ditch again. I'd seen enough. Jane followed me so quickly that she must have had the same reaction.

About fifty yards further along, the ditch drew close to the barbed-wire fence. 'It was here,' I said.

'What was?'

'Where we sometimes scrambled out.'

'Why here?'

'I don't remember.'

Or did I? I found a spot in the wire which was passable and although Jane voiced strong objections she climbed after me. We were higher up in the picnic meadow and the view of Canterbury was similar but better than the picnic spot. This, not the other spot, had been the perfect place. But are picnic spots ever perfect? Aren't there always ants' nests, or stones, or nettles to remind one that life is not entirely a picnic?

'That's strange,' said Jane, as she looked at the view. 'I remember it quite clearly now, but I'd forgotten it earlier. Perhaps that's best,' she added, 'in the circumstances. Best to forget what happened.'

'Happened?' I repeated. 'You mean the murder.'

'Yes, Laura's murder. Let's get the picnic stuff and go,' she said briskly. 'It's getting chilly.'

Memories were rushing back so fast that I could not make sense or order out of them.

'Look, Emma, there's my magic castle.' Laura pointed at the pinnacles in the distance. 'Isn't it lovely?'

'It's a cathedral,' Tom pointed out.

Laura turned on him, hurt. 'It's a castle today, Tom. For Emma, Jane, you and me. Can't you play pretend?'

'Not on magic stuff. It doesn't exist.'

'It does, it does . . .' Laura began to cry. 'You just have to believe in it.'

'It does exist, Tom,' said someone. It wasn't me though. I couldn't read the faces now. In the old pantomimes of the nineteenth century there would be a transformation scene in which a curtain of gauze would descend between the action and the audience. One had now descended on my memory. What had once been clear, no longer was. But in a transformation scene, one knew what was behind the curtain. Here, that knowledge was missing.

Eleven

I parted from Jane at Ducks Green village hall and walked back, shaken, to the cottage. It's said that the last mile home is the longest, and this one most certainly was. I tried to make sense of what I'd seen, but the more I struggled to get it into logical order the more it retreated beyond my reach. Tom had been to the magic place, yet never referred to it. Jane had been there, but couldn't remember it clearly. And I . . . didn't want to remember it clearly, because it must remind me too much of Laura.

I turned into Love Lane, not with a sense of homecoming to Wychley Cottage, which only presented more questions, but with the realization that the answers to them might lie within my own mind.

There was no sign of Jack's car in the parking patch, which was a relief because it gave me more time to think out what to tell him about the day – if anything. So far as the magic place was concerned, Jack was an outsider and so how could I convey to him the import of its rediscovery to me? And yet he had shared the experience of the treasure hunt with me as I related it. Why not this too?

I glanced at the cottage, which looked so placid and innocent, but promptly turned left into Kate's garden, more out of cowardice than anything. It gained me a breathing space. There was no sign of Kate working in the garden, but I decided to knock anyway to see if she was in. I needed a dose of her practicality.

She took one glance at my face as she opened the back door to me. 'Come in. Knocked over an aspidistra, have you?' She was referring to a famous incident in my youth when I had run howling to her for help.

I managed a laugh. 'If only.'

'That bad? Tea or whisky?'

'Tea, please.' The latter was tempting, but what wits I had needed to be in prime condition.

Kate busied herself with cups and kettle. 'Nice dinner party last night. Thank you.'

I watched her, envious of her sorted-out life. 'Do you ever re-enter the past, Kate?' I knew the answer, of course.

'No. Nasty place. It moves around, so you can never quite get to grips with it. Much better to pop in now and again just to pick up a memory or two.'

'I agree.' I began to cheer up immediately. 'That was my attitude until . . .'

'Until you came back to Ducks Green,' Kate finished for me. 'But it's not the village's fault, Emma. It's moved on and left Laura's murder too far behind for your purposes.'

'People who knew her don't seem to have forgotten.'

'Because the murder's unresolved,' Kate pointed out. 'It's covered over and not revisited unless something or someone stirs it up – like you're doing. Ever see those time plays by Priestley? *Dangerous Corner*, for instance. In it time slips back to a watershed moment when if some little detail had changed, the whole course of events could have been different. And, of course, there are people's memories to take into account. Take four truthful witnesses and you get four different stories. Ever see Kurosawa's *Rashomon*—'

'Stop!' I began to laugh. 'I can only absorb one new idea a day.'

'How boring.' Kate pulled a face. 'Now, what was it you came about?'

'I went on a picnic with Jane.' It was easy to talk to Kate and this might help. 'Inevitably, we got back to Laura.'

Kate frowned. 'That's what you came back here to do.'

'Yes, but it's taken a different turn. It may be nothing to do with the murder but it's disturbing.' I hesitated. 'You remember where the Wests lived, in Ducks Green?'

'Appley House. Yes.'

'I know Toby Martin's parents own it now. Have they changed it much? Is the orchard still there? I keep having flashbacks of a treasure hunt there, where I first met Laura.'

'You're worried about that?' Kate looked at me with keen attention, not as if I were dotty.

'Only because there's something I can't grasp, and keep feeling I should.'

'You're in good company there. I don't either. More helpfully, I presume you haven't tried to see it again.'

'What?' I realized how tense I was as the word shot out.

'Don't be so edgy.' Kate eyed me curiously, as well she might. 'Do you want to go back to this orchard of yours? The Martins are friends of mine. I can fix it, especially as Christine said she'd met you.'

'Yes, please.' I was surprised at how eager I was. What on earth was I hoping for? That fifteen little tots would reappear from a quarter of a century earlier and take up their former roles in the hunt?

Kate was already on the phone. 'No reply,' she said, putting the receiver down. 'I'll ring again and let you know.' A pause. 'Is this going to *help*, Emma? Suppose it just brings up more unwelcome memories. This treasure hunt can't have anything to do with Laura's murder.'

'It might help.' Put that way it sounded a forlorn hope, which made me hesitate even more about raising the subject of the magic place. But I decided to go ahead. 'Do you know anything about the owners of the land up behind Ducks Green, including Mereden Wood? I was up there with Jane today.'

'Show me,' Kate commanded. She fetched an Explorer large-scale map from her desk and I pinpointed the place with ease.

'Somewhere around here.'

'I'm pretty sure that's the Belleview estate,' Kate said. 'Mean anything to you? Way back in the nineteenth century it belonged to some lord or other. A lot of rumours grew up around it, which developed into legends, such as that his wife had run off with a lover, he'd murdered her then gone mad, he refused to touch the pleasure gardens she had created because she was buried in them, etcetera, etcetera. It was derelict for a time, and the last couple who actually did anything to the gardens bought the place for a song after the Second World War, convinced it was going to be their life's work to develop it. Their dreams were bigger than their bank balance so they did little bits here and there. The current owner, who inherited it from them about ten years ago, is still living in the house, and still hoping he'll get a lottery grant to restore the grounds. A Lost Gardens of Heligan sort of thing. There'd be no chance of planning permission for building there, so no temptation for developers that way, but meanwhile the gardens slumber on.'

Bits of the story came back to me now: odd comments by my parents, and references to it when Mark and I lived here. I'd paid little attention, even though to find such a place lingering in Kent was unusual.

'Strange your finding your way up there.' Kate looked at me thoughtfully. 'Does *this* have anything to do with the murder, Emma?'

'I don't know,' I answered truthfully. 'Probably not. It's just a place I used to visit with her – and with Jane,' I added. 'Like the orchard, which is where I first met her.'

'Sure you're not getting nostalgically sidetracked?'

'I don't think so. Laura's death was so unlikely, given the kind of person I at least thought she was, that the reason for it could lie in the *sort* of person she really was.' I stopped. 'Does that make sense?'

'No,' said Kate flatly.

That was hardly surprising. It didn't to me, either. So I tried again. 'Jane reminded me that Tom was part of our group then.'

Kate sighed. 'When?'

'Our primary school days, when we used to go to this spot on the Belleview estate.'

'Relevance, please? I might be dim, but I see none.'

'Nor do I,' I confessed. 'And yet there might be a link. Something I'm not remembering. Something to do with Tom, perhaps.'

Kate looked even more concerned. 'Don't remember too hard, Emma. Please. Especially where Tom's concerned.'

Jack came back late that night, tired and obviously worried about something, which from experience I knew he was not going to, or perhaps was not able to, share with me.

'Good day?' he asked, without much interest.

'Yes, thanks.' That seemed the simplest answer.

'Have fun with Jane?'

'Yes.' I decided to goad him out of his detachment, and my previous reservations vanished. He was involved in the Laura story, and I saw no reason why he shouldn't know about this development. 'We found a place both of us had forgotten about. Kate says it's part of the old Belleview estate. We used to play there as children. It used to be a small, secluded garden with a pond. No access except by the stream, now a ditch, and the pond is just mud.'

No reaction greeted this somewhat unusual statement, save for polite interest, and for some reason I was relieved at that. What had I expected? That Jack was going to clasp his forehead and reveal some hitherto forgotten gem?

'Who's we?' he asked. 'You and Jane?'

'Yes. Laura, Jane and probably Tom too. I'd forgotten he was one of our gang then.'

He gave me his full attention now. 'How could you overlook that? Damn chap seems to crop up everywhere,' he murmured. It wasn't like Jack to be sarcastic, and it made me uneasy.

'I suppose the place was lethal for children our age.' I felt I had to continue to prize more reaction from him. 'Our parents couldn't have had the slightest idea what we were up to.'

'Not going to make a habit of trespassing, are you?'

'Not good for the reputation,' I quipped.

'Tom was with you? How come? I thought you only knew him at secondary school.'

'That's what I remembered, but Jane reminded me he'd been there a lot earlier than that. He lived in Cobshaw then, so we were a sort of gang, even if not at the same school.'

'This gang, who was in it?'

I looked at him blankly. 'Laura, me. Tom, Jane—' I tried, but no more faces came to mind. Names of fellow pupils came back to me, but were they in the gang? I couldn't be sure, any more than I could be sure of who was at that birthday party. In adult years, it is easier to pigeonhole facts and faces, but the teens can form an impenetrable barrier between childhood and adulthood. So much is happening in the teens that only the memories involving self and those who most affect one make their way through to adulthood, and even they can get laid aside as interests and circumstances change.

There was no way I could cross that barrier. Somewhere those facts and faces might lie sleeping in my brain, but how to find them? And, even more important, how to recognize them for what they were?

Jack was waiting, and I had to tell him I'd drawn a blank. It didn't seem to matter. He was back in detached mode. 'No problem,' he said. 'Being three years older my gang would have been entirely different to yours.' Then an unexpected switch of tack. 'Emma, the Folkestone job's over so far as going there is concerned.'

'You're going back to Dulwich?' False step.

'Would you like me to?'

'No.'

'Good. Because I'm not. I'm working here for the moment.'

How did we get to this bleak point? I wondered. The distance between us was growing rapidly. '"Here" meaning "in the cottage"?'

'Why not? I've got a laptop and a mobile. What more do I need?'

I would never have believed that I could get quite so involved in the intricacies of name badges, various diets and bottles of bubbly that I could manage to suppress all other thoughts. I managed it, however, as the days passed, and Saturday, the twelfth of July, grew nearer and nearer. It was made easier because I was either at Tolling Bells' office or at Petra's home or Holt Capel, which also made it easier to establish a working relationship with Petra. After a week we were almost matey. On the Friday, with eight days still to go, we decided to lunch together at a local pub. We were sitting in the garden, waiting for our salads and running through a list of outstanding matters, when she commented out of the blue, 'I have to keep an eye on Lee. He's got a thing for Mrs Patterson-Hughes.'

'You're not serious.' Silly thing to say. One look at her and it was clear she was. I'd met the lady in question and she was not just rolling in money, she was a veritable Swiss roll of it – and looked like one, to boot.

'With Lee, of course I am.' She eyed me dispassionately. 'Luckily, you're not his type. And probably not rich enough.'

'Thanks,' I said, amused.

To her credit she laughed and became quite human. 'Sorry. It's actually a compliment, seeing some of the tarts he falls for.'

'So it's never serious then.' I tried to make it sound a statement, not a question, but Laura was very much in my mind.

Petra shrugged. 'At what point does not serious become serious?'

'When you love someone,' I shot back promptly.

'But how do you know that,' she asked quietly, 'when you're in danger of losing him?'

I thought of Jack. 'With me, it's all the time. Not wise, perhaps.'

Petra was there in one. 'Tom's told me about your Jack Scarlet.'

'Has he?' I was not pleased, imagining what he might have said.

'Hardly in glowing terms. He thinks you're in over your head. Are you?'

'Aren't we all when we're in love?' I responded lightly.

'No way. I have my head well above water where Lee's concerned. I need to see what's going on.'

Uneasily, I wondered if by any chance she *did* mean with me, but apparently not.

'Your friend Laura,' she continued. 'That *was* serious. I had to try to sort out whether I wanted Lee as a fixture or not. We had two kids by then, so that helped me decide, but at one point I thought we were heading for the courts.'

I felt a curious mixture of relief that Laura's death could be more straightforward than I was fearing, relief that Jack was therefore probably not her lover – and dismay that this was confirmation that Laura could have had an affair with someone so seemingly superficial as Lee.

'He had an affair with Laura?' I asked baldly. The time for discretion was past.

'Must have done. Lee doesn't waste his time if there's no bed at the end of it, and preferably at the beginning too.'

'Suppose,' I thought of Jane's words, 'she was a tease, a frigid ice-queen?'

Petra hooted with laughter. 'If you believe that, fine. I'd quite like to think of Lee chasing a tail that didn't stop and wag for him. Wasn't there a US president who said he'd committed adultery in his heart? Lee doesn't have a heart, but if he managed to find one, it would be either for me or for Laura. There was just a moment when our marriage looked as if it was crashing on the rocks. Tom says you're divorced, so you must know all about that.'

'I do.' For me it had been the day when Laura had put Mark's affair with Anna into hesitant words. Before, it had only been a sinking feeling that I could manage to dispel. The pain had been bad.

'Did Tom know about Laura and Lee?' I asked. Interesting that it had been Jack and not Lee whom Tom had picked on as Laura's lover.

'I don't see how he could have missed it, so I'm sure he did.' Petra hesitated. 'I'm sorry, because you were Laura's friend, but she was killed and there had to be a reason. It couldn't have been Lee, if that's what you're thinking. He's far too fond of his own skin. If Laura had played him up, he'd just have come crawling back to me. As for Tom, I like him, but having him in Africa was a whole lot easier than working with him here after her murder. I was glad when he left. And now he's back I'm still not too sure about it.'

On this uneasy note, we tacitly decided to get back to arrangements for the twelfth of July.

When I reached the cottage that evening, I saw the laptop on the table, but no Jack. He was sitting in the conservatory, and as I approached I could see Kate's copy of *Good Wives* on the table. No mistaking that jacket. Curiouser and curiouser, as Alice in Wonderland said. This indicated he'd been so delighted with *Little Women* that he'd picked up the sequel. *Very* odd, even if at the moment he was just staring out of the window, and was unaware of my arrival. I crept up unnoticed behind him.

'How's Beth doing?' I asked cheerily. 'Is she dead yet?' That was the scene everyone remembered.

He jumped a mile high. '*What?*' Then he saw me looking at the book. 'Oh yes. I've finished it now. How did you get on?'

I told him about the arrangements for the big do, and he asked a few questions about the guests, even offering to come along and help. So I took a step forward. 'Lee and Laura appear to have been an item?' I tried to look casual and not as though I was scrutinizing him for his reactions – which I was. 'Do you think that's possible?'

He seemed almost bored by the subject. 'Who knows?' he said wearily. 'I'm constantly surprised. I'm supposed, in my job, to be able to spot a con man at a hundred yards, but I can't. It's a lot harder than that. Emma,' he asked abruptly, 'do you like this place?'

'Cobshaw or the cottage?' I asked, surprised. 'Yes to both, in fact. Why?'

'You don't feel, well, threatened here?'

'What do you mean?' I trotted out this inane response, but I knew very well what he meant.

'With these woods around us, I have the oddest feeling that we're not alone. We're being watched.'

'It's the trees,' I managed to say, trying to hold on to a rational explanation. 'They give you the feeling they're about to close in. Laura—'

He made an impatient gesture and I quickly shut up, remembering Mark getting infuriated during our marriage if I went on too long about her. Perhaps rightly so, in hindsight. 'No. It's happened in Canterbury too.'

'*Canterbury?*'

'Oh God.' Jack stopped pacing around the conservatory and threw himself down in his chair again. 'I should have explained. The job's still on, but it's moved back to Canterbury.'

It was too quick, too glib a response. 'No, it hasn't. It's been there all the time, hasn't it? Folkestone was to put me off the scent.'

'If you want to put it that way, yes.'

'Why didn't you tell me?' I shouted. I took a flying leap into the dark. 'It has something to do with Tom, doesn't it?'

'Partly. I can't discuss it. You know that.'

'A bloody convenient excuse. What the hell's going on, Jack? *Tell* me. You know you can trust me, and I am involved in this.'

'I could trust you *once*. Now I hardly recognize you, Emma. You belong more to Laura, or even Jane or Petra, than to me. And as for Tom—' He shrugged.

I felt poleaxed by this unfair attack. 'And what about you?' I retaliated. 'You've stonewalled about Laura on every occasion. You admit you knew her, but you won't tell me anything more. *Or* anything more about a job that includes the man I'm working for. How do you expect me to feel?'

'To trust me when it's essential.' He stared me down, and I was looking at the face of a stranger. The muscle in Jack's cheek was working furiously. 'I'd better leave, Emma. Tomorrow – tonight. I'll go back to London.'

Then, before I even had a chance to react, he changed again. 'Hell, no, I can't do that, Emma. I can't leave you here alone. No way.'

'Because you love me, or because of what I'm finding out?'

Jack flushed with anger. 'You're on the wrong track,' he threw at me. 'Because it's not safe here, that's bloody why. Even if you moved back into Kate's house, I couldn't leave. That's why I came here, for heaven's sake.'

'Why should anyone attack us?' I stammered, taken aback by his vehemence and clutching at common sense. 'Because of Laura or because of this job of yours, Jack?'

'I don't know the answer, Emma.'

Which is worse: to have one's partner sleep in another room, or in the same bed but not communicating? We opted for the latter, but not through love. Out of need. It seemed to me we were both stepping into the darkness but each choosing our own route.

'If you still have this fixation of yours about orchards,' Kate said, when I saw her the next day, 'the Martins have suggested we come round on Monday evening. Is Jack coming?'

My first reaction was that I wanted to go alone, but my second was that, as his mother had been present at the treasure hunt, Jack should be there as well. Even though he must have been present, he'd forgotten it. This might jog his memory.

When I asked him, he was keener to come than I had expected. 'But what do you expect to find,' he asked, 'except for a few trees in an orchard?'

'I don't know.'

He looked at me thoughtfully, but his comment was surprisingly reasonable. 'It can't have anything to do with Laura's murder, only to do with your friendship with her.'

'It might have,' I said, against all reason. 'You never know. At least I'd like to pin my flashbacks down to reality.'

He said no more, and I felt diminished. I was firmly defending my corner, and clearly everyone else was merely humouring me. The best way to keep me quiet.

When we arrived, I was disappointed that Toby wasn't there, but Christine and her unexpectedly jolly husband Ken welcomed me as though it was the most natural thing in the world for someone to demand to see your orchard. We began with polite chat and drinks – not smoothed by the fact that I could see a framed photo of a young Toby, aged about thirteen or so, seated at what was undoubtedly Laura's piano. I did my best with the conversation, but was grateful when we set off down the garden.

At first I thought I was making a terrible mistake. I recognized nothing here, not in the borders, the lawns or the paths. Nor did I recognize anything in myself; nothing stirred memory, and I thought I was on a wild goose chase, as we filed along behind Christine and Ken towards the garden gate at the far end. Ken opened the gate and I followed him through. I was in the orchard once more.

And it was just that, an orchard.

It was going to be me! With a thrill of excitement, I realized that I had managed to unwind my blue thread from the last tree first. I would run up to Laura's father and win the special prize. But then I saw Laura behind me. She should win it. She was shy, she knew no one here, it would please her and she'd been kind to me. So I let her overtake me, and I watched in pleasure as she took the prize.

But no, none of this could have happened. I fought in vain against the cobwebs veiling the truth. It couldn't have been Laura who won that special prize because her father had said she should let one of her guests do so as it was her birthday . . . The cobwebs were winning, choking me, victorious over memory.

As I looked around the orchard in a daze of disappointment, I heard Ken say apologetically to Kate, 'We don't do much to it, just pick what apples bother to grow here.'

I didn't hear what came next. The past plays tricks with us. The orchard was much smaller than I remembered, perhaps a dozen trees grew there. It wasn't particularly wide, though the field beyond it might have made it seem so when I was younger. Now I saw it was not the endless expanse of wild nature that lived in my memory. I tried to recall my image of the coloured wool strands wound round these trees, but neither that nor my other memories added up. I thought of Laura coming across to help me find my thread . . . here? . . . there? No. I could not relate this place to any of my recurrent flashbacks. Besides, Laura had apparently thought it was me helping her, not the other way around. Or had that been my holding back to let her win? No, that wasn't right either. There was nothing in this place to guide me further forward. Laura, Jane . . . nothing. Except that I had an odd conviction now that Jane was most certainly not the other girl I kept seeing. I thanked the Martins and turned to go. There were no ghosts left here.

But then one stole upon me, terrifying me. An apple tree, with the sun behind it and beneath it three girls: Laura, myself and another fair-haired, shy little girl. Just for one second the blur lifted from her face.

'*Beth*,' I cried out. 'What happened to Beth?'

It was over. I was back in the cottage and Kate had returned home. I was lying on the sofa, alone with Jack as an anchor at my side to fasten me to the everyday world. I must have blanked out for a while because I was only dimly aware of apologies being made, of people with alarmed faces and of being helped into a car and back to the cottage by Jack and Kate. Somewhere in the fuzzy distance I knew Kate had been fussing over me, but then nothing until now.

'I'm sorry,' I said as I stirred and shakily sat up. 'I don't know what happened.'

Jack was looking as shaken as I felt, and wore no mask now. He was drawn and white-faced. 'I was wrong,' he said. 'You did have a memory of that place. I shouldn't have let you go. You shouted something out. Do you remember that?' Then he added quickly, 'Don't push it, darling. Don't push. Take time.'

Almost as if I were having a baby, I thought hazily. 'Yes, I remember.' It puzzled me because what I had cried out meant nothing. 'It must have been the result of seeing you reading those Louisa May Alcott novels and making that stupid joke about Beth. So in the orchard, I must have meant Jane when I called out and gave her . . .' And then the panic returned.

'Be careful, sweetheart. Be careful. Wait . . .'

'No,' I whispered. 'That's wrong. It *was* Beth. She was the other girl. How could I have forgotten her?' I was seized with terror. Who was this Beth? Why did it seem so important? It was only another memory trip.

'I wasn't at that treasure hunt of yours, Emma,' Jack said. 'So while you were unconscious, I decided to ring my parents.'

'Why?' Then I remembered that his mother had been at the party. 'Why ring them?'

'My mother knew about the other girl,' Jack said slowly.

'Who was she?' I could hear my heart beating. This was something I wanted – no, that I *didn't* want – to hear.

'Beth was my sister.'

Twelve

I watched Jack pacing around the room. Time seemed suspended. Stop the world. Everything's changed and I don't understand what's going on any more. Jack and I had reached a watershed and there would be no going back. Only, I desperately hoped, forward. I swung my legs off the sofa, and went shakily up to him to put my arms round him. The comfortable atmosphere that I had thought had vanished forever returned, but the silence between us remained.

'Drink?' he asked at last.

So it was going to be a long session. I shook my head, and he sighed — not in resignation, but more, I hoped, with relief.

'I'll tell you about Beth.'

It was still warm in the conservatory as the last of the dying evening sun caught it. It was the best of all times for lovers to speak openly, now that the day was done. We sat in the two armchairs and I waited, content now that I knew something between us had been resolved.

He began awkwardly, as though not knowing how to part with this information after so long, and indeed I wondered how we could have ever lived together without this knowledge between us. Proof, I thought, that onward is never on sure ground without knowing where the journey had begun.

'Beth was your age and Laura's, three years younger than me. She went to Lilleybourne primary school, so she wasn't in with your lot at Ducks Green, or with the Cobshaw school groups. Isn't that the school Tom would have been at? My parents knew the Wests though, and so Beth was invited to Laura's party, just as you were. That's why my mother was there, but not me.'

'And after that?' Still I couldn't remember Beth with my conscious mind.

'She sometimes joined you and Laura and the rest of your group at weekends or after school, not exactly part of the gang, but a recognized visitor, as I'm pretty sure Tom was. At the time she met you all, I was at the Junior King's School in Canterbury, and was far too superior to join in the kids' stuff, especially with my baby sister.'

I saw the expression on his face, read it correctly and took his hand in mine. 'What happened, Jack?' I asked gently. 'You said she *was* your sister.'

He had to make an obvious effort to continue now. 'Beth disappeared. It was a Friday afternoon, the seventh of June, 1985. My parents didn't worry too much when she was late home; they assumed she was either with her friends from Lilleybourne or with Laura and you. When the hours passed and they discovered she wasn't, they naturally panicked. They checked all round. Laura was with you at Cobshaw, and maybe even Tom.'

'*Even* Tom?' What was he implying?

He hesitated. 'Sorry.'

'What happened?' I asked again after he stopped. I couldn't press him on Tom. Not at this point.

'Beth had disappeared. Not a whisper, not a clue, though I think she had been seen in Ducks Green by someone. There was a police hunt of course, and they talked to all her friends, including your group.'

I was aghast. 'But I don't remember . . .' I came to a stop, feverishly thinking that perhaps I did recall something. Or was I conjuring up an image of policemen – no, policewomen – coming round to talk to me? I gave up. I simply could not be sure of disentangling truth from imagination. Disentangling – that made me think of those woollen threads of the treasure hunt again and of the fair-haired girl I must have confused with Laura. But why?

'Did you have no more news at all?' I asked.

'No. There were rumours, naturally. Paedophiles seen at the school gates, strange cars had been spotted, rumour piled on rumour as the power of suggestion mounted. None of the cars that were checked out produced any leads, nor did the known paedophiles. There's been no firm lead from that day until this.'

Jack's voice was flat and unemotional, but I was battling with the horror. 'That's terrible. Your parents, the not knowing. The daily hope . . .' Words were inadequate but communication depends on more than choice of words, and I think Jack understood what I was feeling.

'Hope lasts quite a while,' he said sadly. 'We stayed in Ducks Green for a year or so, then moved to Canterbury. My mother was against it because she said that Ducks Green was Beth's home. One day Beth might come back. Eventually, my mother agreed to move though. Beth was a sensible girl, she realized, and if she didn't find us then she knew how to do so. Neighbours and the police would know. The whole time was hell, Emma. Even in the Canterbury house, my mother set aside a room to be Beth's, with all her familiar things in it. Just in case . . .'

'That must have been rough on you, Jack.'

He looked at me in surprise, as though he had never thought of it that way. 'It was. It was a tough time. Luckily for me there was enough going on at Junior King's to distract me. It was worse for my parents. Although they've moved to France, I'm sure my mother secretly hopes that one day there will be news.' He saw my look. 'Of whatever kind,' he added. 'Once the shock is over, certainty, even of death, can be better than the not knowing.'

'Why can't I remember her, Jack? I only remember the name Beth and have fleeting memories of her face. And yet it was an ongoing friendship for –' I calculated – 'two years or so. Forgive me, but could I have disliked her?'

'No. Not possible. But don't blame yourself too much. The division between primary and secondary school at eleven is a big one. Everything that happened before that is apt to become dimmed with the change of approach to life. With Beth no longer present to remind you, you moved on. It's natural for children.'

'Agreed, but it isn't a complete answer to it, is it?'

'No.' A pause. 'Emma, when we met, I didn't know who you were. Your name was Cardale by then, not your maiden name of Haywood. Even if we'd met as children, I had no recollection of that. It was only when you told me about Laura that I realized you were *that* Emma. My parents had heard about Laura's death immediately from the Wests and told me, but they were living in Canterbury then, so I never caught up with the Haywood change. When I realized who you were I could hardly believe the co-incidence, but I decided I had to keep quiet and not to tell my parents of it. Maybe that was wrong, but Laura West and Emma Haywood brought back too many memories of Beth. It's a taboo

subject – we've none of us forgotten, but it's only a silent aware-
ness. There's never been anything to discuss, so I didn't want yet
another unwitting reminder of those days in you. I figured once
you had poured your heart out to me over Laura, you'd be glad
enough to leave it behind too.'

'I was,' I admitted. 'But then Tom Burdock came back.'

'You can't blame me now for my lack of enthusiasm.'

'I attributed your silence to other reasons though. I'm so sorry,
Jack.'

'That was natural enough. We both blundered around this.
Laura is a touchy subject all round. I did know her as a child. I
also met her on occasion – later, after I'd left home – because
when I visited my parents in Canterbury she was sometimes there.
I met Tom a couple of times too, after they were married. We
didn't get on even then.' He hesitated, but then added, 'When
we met in Africa, we still didn't, especially as he refused to believe
me when I said who I was with in Canterbury the day he claimed
he saw me kissing Laura. It wasn't Laura. It was my current girl-
friend, Gina, who happened to be blonde. That to Tom merely
meant I was admitting to an affair with Laura.'

Jack had that familiar don't-ask-any-more look about him, but
that didn't stop me thinking. 'And how come this coincidence
of your meeting in Johannesburg?'

He shrugged. 'Just that. Coincidence. I often have work in
Joburg.'

I was still puzzled. 'It seems odd to me that you don't get on.
I would have thought Tom was fairly innocuous to meet casually.'

He glanced at me. 'Are you busy concocting a theory that I
was jealous of his marrying Laura?' He said it lightly, but I trod
carefully.

'No, but it's strange because he's a likeable man.'

'Perhaps it was because he was swanning around in your group
so smug and self-satisfied, when Beth had been deprived of the
same chance of growing up.'

'Doesn't wash,' I said briefly. 'Did you think that about Laura
or about me?'

'I didn't know you then, so absolve me from that. But as for
Laura – I can't answer that or for my subconscious. It doesn't
ring any bells for me as a theory, but then it wouldn't.' A pause.

'She and Beth both had long, blonde hair. Beth took after our mother; I inherited Dad's looks.'

I thought of the grey-haired elderly man I'd met and couldn't imagine him as an upright, active man of Jack's age. Had that quizzical and patient manner come about because of the tragedy of Beth's loss? 'Tell me about her, Jack,' I said impulsively. 'You've told me her sad story but not what she was like. I must have been confusing her with Laura because of the blonde hair.' Jane's hair was dark, so I realized now that the other girl I kept glimpsing in my flashbacks of the treasure hunt could not have been her.

I couldn't remember my parents speaking of Beth. True, they no longer had any reason to do so, and yet something should have lingered if it had been a cause célèbre at the time. Nor had Jane mentioned her – and nor had Tom. And yet it seemed we'd all known her to some extent. Seeing Jack hesitate, however, I guiltily said, 'Don't answer if it's painful.'

He managed a smile at that. 'The whole subject is, but not to describe her. Sometimes when you talked of Laura, sweetheart, it did seem to me it was Beth you were conjuring up. I could say she was kind, she was gentle, she was loyal, but that wouldn't add up to a person, only to a few qualities strung together.'

And Laura was a stirrer, I thought, not the girl I'd thought. Could it be that Laura had never been the little girl I remembered but that I had transposed Beth's image for hers? I wasn't happy with that. And yet, where *was* Beth in my mind? Which particular brain cells had to be reactivated to bring her before me?

'She was a shy girl, which I don't think Laura was,' Jack continued. 'She watched from the sidelines because she was nervous of joining in, but she was the one who comforted me when my pet mouse was eaten by the cat next door, and she was the one who made the peace when I was rowing with my parents. I saw a lot of my Beth in the Alcott series. She was the loving spirit of our family too. Sentimental?' He cocked an eye at me. 'You must have thought I was nutty reading those books. But it concentrated my mind wonderfully.'

'Until I barged in and asked whether Beth was dead yet,' I pointed out ruefully.

'You weren't to know.'

I hesitated, not knowing how far to probe. I could go on a

cautious step further, though. 'Where does the pain lie now, Jack? You said it was still there.'

'In guilt. I always think that if I'd been there, I could have prevented her disappearance. I was out doing my big, macho brother stuff with my own gang in Canterbury the day she disappeared. And all the while . . . It had been rammed into me that it was my duty to protect her, but the attention always centred on her. I loved her – no problem – but I resented it sometimes. After all, even Alcott's winsome brood had its differences.'

My turn to say, 'It's natural enough. Jack, you said those books concentrated your mind. What on though? Is that why you came down here?' I began to see now. 'It wasn't just a job or guarding me against nameless dangers. It was Beth. Tom's visit stirred it all up for you too. If I was checking into the past over Laura you thought I might find out – or *you* might – more about Beth's disappearance.'

'You're right,' Jack admitted, 'and I'm sorry. I just couldn't get my head round telling you about Beth while you were full of Tom and Laura. Nevertheless, there *is* a job. But guess what? I still can't tell you about it. I should be able to very soon now – probably.'

I'd think about jobs tomorrow, I decided. I was still on Beth. There was a yawning hole in my mind where she should have been. 'You said you rang your parents earlier this evening. Did they know you were here, looking into Beth's disappearance?'

'No. They do now.'

'Were they upset?'

'Yes. But worse, they hope I'll find something out. Kinda puts the pressure on, don't it?' He grimaced and I silently wept for him.

'And now for the big question. *Have* you found anything out?'

'I'm not sure, but the more you probe into Laura's past, the more it might throw light on Beth.'

I jumped in with all guns firing – stupidly. 'Beth disappeared aged nine. The party with the treasure hunt I've told you about was two years earlier than that and Tom wasn't at it.'

I immediately realized the implication of what I'd said, and could have kicked myself. Jack realized it too. 'So you see a connection between the two statements, Emma?'

'No . . .' I half choked.

'Sweetheart, you nearly passed out in that orchard and you blanked out once back here. There has to be a reason. Are you implying it's to do with Tom?'

'I don't know,' I whispered. 'How could it be? It must have been remembering Beth that brought on the shock. Only that. She must have been important to me, and I'd forgotten her.'

'That's enough to do it, but was there more? Careful now.'

'You mean, am I sure Tom wasn't there? But even if he was, Jack, it was another *two years* before she disappeared.'

He slumped back in his chair. 'I know. I'm sorry, Emma. I wanted to stay detached, not get worked up over this, so that I could help you over Laura and maybe just think about Beth logically. It would be a kind of recompense for being so useless to my sister at the time. But look at me. I'm groping in the dark as much as you are.'

'Is that why you imagined this cottage is being watched?'

'It is. I can't be wrong over that. After all, think of the hell holes I've been working in for years – I'd hardly be frightened of a dark wood for nothing.'

'You might be if it's the unknown challenging you, not the known.'

'Not even then.'

I thought for a moment. 'Do you think we should move into Kate's house?'

'No. Besides, just in case I'm not bonkers and there is something nasty in the woods, it's not fair to put Kate in the firing line too.'

'You're serious, aren't you?' One look at his face convinced me.

'Yes. After this big affair of yours on Saturday, let's move back to Dulwich. My job should be over.'

'But mine won't be.'

He mistook my meaning. 'With Tolling Bells?'

'I meant Laura.'

'Do they go together? Don't forget that possibility.'

I grasped the nettle. 'Tom?'

'He always seems to be *there*,' Jack said in anguish, 'but I've no idea whether he's involved in Laura's death. All I know is that I had no arrangement to see Laura that afternoon, that Tom is still the most likely person to have murdered his wife and that you're working for him. And what's more—'

I faced this head on, and finished it for him. 'Tom was around in Laura's group as a child, at the same time as Beth. But how could there be any connection between her disappearance and Laura's murder?' Wild scenarios flew through my head: Tom knew what had happened to Beth; Laura had discovered that. No, there was no foundation for either of these.

I struggled for a rational approach and began at the beginning: 'You said Beth was a visitor to the Ducks Green gang. Did she ever mention Tom? Was Laura her special friend? Did she *have* a special friend?'

Jack looked at me compassionately. 'Yes, she did. It was you, Emma.'

Me? I lay awake that night long after Jack had tried to comfort me, first with words and then with love. Both worked but not for long enough. I woke up in the dawn to hear the birds singing and to face the fact that someone who had loved me had vanished from my memory. I tried so hard to bring back that shy and loving little girl, but I had mentally turned my back on her. I must have done. Beth had vanished without trace, both physically and, worse, from my mind. What must Jack have thought when I told him about Laura's death – but with no word of Beth?

'You're crying.' Jack had woken and his finger was tracing the tears on my cheek.

'I can't help it.'

A kiss on my wet face was as gentle as the touch of thistledown.

'Do you think you could have cared too much?' he asked. 'And that's why you've blotted her out of your mind?'

Could that be true? If only . . . I clutched at this straw, but honesty compelled me to say, 'Perhaps, but why then did I remember Laura so clearly from my childhood?'

'Love has room for more than one friend at a time.'

Had that been true for me? And more importantly, had it been true of Beth? Slowly, slowly, as I slept that night, Beth returned to me.

She smiled at me, this other girl. Very shyly as if, like me, she felt out of place at this birthday party. Not part of the crowd. But then I'd met Laura, however, and so I was happier. Although this girl had long, fair hair, she was thinner than Laura and seemed a different sort of person.

'My name's Beth,' she volunteered, stealing a look at me as if to sum up whether I had interest in this.

'I'm Emma.'

'This is a nice party, isn't it? Where's your piece of wool, Emma?' Her yellow thread was in her hand.

I looked down at mine in dismay. 'It's broken.' I could see Laura now, waving at me happily and I waved back. But it was Beth who was searching for my loose thread of wool. Then I saw her running towards me, a blue thread in her hand.

'Here it is,' she called. I ran up to her and took it, but my hands were trembling. 'Don't worry, Emma. I'll do it. Look, it's easy.' She took the two ends and tied them carefully together.

'Thank you' I whispered, suddenly shy myself.

Beth flushed with pleasure. 'Have you lots of friends here?' she asked diffidently.

'I know Laura,' I said proudly, 'and some of the others. We're at school together.'

'I know Laura too. I like her very much. I hope she wins the prize.'

I was happy again. 'Come on, Beth. Let's all race each other for it.'

And so three threads were disentangled at last in my mind. Laura, Beth and me.

But what happened next? And what happened after the party? Memories began to come back one by one: Beth on a hillside; Beth, Laura and I playing in Laura's garden; Beth by the duck pond. Laura and Beth dissolving into one another as I struggled to fight my way back.

And then came a memory so unexpected, so frightening, that I had to sit up in bed and stop myself from crying out in fear.

'What is it?' Jack's arm was round me. 'My sweet, what's wrong?'

I shook my head violently. 'Nothing.'

'Tell me about nothing.'

I tried, but it had gone. 'I was going to Mereden Hill.' The picnic field with the view over Canterbury.

'What's frightened you there?'

'I don't know. It was just frightening.'

'Was Tom there?' Jack asked.

'Yes. He was running. *We* were running, Laura and I.'

'Where to? And why?'

'I don't know. I *don't.*'

I'd been due to meet Petra at the Tolling Bells office on the following morning, but when I arrived neither she nor Lee was present, only the receptionist and Tom. I didn't feel up to facing him yet, but fortunately by the time I saw him, my wilder notions had disappeared, and the nightmares had mostly been dispelled. But there was just enough left to make me feel distinctly uneasy about being with Tom – which was very unfair, I told myself. I had to remember that there was not one shred of hard evidence that Tom had anything to do with Laura's death, let alone any involvement in the Beth story. I was determined not to mention Beth to him. I needed to mull that over more, and it seemed wrong to involve Tom in what was between Jack and myself.

'You look harassed,' I told Tom, after he'd explained that Petra and Lee had been held up, but he was fully in the picture with what I needed to know.

'So do you,' he returned. 'Working you too hard, are we?'

'On the contrary.'

'Ah, takes your mind off Laura and Jack, does it?'

I refused to get riled – assuming that's what he intended by linking the two. 'Yes.'

'Me too.' He did not pursue the subject and I was grateful. 'Petra wanted you to have the final list of additions to the guest list. I've printed it off for you, and emailed it too. Can we leave you to do the necessary?'

By which he meant notify caterers, write name badges, etcetera. 'OK. Are there likely to be any more?'

'Nothing's a final list until it's over on this job. It's not easy.'

I noticed he was looking downhearted. 'What's wrong, Tom? Jamie, or work problems?'

He grimaced. 'At the moment, the latter. If it weren't for Jamie, I think I'd head back to Africa. Bloody paperwork. Reams to print off on stuff like due diligence and governance. I spend all my time keeping in touch with the board and not doing the job the charity's set up for, which means that those who need it most don't get the cash.'

'Board not pulling its weight?'

'It's doing a good job over the fund-raising, with Lee continuously prodding. It's my side that's floundering. At the moment it's money-laundering rules that are getting me down.'

'What about them – apart from the fact that you can't do it?'

'Rules brought in a year or two back. We have to bend over backwards, with strict policies in place to minimize the risk of picking up criminal cash. Fund-raising is hard enough at the moment without having to demand proof of identity from donors and so on. It's a full-time job trying to keep track of every donation's source and destination, let alone checking the donor's bona fides.'

'Must be difficult considering you're sending cash through to Africa all the time.'

He gave me an odd look. 'It is. Anyway, all offices have their problems. I saw Jane yesterday, Emma. She told me Jack's back in Cobshaw with you.'

Not a subject I wanted to pursue, so I went off on a tangent. 'Did she also tell you about our picnic up on Mereden Hill?'

'No.'

'She and I had one there recently. There's a good view of Canterbury in the distance if you peer hard enough. And quite by chance we came across a place on the old Belleview estate where we all used to play as children – you might have been there too,' I added as casually as I could. 'I hadn't remembered that we all went back so long. I mainly remember you as a gangly teenager.'

'Thanks. Yes, we do go back further. I remember you as a delightful adventuress in the way of explorations and tree-climbing. What sort of place was this?'

I described it to him as best I could. 'It's only a ditch now,' I finished. 'The pool is just mud, and stagnant.'

He frowned. 'Yes. I remember it, I think. I went there once or twice. Pushing at the edges of memory though. Who else knew about it?'

'Laura of course, and Jane. And others.' I would wait for him to mention Beth.

'I'm pretty sure I remember the view of Canterbury. That sloping hill and meadow.'

Tom running . . . running. My nightmare came back to me. But it *was* only a nightmare, I told myself.

'Maybe I'll go back. If I ever get custody of Jamie I'll take him there.'

'Stick to the hill,' I suggested. 'The other place is only of interest to us. He'll see it just as a ditch and wonder why his father and mother used to play in it.'

'Just a ditch.' Tom stared at me, but he did not share his thoughts. And there was not one word to suggest he remembered Beth.

I couldn't get Jack's words out of my head. His parents had assumed Beth was either with her Lilleybourne friends or with Laura and me on the day of her disappearance. But she can't have been, or I would have told someone. Why had I no memory at all of that day? On an impulse I decided to stop at Mrs Grenier's house, behind the village shop where the former village hall had stood. Friday the seventh of June had been a school day, and so it was possible, even probable, that she would remember it very well. I should have rung first, but to my surprise I was greeted with, 'I wondered when you'd come, Emma.' The faintest note of disapproval took me right back to schooldays.

'I'm sorry to come unannounced.'

A smile. 'I expected you much earlier than this. Come in, please.'

She led me through the hall into the small sitting room at the rear of the house overlooking the garden, and sat me down as though I were a six-year-old waiting to be instructed. 'Laura West,' she said briskly. 'What exactly did you want to ask? If it's who murdered her, I can't help.'

'No. It's more than that. It's the kind of person she was.'

'Now that is a most surprising question coming from you – although perhaps not in the circumstances. I suppose one can be too close to judge someone.'

'I thought of her as the kindest, most loyal friend there could be.'

'Thought?' she picked up immediately.

'Looking back, and from what others have suggested, I wonder whether that was true.' I fought to keep my fears of disloyalty to Laura at bay. I had to examine everything if I was get anywhere.

'Of the child Laura or the adult?'

'Both.'

'I can only speak of the child. I saw nothing to suggest you were wrong. People can change. Or at least appear to change, conditioned by events. Could that be the case here?'

Relief was tempered with doubt. 'It could,' I replied, 'but I can't see anything in her life that could have made her change. She was happy. She had a child she adored. She had a husband she loved.'

'You're sure of all that?'

'Yes – no. I can't be any longer. So many rumours.'

'Ah yes. Her purported lovers. I discounted them. So very unlikely. But even so, are you sure she was happy?'

I began to think. Why else would Laura have turned into a stirrer, save through her unhappiness? And yet why not discuss her problems with me? 'I thought she was.'

'You still look worried though.'

'I'm busy disentangling threads, but they keep muddling themselves up.'

She laughed. I didn't think I'd ever heard Mrs Grenier do that before. 'Never good with your hands, were you, Emma? Nevertheless, you've charged ahead and very effectively so.'

'But Laura was the leader.'

'Emma the lion, the rock. Laura the pussy cat. Beth the fawn.'

I was shaken at hearing that name, as if I hadn't really believed she existed before, as if she was just a name between myself and Jack. 'Beth,' I said. 'You talked of Beth.'

'Is that so surprising? My dear Emma, you've gone white.' She looked most concerned.

'No one else talks of her. I'd forgotten her. Can you believe that's possible? I've only just found out. No one talks of her. Not Tom, Jane—'

'That's because she vanished with no answers. There was no ending. At what point does one stop saying "she is" and start saying "she was"? Far easier for those still here not to talk of her at all.'

'Perhaps, but there's more. There has to be.'

She sighed. 'Of course. I told the police I'd seen Beth Scarlet that afternoon. She was waiting for you and Laura at the school gates.'

'Waiting for us?' This was getting worse. Jack hadn't known that. 'What happened then? Where were we?'

'I don't know. I just saw her as school ended waiting there.'

'Jack, her brother, told me Laura and I were at my home in Cobshaw after school.'

'The police decided someone had persuaded her to leave with them, probably by car, but whether that was before or after you left is not known. On the Monday following her disappearance the police came to speak to the whole school. They asked for anyone with any information to come forward. Not you or Laura, because they went to talk to you at your homes individually. But they got no further. Your parents confirmed that you and Laura had walked home to Cobshaw and stayed there. You weren't able to tell them anything about where she was or what might have happened. That's the trouble with best friends, of course. I should have seen the signs.'

'I don't understand,' I said dully.

'Best friends see nothing.'

There was something wrong. Odd how one's hackles go up, a natural antenna in the face of trouble. As I reached the cottage, the front door was open and I could hear raised voices. I rushed straight inside, and stood appalled at the sight of the living room. Every drawer had been emptied; books were ripped up and the torn pages scattered. Kate's photos smashed. Kate was screaming abuse about the vanished vandals, and Jack was little better. He wasn't so much angry, as tense with worry.

'Believe in our watcher in the woods now, Emma?'

I looked round at the chaos. 'What's missing?'

'My laptop with my work stuff on it.'

'Oh Jack.' I was poleaxed by this new blow. 'How bad is it? Are the police coming?'

'Burglary is hardly high priority, but in theory yes. I rang Paul anyway. He popped in on his way home and has come and gone.'

'How did they get in? The door? The windows look all right.'

'Probably a bump key, Paul says.' He saw my blank look. 'Master key to every kind of lock. Sophisticated vandal, eh?'

'He'll be an ex-vandal, if I catch him,' Kate said grimly.

'We'll try to make it up to you, Kate. I think we're the target, or rather I am,' Jack said. 'Certainly not you.'

'You could have fooled me,' Kate retorted tartly, picking up a smashed photo of her mother.

The police, perhaps egged on by Paul, duly arrived, inspected the broken window entry point, noted the damage down without comment and left. Kate nobly cooked us some supper, and then we all did a brief clear-up so that Jack and I could at least go to bed without stepping on broken glass.

'Is the laptop secure, Jack?' I asked. 'Is this attack to do with your job?' I longed for the answer to be yes.

'I'd think so, if it hadn't been for these books and pictures. That's pure personal hatred.'

'Or to disguise the real motive?' Kate suggested.

I didn't agree. Looking at the chaos around me I thought it too vicious for a mere cover job. It took real hatred to do this. The sooner we were out of there the better and Kate would doubtless agree. The show was only four days away now, and we promised her she wouldn't see us for dust after the weekend. She pointed out that she preferred us to dust, but we gently refused her suggestion that we move in with her.

Jack and I spent the Wednesday morning clearing up, sorting out insurance and how to deal with the damage to Kate's property. In the afternoon Jack went out and I was alone. It was time to ring my parents, I decided. They knew Beth, they knew me. They would know what had happened in 1985. I couldn't understand why they had never mentioned her, even when I moved in with Jack, although Scarlet isn't that common a name.

My parents are delightful people. I get on well with them, and am extremely grateful to them for being such reasonable folk. But they can be definitely on the scatty side, particularly my mother.

'Beth Scarlet, mum,' I said after the preliminaries of the call were over.

'What about her, dear?'

'Why did you never talk to me about her disappearance?'

'Well—'

'Or,' I added quickly, determined to get this in the open, 'when I moved in with Jack?'

'We didn't want to upset you, darling, by bringing it all back to you. You were in quite a state at the time. And Beth was your best friend.'

Thirteen

Emma the rock, Mrs Grenier had said. I felt more like Emma the sponge – wet and soggy. I woke up at four on Thursday morning, feeling just that way. Four in the morning is peak panic time, when one thinks one is seeing the world in stark clarity. Wrong. One needs to be vertical to see matters in context. But *was* there a context over my dilemma? Stretching back as far as I could remember, I'd always looked on Laura as my best friend, but now my mother had confirmed what Jack had said, that Beth had once filled that role.

Memories of Beth were floating back in mere wisps. They no doubt fitted into some kind of frame but along the way I'd lost it. In its place I could only put the orchard treasure hunt and something that was only now coming into focus: a police-woman talking to me. Slowly, I recalled a blur, an enormous kerfuffle of anxious faces and adults whispering in corners, while Laura and I clung to each other, sharing our fear of the unknown.

I did remember now that Laura and I had picked up from the adults' behaviour that Beth's disappearance was due not to some unexpected holiday or visit to a faraway aunt, but to something terrible. But what? No one had ever explained, and so, scared, Laura and I had buried the matter in self-defence and got on with our lives. Perhaps it was from that time that the two of us had cemented our friendship. No, that couldn't be right. There was Jane and there was Tom and there were others. How did the rest of the gang fit into the Beth story? There were no answers, and I gave up the struggle to make a coherent picture. It was easier to deal with the present.

'How did you manage without your laptop yesterday?' I asked Jack anxiously. I had decided to assume that it had been a straight-forward robbery because the alternative took me further into that dark wood. 'Was it stolen because of the information it contained?'

'No way of knowing.' Jack looked glum. 'If it was for its content our chum could find a lot to interest him. On the other hand, if the burglary was simply malicious there'd be no problem.'

That took me aback, and I felt I wasn't getting the full picture here. 'Why not?'

'Big confession time again.' A half-hearted grin. 'I trusts nobody, see, miss. I tugs the old hat over me eyes, and pulls a fast one.'

'Make it faster,' I said impatiently. It was all very well to fool around, but I knew Jack. He was trying to convince me all was well – which meant it wasn't.

'Right away, ma'am. It was my back-up laptop that's gone with the fairies. I've got the main one safe and sound. Kate's guarding it for me.'

'*Kate?* Is that because she's the one person who couldn't be our watcher in the woods?'

'Agreed, Sherlock. She can just peer out of her bedroom window to see what we're up to. Not all of it, I trust.'

I dutifully laughed, but inside I was a mass of confusion. Jack had taken the phantom watcher seriously enough to concoct a plan, and he'd been right about the threat to us. 'If the laptop was the prime motive,' I argued, 'our thief was hardly likely to have wasted time trashing the cottage. If it wasn't, it was either a casual drugged-up vandal who rampaged through the cottage, or someone who was sending us a personal message.'

Jane had rung me to announce she was cooking lunch for me and that I was coming, like it or not. I did like it, and a break from the cottage would be welcome, especially with a dose of Jane's rational approach to life thrown in with the lunch. Before that, however, there was the clearing up to be completed. Jack had had to leave for Canterbury, via a visit to Kate, and so I'd offered to finish it. Ten minutes later Kate arrived, like a whirl-wind, to give me a hand.

'It's not until you see something you love treated like this, that you realize how personally you feel about it.' She had picked up a book and was hugging it to her. 'Henry Kendall's memoirs. I'll never forget his story of dear old Marie Tempest. Now that lady really would have objected to being torn up and thrown on the floor. Definite lèse-majesté.'

Lightly though she spoke, I could see there were tears in her eyes at this destruction of her beloved books.

'Marie was a tigress,' she continued, 'but a pussycat when you got
to know her. Mum met her in the late thirties when Marie was well
past it as an actress because her memory had gone. She just would
not give up though. Finally, crunch time came. Rehearsals went
on and on but she could not remember a single line, although
she swore it would be all right on the night. Kendall was the
producer, and he had to lead her gently away and explain that
she had to give up the stage. She left that theatre like a queen
without a word of protest. I hope I go out like that.'

'You're far too lively to go out at all.' Kate, I thought, would
be protesting at the gates of Heaven. I might just as well not have
spoken, for Kate was oblivious. She was standing there with Henry
Kendall still clasped to her bosom.

'Dan Leno too, poor old sod,' she added. 'All that happiness
he brought as a comedian, and all he wanted to do was play
Richard the Third. He lost his marbles too. Talking of Richard
the Third, was Tuesday night's winter of discontent to do with
Jack's work or yours – by which I mean Laura West?'

'Don't know. Wish I did.' A wild idea came to me. 'Unless it's
both.' Where had that idea come from? And, more importantly,
where did it lead? To Jack, his job, Beth or Tom? I swallowed,
hoping to return to safe ground.

'Ah.'

'Kate?' She was up to something. 'Stop looking like a wise old
witch and tell me.'

'You were worried about Jack's possible involvement with
Laura's death at one time, Emma. Are you still?'

'No.' That seemed a world away in time.

'The diary entries must therefore have been faked.'

Must? I thought. Had Tom deliberately faked them? *And* lied
about Jack admitting to an affair with Laura? If so, where did
that take me? Answer: somewhere I didn't want to go.

Kate was looking thoughtful. 'And you know about Beth now.'

'Oh Kate.' I sat down, overcome. 'You knew all the time about
Jack and Beth.'

'I don't know what you mean by all the time,' Kate answered
crossly. 'It was only your dramatic exit from the Martins' orchard
on Monday that reminded me about her and of her surname. So
I made the connection with Jack. After all, I only arrived in

Cobshaw a month or two before Beth disappeared, and so I was not close to the story. I didn't remember her name until you screamed it out in the orchard. I do remember your parents being worried about you at the time. They said you'd retreated inside yourself and wouldn't talk about Beth. You spent all your time with Laura or Jane, but mostly with Laura, which your parents thought was good for you. You were sharing the trauma with each other. I'm not so sure your mum and dad were right.'

In hindsight nor was I. 'Do you remember Tom from that time, Kate? I seem to have blotted that out too. I remembered him only from teenage years.'

'Oh no. He was there earlier. Likeable enough, but had a few problems.'

As we all have, I thought. Amazing how I could be seen as a leader by some people, whereas I remembered myself as a follower.

The cobwebs were clearing. The memory became clear at last, no puzzles left. I could see Laura's father standing by the far gate, ready to present the winner with the special prize. So far no one had claimed it. Everyone seemed to be yelling in excitement. I knew Laura and Beth were behind me, and as I looked round at them both, I suddenly realized that I would reach him first. But what about Laura? It was her birthday, so shouldn't I let her be first? Laura saw me hesitate. 'Go on,' she whispered. 'You have it. Daddy wouldn't let me win. It's my birthday. It would not be fair.' I saw the tinsel paper round the prize he was holding; it was glittering in the sunshine, and I longed for it. Then I saw Beth, who had fallen behind Laura and me. Beth, who had tied my thread together again so painstakingly. I would reach Laura's daddy before Beth unless I did something to prevent it. So I did.

I snapped my thread off, and watched Beth take the prize.

I couldn't explain to Kate why I was crying and she didn't ask me. 'Coffee,' she said briskly. 'And a ginger nut. Excellent for putting oneself back on one's feet. Do you have any?'

I managed a strangled giggle. 'Feet or ginger nuts?'

'Ginger nuts. Come over to the house,' she ordered me and I meekly obeyed. I was commanded to sit down while she made coffee and produced the biscuits, and then Kate duly put me together again, like Humpty Dumpty.

'I'm ready now,' I told her gratefully, once I was fully 'mended' and back on Humpty's wall.

'For what?'

'Tom's do on Saturday.'

'Is Jack going?' she asked casually.

'Yes.' I didn't want to ask her why she wanted to know. I kept my blinkers on. I had my own journey to accomplish.

'I expect he wants to be your guardian until you leave on Sunday.'

I gratefully accepted this explanation. After all, it could be the right one, even if Jack hadn't minded leaving me alone.

'You need a guardian, Emma.' Kate looked serious.

'It was Jack and you who suffered on Tuesday night.'

'How did the vandal know that? You're living in the cottage too.'

True, but the blinkers were very effective.

As I reached Ducks Green, it was beginning to feel uncannily like the old days, popping into Lark Cottage to see Laura, hearing her playing the piano, and greeting Jamie and Tom. Once I was inside Number Twelve, however, it became Jane's domain again, as she fussed over me.

'Billy and Alice are staying to lunch at nursery school today,' she told me. 'I should think you need a quiet natter after what you've been through. Paul told me what a mess it was.'

'Kate and I have tidied it up now.'

'You should have rung me,' she lamented. 'Stupid of me not to think of it. Did you lose much?'

'Jack's laptop. Mine was in the car, fortunately.'

'I'm so sorry. Any hope of his getting it back?'

'I doubt it.'

'Jack can't be too impressed with Kent. I hope it doesn't put him off being in Cobshaw. I have hopes of you both settling down here forever.'

I smiled. 'Maybe some day, when this is all over, Jane, but Jack has to go back to Dulwich after the weekend.'

'Leaving you alone?' Jane's concern was evident.

'No, I'll go too.'

'Just as we got to know each other again,' Jane wailed. 'Why don't you come here, if Jack doesn't want you to be alone?'

'That's sweet of you, but, sometime or other, I have to return, and I want to be with Jack. Difficult to start a family while we're forty miles apart.' And, having got Jane's grudging agreement, I added, 'I'm not giving up on Laura though. Far from it.'

'But you are happy enough about Jack to go with him?' Jane looked doubtful.

'Yes,' I said firmly.

She still looked doubtful. 'Which leads us to Tom again. Where it all began.'

'Yes and no.' I sipped a glass of wine, glad I'd walked there because the drink was certainly calming. 'Can I help you?' I asked, seeing her preparing to move to action stations. I followed her into the kitchen, but she refused to let me help.

'You sit there and talk,' she commanded me. 'I'll do the buzzing about.'

I did as I was bid, and reverted to the subject of Tom again. 'I'm a little further forward on that front.'

'With new evidence?' Jane frowned.

'Not exactly.'

'I don't understand.'

'I'm not sure I do myself. Everything still points to him, but I know there's a missing factor.'

'You mean you can't pin down this lover?'

'No, but, on that subject, I think the ice-queen and Lee Hunt-White theory is out. I can't see Tom going on working with Lee if he suspected him of having an affair with Laura.'

'He didn't,' Jane pointed out practically. 'Tom went off to Africa.'

'That's true.' I stared at her. 'But he thought it was Mark to begin with, and then Jack. Why suddenly switch to suspecting Lee, unless he's really out of his mind? He doesn't strike me that way though. And if he's guilty of Laura's murder, why risk coming back here?'

'There's Jamie,' Jane instantly pointed out.

'Yes, but he'd been apart from him for years. He could have left it like that.'

'I couldn't in his shoes.' Jane shivered. 'Could you?'

'I don't know,' I answered truthfully, 'for obvious reasons. But some women have little or no maternal instinct so perhaps Tom deep down doesn't have paternal instinct.' Then I remembered seeing him with Jamie and realized I was talking nonsense.

'Let's have lunch,' Jane said abruptly, and I realized I might have offended her.

I helped her carry plates into the dining room and, once we were settled, I apologized. 'Sorry, I didn't sleep well last night, and I'm not thinking straight.'

'I don't sleep well either. Billy and Alice are enough to ensure that.'

'They're so lucky to have a mother like you.'

'Do you think so?' Jane looked wistful. 'I try my best, but I sometimes wonder what they'll be like as teenagers.'

'I'll have to build my relationship with Jack again before we turn out our own Billy and Alice. You have a good one with Paul, and that's the vital factor, isn't it?'

'Yes, it's like having a best friend, isn't it?'

I had my opening. I'd been wondering how to broach the subject of Beth. 'Our group, Jane. How many were in it in our primary school days?'

She laughed. 'You're asking a lot. We met about twenty-five years ago. And we were kids then. I tend to remember the later years when we were teenagers: going to discos, clothes, listening to Take That and Sting on our Walkmans. Amazing that Tom stuck around with us, but I suppose he was at the same school as us by that time.'

'Were there other boys in the extended group?'

'Oh yes.' She reeled off two or three more names, one of which I remembered. We discussed him for a moment or two and then I asked:

'So what kept Tom around all that time?'

'You.' Jane grinned. 'And Laura, of course. He was a faithful little puppy dog. I remember that but not much else. That magic place we went to during our picnic? I didn't remember that at all until we reached it, and now I can't sleep for thinking about it. Eerie to think that part of our past was just lying around there.'

But which part? I wondered. 'Were there other girls in the group?'

Jane reeled off a couple more names. 'It all changed once we were at secondary school. Some left and newcomers joined in.'

'I talked to Mrs Grenier yesterday.'

'The Great Grouch herself. Sometimes I still find her difficult to talk to.'

'You were right though. She's a nice old thing now.'

'You didn't say that at the time, although it was me she had it in for.'

'Why was that?'

'Couldn't keep up with the rest of the class. She liked bright girls and boys, did Mrs G. She couldn't be doing with stragglers, but I haven't done too badly for a straggler, have I?'

'You've done splendidly. You ought to build a business around these quiches, Jane. Local trade. Ever thought of that?'

'I have my hands full at the moment.' She looked pleased, however. 'It's an idea though. Thanks. You can come back and help me.'

'I'll do that, if the planned brood fails to materialize.'

'If it does, we'll leave it until we're matrons, with our kiddies grown up.'

'Nonsense. You'll be full of grandmotherly duties then.'

'Nonsense yourself. You'll be looking forward to a life of freedom again.' She paused. 'What did you want to know about the group for? What connection could it possibly have to Laura's murder? Ah.' She answered the question herself. 'I see. Every road leads back to Tom, the faithful puppy and later husband. Or perhaps not so faithful.'

For a moment I thought Jane was hinting that Tom and I had indeed been an item – no, Jane was far too sensible. Anyway, I had other fish to fry. 'Tom didn't quite belong to the group, as I remember. He was a casual visitor – like Beth.'

'Beth? Who was Beth?' She looked completely blank.

I could hardly believe her reaction and greeted it with relief. So Jane had forgotten too. An immense weight of guilt seemed to roll off my chest.

'She joined our group from time to time in our primary school days.'

Jane frowned. 'I can't picture her. Describe her.'

'Long fair hair, shy, thin—'

'That's Laura or that other girl. What's her name – Susie or something?'

'No.' I remembered Susie. 'It wasn't her.'

'Are you sure?' Jane was looking as worried as I had felt, and having raised the subject I had to reassure her.

'I think we're both subconsciously suppressing her memory, Jane.'

'Suppressing? Have you had a spot too much of that Chardonnay, Emma? Why on earth would we have done that? Didn't we like her?'

'We did, but Beth vanished without trace one day in 1985. There was a big police hunt, but it led nowhere. We didn't understand what was going on. She must have been abducted and probably killed. There's been no news of her since.'

Jane's face was full of horror. 'We didn't understand?' she repeated. 'Oh, that rings true.' She must have caught sight of my face. 'Or does it?'

'Yes. Mrs Grenier says Beth was waiting for us outside the school the day she disappeared.'

'At the gates?'

'Presumably.'

'That's just terrible.' The reply was perfunctory, as Jane was clearly desperately trying to remember Beth, just as I had done. Then she too began to remember. 'Really skinny? And pale, wasn't she? Never said much. Oh Emma, talk about the waters of time. They seem to have closed over her head so far as we're concerned, poor girl.'

I swallowed. 'My mother and Kate seem to think I was very close to Beth, even her best friend, but I can't believe it. Do you remember it that way?'

'No, and I'm sure I would have. Tom wouldn't have liked that – or Laura.'

'Why Tom?' Here we went again, round and round the mulberry bush.

Jane stared at me. 'As I said, everything does come back to Tom, doesn't it? He liked being top dog with everyone. What was Beth's surname? Do you know?'

I hesitated, but Jack wanted information about Beth in case it led to anything new about her disappearance. 'Scarlet,' I told her.

'*Scarlet?*'

I thought Jane was going to faint, she looked so white, and I was sorry I hadn't explained at once.

'He was her brother. That was why Jack knew Laura and her parents. The Scarlets and the Wests were friends.'

'You realize what this could mean, Emma?'

I stalled for time. 'In what way?' I had a nasty feeling I wasn't going to like the way, whatever it was.

'Tom and Jack don't get on. Do you think – oh God, Emma, I can't even say it.'

I could. I *had* to. 'Do you think that they met as children at the time of Beth's disappearance, and that there's something we don't know about. Jane – is there? Could there be?'

She looked scared. 'I'm frightened, Emma. I don't know why. I suppose it's because I can't remember.'

'Only bits and pieces have come back to me, so we're probably seeing bogies where none exist, Jane, making a tapestry out of nightmares.'

'Nightmares . . . Emma, please don't leave me until I've remembered too.' Her eyes looked terrified and I had to go carefully.

'I do have to go back to Dulwich on Monday,' I said gently. 'I owe it to Jack. But I won't leave you in spirit, and I can be back down here, or you on a train to Dulwich, in a flash.'

She began to recover, and I cursed myself for putting her through the same kind of experience as I'd been through in the Martins' orchard, when Beth's name had come back to me.

'Stupid of me,' Jane said weakly. 'If only I could remember more. Now I'm over it, I'll try to get a clearer picture of Beth and Tom at that time and see if I can make sense of it all. Even so, I can't see what it has to do with Laura's murder. Oh Emma, ring me before you leave, won't you? I'm beginning to feel damned glad I live with a policeman.'

Tolling Bells did need my services on the Friday and Tom and I were both counting the hours, although for different reasons. Tom was pinning his hopes on Lee producing enough potential donors to make the charity viable for the next year at least; I saw the event as a hurdle to surmount before I could return with Jack to Dulwich. Such a retreat wasn't going to resolve anything, but it might be a lot safer, and would give me a breathing space to work out where to go from here. Jack had still been worried last night that our chum, as he still called the burglar, might return.

'Why should he?' I had asked.

'Because it's not over yet.'

I had stared into those impenetrable woods and believed him. Nothing had occurred during the night, however, and Kate had said firmly that she would be watching to ensure that nothing did.

Holt Capel Manor seemed a comfortable distance away from it all, even if the first person I saw there was Tom, who greeted me awkwardly. I found out the reason once we had retreated to the pub for an early lunch. 'Jane rang me last night,' he said. 'She was in quite a state.'

My heart sank. Why ring Tom? The trouble with Jane was that she always wanted to get to the bottom of things immediately. No holding back. She never saw the finer points of a situation. A big advantage sometimes, but not at the moment.

'You've been talking about our childhood, I gather,' Tom continued.

'Yes.' I reminded myself I had nothing to be defensive about.

'She said you'd mentioned Beth's disappearance.'

'Yes,' I said again, irrationally glad that we were in the pub, not somewhere on our own. Stupid of me, but I was aware that the burglary had had its effect and I was seeing bogeys where none existed. 'You never mentioned Beth to me,' I added.

'So what? I haven't mentioned other members of the group either. But Jane reminded me of Beth's surname, which gave me quite a turn.'

'Didn't you remember it?'

'Why should I have? We didn't deal in surnames unless we knew them through being at the same school. She was just another kid called Beth.'

'Not just another kid. She disappeared and there's been no news of her since.'

Tom flushed. 'Dreadful for the parents. But we were children. All we knew was that one of the group wasn't there any more. We didn't know the word disappearance meant anything other than the literal words. You knew her best, Emma. I remembered her; Laura did too, I'm sure. We probably talked about her. Her parents never mentioned Beth though, and nor did the Scarlets when we met them. I suppose that's natural enough. Why didn't *you* remember her, Emma?'

He leaned forward across the table, and his face was close to mine: red, angry, demanding.

I struggled with an answer. 'I didn't—'

'The reason is because her name was Scarlet, wasn't it? You didn't forget Beth at all, but you discovered that your beloved Jack was her big brother. I knew Beth had a brother; I saw him a couple of times. A great tyke throwing his weight around. I didn't know his name, but I hated his guts. And then as well as haunting my marriage he bloody well turns up at the Tolling Bells office in Africa.'

So my wild idea was not so wild after all. Forget about the party in Johannesburg. Jack's job and Tom's charity could be one and the same. 'To see *you?*'

Tom looked embarrassed and hastily sat back. 'Office business, but he knew who I was all right. It went back a long way. If you knew Beth, you knew the brother. Jealousy was his second name, not Scarlet. He was there in our group all right. Sent by his parents to look after her, he said.'

'He loved her—'

'*Loved* her? Good grief, no. He hated her. He resented her even being born because it spoiled his limelight. Big brother Jack had to be number one. Oh Emma, why the hell did you have to go and fall for him? Talk about history repeating itself. If you're looking for reasons why Beth vanished, try asking brother Jack where he was that day. *And* whether Laura knew something that we didn't.'

Fourteen

Fear. Where does it come from? It must live close to us because it comes quickly, sweeping in to overpower sense, emotions and logic in one overwhelming wave. It came for me that evening with Jack's phone call. I'd all but dealt with Tom's outburst by then; there were reasons for it, I told myself. Jealousy of Jack, distorted vision of the truth – reliving the same emotions that had clouded him when Laura was killed. They could also be consistent, I told myself, with his being involved in her murder. Yet that too seemed unreal. The more I was caught up in this battle between Tom and Jack, the more Laura seemed to retreat from me; never had she seemed further away than now. I was both physically and emotionally alone in a dark cottage surrounded by the silence of the woods, facing the unknown, the missing factor, which was awaiting its own choice of moment to strike. And strike it would. I knew that.

'Emma?' Jack's voice on my mobile brought me back to reality. I had been dreading his return, knowing I would have to tackle him about Tom's accusation. You know Jack too well, I told myself. There's no way Tom could be right in his accusation that Jack resented his younger sister so much that he could have killed her. But then the worm inside me had its say: is eighteen months so very long to know someone through and through? Did I really *know* Jack?

'All present and correct,' I answered him as gaily as I could. I only sounded as if I had laryngitis, and I could 'hear' his pause at the end of the line.

'Look, I won't be back tonight, sweetheart. I've been held up.'

'Oh.' Relief tangled with guilt, and then suspicion. Late night at the office? Come off it, Jack. 'Why?'

'Work, I'm afraid.'

'What about tomorrow? Are you still planning to come to the manor?' I held my breath. If he said yes, I could at least rule out Jack's antipathy to Tom being as strong as Tom's clearly was for him. But if he said no, then I'd have to continue stewing over the question. As so often in life, however, it was the unexpected that caught me out.

'I'll probably have to forgo the pleasure of mingling with the rich and famous,' Jack said. Then with a rush, 'Emma, look, I may be at the manor, but you won't see me. I hate to use the old words "trust me" but I want you to.'

What on earth was going on here? More mystery, more secrets, although he was surely giving me a strong hint that the 'work' was centred on Tolling Bells. 'Won't see you? Are you going to be dressed as a clown, or a waiter?'

He didn't bother to answer that. 'Do something for me, will you?'

My hackles rose. *Of course*, I thought mutinously, *anything*. Once I would have meant that, but now the hackles began to tingle with apprehension. 'If I can.'

'You can all right. Stay with Kate tonight. I don't want to think of you alone in that cottage with our chum waiting for another chance.'

'He came during the day last time,' I reminded him, relieved his request was so simple.

'Let's be on the safe side, eh?'

That suited me, though after Jack had rung off, I felt a wimp at having to call Kate up and plead for sanctuary.

'Of course you can come.' The sound of Kate's vibrant voice, even over the ether, was a boost. 'I always keep a bed made up in case Mr Pim passes by.'

'Who's he?' I asked blankly.

A reproachful, 'Oh Emma,' put me in my place. 'A.A. Milne's *Mr Pim Passes By*,' Kate kindly explained, 'opened January 1920 at the New. Mr Pim was a mysterious figure who strolled through people's lives making everything all right for them.'

'Sounds good. I could do with a dose of him right now.'

'You'll just have to put up with me,' Kate said briskly.

Going to Kate's now felt less like a retreat than taking my seat before the curtain went up. Tomorrow's event at Holt Capel Manor had theoretically nothing to do with Laura, the reason I'd come to Cobshaw, or even with Beth. It could have everything to do with the tension between Tom and Jack, however, which

was a vice that had gripped me in its middle. Jack had said he
might be present, but 'you won't see me'. Thanks a lot, I thought.

Saturday proved to be reasonably fine. That helped. At the very
least, rain didn't look as if it would be bucketing down. What to
wear? I wasn't one of the guests, only a service provider. I made
myself pin my thoughts on clothes and not on where Jack might
be. I didn't exactly need a black dress and apron, so smart casual
would do, I decided, and rushed back to Wychley Cottage to
change into trousers and blouse. The guests were not due to arrive
until five or so. The programme was to allow a couple of hours
for drinks, nibbles and social networking, followed by a buffet
dinner and speeches, and then dancing for those who wished or
skulking for those who didn't. The proceedings would conclude
with a final word reminding the probably now glassy-eyed guests
about the virtues of Tolling Bells. All very traditional.

I arrived at midday, as Petra had requested, and found a designated parking area in a field a short way further along the lane
from the manor entrance. I walked back to the manor, stopping
briefly to admire a small pond by the side of the lane, where a
family of ducks had taken up residence. When I reached the
marquee, Petra was already there, looking worried, to say the least.

'Things going wrong?' I asked anxiously. 'Drinks not arrived?'

'No. Lee's not here yet, that's all. Nor Tom, so I'm damned
glad you are. Look, could you take care of . . .' She reeled off a
list of tasks, which I hastily committed both to memory and a
notebook.

Lee and Tom had arrived by the time I'd worked my way
through the list. I'd glimpsed them walking together into Sir
Neville Wilson's conservatory, which was so large it ran the length
of the house. I was on my way to report to Petra, who had also
disappeared into the house, when Tom emerged, having, I guessed,
spotted me.

'Everything all right with you?' He looked so preoccupied that
I could tell he wasn't concerned whether it was or not.

'I've got over the shock,' I said lightly.

'What shock?'

That took me aback. He really had got something on his mind.
'The one about Jack that you gave me last night.'

His expression changed to wariness. 'Is he here?' he asked.

'He isn't tied to my coat-tails,' I replied, uneasy because this seemed so important to him.

'I thought he might be coming as your partner. Petra said something about it.'

Tom was searching my face as though a lot depended on my answer, so I fielded the inquisition as best I could. 'I thought about suggesting it to him at one time, but I'm here to work. Jack isn't in with fund-raising crowds, so there didn't seem much point. Anyway, he's not around at present.'

The minute I said that, Tom looked more cheerful. 'Good. Sorry, Emma, I meant what I said last night, and the thought of you sharing that remote cottage with him worries me.'

This riled me to say the least. 'I'm in no danger from Jack, Tom, so forget that. Jack and Kate are the ones who suffered most from the break-in at the cottage, not me.'

'Were you actually there when this so-called burglar broke in?'

Here we go again, I thought angrily, but struggled not to get involved in this. He seemed to be implying that Jack was in some kind of plot against me, and had faked the burglary. The idea that Jack would trash Kate's beloved possessions was crazy. No, I told myself. *No*, I would not even consider it.

'Excuse me, Tom. I've got to find Petra.'

I was aware of his eyes on me as I walked away, and I thought again of the ridiculous idea that Tom had been in love with me. Whatever Laura might have heard, it was certain there were no vibes between Tom and me then, and if he had imagined them present in our schooldays when he asked me out on that one occasion that time had long since passed. Any vibes around now had far different causes.

I was so busy over the last minute panics that occur at events like this, such as missing glasses, one too few tables, non-arrival of the ice cream, etcetera, that the hours passed quickly, and my personal dilemmas retreated. Even when Lee strolled over to thank me fulsomely for my tiny contribution, I didn't stop to think of him in conjunction with Laura until after he'd gone. I couldn't believe this smooth operator was her type – and yet could I now be sure what her type was?

'It's been good to have you around, Emma,' Lee had said.

'I know Petra's very grateful. I hope you'll stick around because Tolling Bells could do with you. It would be great for Tom, and if he gets custody of Jamie, for Jamie too.'

What on earth had Tom been telling him about his relationship to me? There hadn't been much point in retorting that I had a permanent partner of my own, so I'd replied merely that it had been a pleasure to help the charity.

Had it been a pleasure? I wasn't sure if I'd achieved anything, save as a cog to help the wheels spin. Had it achieved anything as regards my personal problem? I wished Laura had been there. She could have played a far more useful role than I was doing. It would have been her organizing the do. Then the worm inside me asked me how I knew that. Laura wasn't the woman I had thought her, quoth the worm. Laura had worn a mask, below which was a woman I didn't know. But then don't we all wear masks according to the occasion? Laura, Jack, Tom, Jane and myself – all of us had roles to play about which the others knew little or nothing, each one requiring different facets of our personalities.

By four thirty the gardens and marquee were ready, even though no guests had yet arrived. Was Jack there though? Was he in disguise doing the washing up or as one of the gardeners? Why was he so sure I wouldn't see him? As I had no jobs left to do, except to be generally available if and when, the uncertainty over whether he was going to pop up like a true Jack-in-the-box made me edgy. I strolled down the drive, back to the lane leading to the parking field, in case I could spot his car.

There were two men stationed at the gates directing cars to the car park, and presumably checking invitations. Christine Martin was also there. She greeted me with a friendly hallo, asking whether I was recovered following my dramatic exit from her orchard. I assured her I was. Her role was to greet guests and hand out name badges, as networking was to be the order of the day. I walked up the lane to the field, where there were already quite a few cars and vans, including mine of course. The pond I'd noticed earlier was now blocked by a delivery van parked on the verge right by it, and so I was unable to give the ducks a progress report on events at Holt Capel.

I watched as the first guest cars began to drive past me: a BMW 750i, and a Lexus . . . very nice. Jack had given me an eye for such things, and he would have loved to see this array of dollar signs driving past him. I made my way back to the manor and the marquee, a volunteer temporarily bereft of work. I felt like a cameraman, as I watched people arrive and move around like extras on an Agatha Christie film set. Only this set was real.

Lee, Petra and a man I recognized from photos as Sir Neville, with presumably his wife at his side, had formed a greeting line. Champagne corks were flying, and glasses of it were being expertly delivered to the guests. The champagne was being sponsored; so Petra had kindly explained to me when I'd queried how a small charity could afford this lavishness. Once upon a time the high fliers would have been solely male, and the spectacularly dressed women merely wives and daughters. Not now. Many of the high-flying philanthropists were women now, Petra had explained, somewhat bitterly, as that was where Lee's extraordinary talent in fund-raising achieved its best results.

I could see no one I knew and certainly not Jack. I spotted Tom though, looking rather lost. Unfortunately, he also spotted me again, and came over to me with the air of a dog who'd found an unexpected bone. Harsh of me, perhaps, but that's what it felt like.

'Amazing, isn't it, to see the wealthy at work?' he grunted.

'Don't you enjoy it?'

'Not much. Lee does this side. I only deal with paperwork and the administration of money to worthy causes abroad. But the charity's mission is small beer beside the job of getting the cash rolling in.'

'How can you tell the potential donors from the existing ones unless you've met them all before?'

'Not my job. Petra, Christine and Lee know who's who all right. Petra will go on a charm offensive, Christine will keep them happy by assuring them how valuable they are, and Lee will be busy winkling out the potentials and introducing them to the existing donors in the hope of making them realize this is a club they need to join.'

This sounded cynical to me, but I supposed that everything has a cynical side if you look at life that way. I looked round at the sea of faces, all strangers to me.

Correction – all but one. I could see Anna, Mark's wife, to my amazement, and I hurried over to her, uncomfortably aware that I hadn't invited them to the cottage as promised. Anna was visibly pregnant and I congratulated her warmly.

'Is Mark here?' I asked.

'Over there.' She pointed. 'But what on earth are you doing here?'

'Just a humble servant, madam.' I bobbed a curtsey.

She laughed. 'That's odd. Mark said you were down here on a quest into the past.'

'I was, but I thought I should widen my scope into the present.'

Mark came across to greet me. 'I've only just heard you're working for this outfit,' he said. He looked worried about something, but I couldn't believe it was to do with me.

'My last working day,' I told him. 'I'm heading back to London on Monday.'

'Good.'

Anna burst out laughing. 'Not very gallant of you, Mark.'

He flushed and managed a grin. 'Sorry, Emma. But I think it's in your own interests. I'm glad you're finishing with Tolling Bells.'

'Why?' I asked suspiciously. 'Because of Tom?'

'Well, maybe – um. Can't say. You understand.'

'Everyone is always telling me I understand, but I seldom do.'

'I'm in accountancy,' he said with an air of great mystery. 'Remember?'

Oh yes, I did. It had been the most important thing under the sun to him – once. Thanks to Anna, no longer, I hoped.

'So—' I began, but broke off. I can, at a pinch, add two and two. Accountancy involves client accounts; client accounts involve the need for secrecy. If the said client accounts have anything dodgy about them it involves big problems. That added up to four in my book. So I added one to make five.

'So Tolling Bells is connected to Jack's work.' The advantage of exes is that one can interpret the expressions on their faces. I was a little rusty over Mark's, but the knack came back quickly enough to tell me I'd scored a bull's eye.

'Is Jack here?' Mark was trying to sound casual.

'He didn't come with me. I'm only a volunteer not a guest.'

The disadvantage of exes is that they can read *your* expressions. 'So he is here.' Mark gave me a sudden smile, which reminded me of why I'd married him. 'Sorry, Emma. Useful to know, that's all. But you know me; I'm on the side of the good guys.'

I believed him. He needed Anna, children and a life. Not trouble.

As the evening wore on, and the noise level grew, there was still no sign of Jack – or at least any sign that I could puzzle out – so I strolled down to the gates and wandered up the lane again to the car park. The sun had gone down but it was light enough to see that the delivery vans were still there. That was natural enough, but closer inspection revealed that the names painted on the sides of one or two of them, including the one by the pond, had nothing to do with the caterers I'd booked. I saw no sign of Jack, however, just as he'd wanted.

I didn't get home that night until one thirty. On the cottage door was a large note in Kate's inimitable handwriting: *Jack rang. Not returning until tomorrow. Mr Pim not yet arrived, so come immediately*. The last word was underlined.

I obeyed. Kate had given me a key and so I slipped into her house, tiptoed upstairs to the Irving room and slept.

'Jane rang,' Kate told me at a somewhat belated breakfast. She had insisted I stayed to eat something because she needed to talk to me. 'She called not long after you left yesterday. She couldn't get a reply from your mobile.'

Guiltily, I remembered I'd left it on voicemail.

'She sounded in quite a state,' Kate continued, 'especially when I told her where you'd gone.'

'Why?' I asked carefully. In a state over Tom? Over Jack? What had set Jane off?

'She kept saying she was having nightmares about you, and was scared something would happen to you.'

In the cold light of morning, I laughed at this. Well, almost laughed. 'I'll give her a ring to assure her all's well.'

'It's Sunday. She'll be at church.'

'Tonight then.'

'Will Jack be back?'

I hesitated. 'I expect so.'

'You don't sound full of joy at the idea.'

I surrendered. 'I'm all mixed up, Kate. Some of me is doing

all right, but some of me isn't, simply because I don't understand what's going on or what *went* on. However hard I push it into the open, I keep coming up against a brick wall marked "passage barred".'

'Pyramus and Thisbe had that problem too. They solved it by making a hole in the wall.'

'What with?' I asked sourly.

'I believe it's called love.'

Love came home to me with a screech of brakes that Sunday evening, and found me patiently waiting in the cottage, unharmed by nameless intruders, watchers or wicked witches. I wondered what on earth I, and everyone else, was worrying about. Did I have doubts where Jack was concerned? No way. Any problem between us was simply a little local difficulty that could be ironed out.

'Were you there yesterday?' I asked. Jack was looking worn out but, I thought, more relaxed.

'Yes.'

'I didn't see you.'

'I didn't intend you to. I saw you though.'

'You were in one of those delivery vans, weren't you? Probably the one by the pond.'

'Some of the time. The rest of it I was crawling through fields with a telescope and Boy Scout penknife.'

'Very funny. Don't believe you.'

'As usual.'

He grinned, and we were back to normal. Or as normal as possible in the circumstances. 'One more day. That's all I need. Can you bear it?' he asked. 'I promise you we can both go back to London on Tuesday.'

Another twenty-four hours here. Kate was going to love that. She would feel it her duty to keep an eye on me, just as she had earlier in the day. I'd seen those curtains twitching, and the little journeys she made into her garden.

'You make it sound as though that's the end of the problem,' I said to Jack.

'It's the end of one of them. With luck both.'

'Which one's ending? The delivery van problem?'

'That was the cure. Or rather a vital stage in the proceedings. Thanks to it, there are various warrants out now, plus various premises being more thoroughly searched.'

My heart sank. 'I take it one of them is the Tolling Bells office.'

'I'm afraid so.'

'Tom?' I asked with trepidation. 'Is he going to be arrested?' Despite our differences I just could not believe the idea of Tom as a fraudster.

'I wish,' Jack said fervently. 'You'll be pleased to know, however, that so far he's in the clear. It's his chum Lee who's being questioned. Serious Organized Crime Agency stuff. That's whom I've been working with for the last few weeks. Not for the first time. That's probably how Paul knew my face. The current job was originally sparked off by the OECD and the Charity Commission. There was a sniff that all wasn't right with the charity, which has some interesting sources of revenue in this country and equally interesting recipients in Africa. Not being a fan of Tom's, I didn't think he had the wits to think this money-laundering operation through on his own, and came, rather reluctantly, to the conclusion that he was being kept in the dark.'

'He told me he was weighed down with charity rules.'

'He was right, although it wasn't so much the rules as the way they weren't being applied that might have been worrying him. As fast as Tom tried to set the rules, Lee seemed to have been breaking them, and once Tom got back here it seems pretty obvious that he began putting the facts together and came up with the magic words "money" and "laundering". That's the charitable view on Tom.'

'And the uncharitable one?'

'I'd like to say he was in it up to his neck, but I don't think that's the case. Inadvertent accomplice is as far as I'd go.'

'But will Tom be arrested?' I was horrified. That would put paid to his chances of custody of Jamie for good.

'Questioned, certainly.'

'He'll be unemployed at the very least.' That would be almost as bad for his hopes.

'It will be up to him to show some gumption. That crowd yesterday was an interesting mix of people, which I dare say is what Lee intended. Some of them are under scrutiny but haven't yet been nailed, and quite a few were genuine philanthropists. It was bad luck,' Jack added, 'that this job cropped up just as you decided to come down here.'

'Not bad luck,' I pointed out. 'Tom came to see me because he knew I was living with you. *How* did he know, that's the question.'

'Confession time. I told him that,' Jack admitted ruefully. 'I thought it would *protect* you. I knew who he was. You'd told me, and so had my parents, that he was in the frame for Laura's murder, and I didn't want him tracking you down. I keep the Dulwich address to myself for work reasons anyway, so it never occurred to me that he could track you down through me. Goodness knows how he got hold of my Dulwich address, but if one's determined enough anything's possible. There was no party in Johannesburg, incidentally. I visited his office there, and he told me he was thinking of returning to the UK. How could I have dreamt that he would fake evidence to suggest I'd murdered Laura? Why should he – I still don't understand. I thought at first it must have been a defence measure because he had something to hide over Tolling Bells. And then something worse reared its head. I began to wonder whether Beth could possibly be linked to the Tom and Laura situation.'

'You mean . . .?' I couldn't even put my fear into words. Was Jack implying Tom could be involved in her disappearance? That had been a nightmare lurking in my mind. Tom running . . . running . . . down that hill. Running from what?

'I'm sure she didn't get abducted,' Jack said. 'Someone would have noticed something significant. I let my parents still go on thinking that's the case, but I think she was murdered here in Cobshaw or Ducks Green. Now do you see why I'm scared that you're running around stirring the story up?'

'But why should Tom have deliberately killed her?' This was getting to be a witch's cauldron of horror. 'He was only a child of nine, for heaven's sake.' I hesitated, but I knew I would have to tell him. 'He tried to warn me about you yesterday, Jack. He suspects you not only killed Laura, but also Beth.'

I held my breath as Jack's face turned from shock into being white with fury. 'Why?' The word fell out like a stone.

'Because you resented her as the favoured younger child.'

I could see him swallowing, trying to hold on to control. 'He's further round the bend than I thought. Resentment? Sure, on occasion. She resented me too, but only on occasion. I thought Beth was the cat's whiskers most of the time and vice versa. You do realize Tom's putting the blame vicariously on to me, Emma? He was jealous. He's an only child, isn't he? Probably he had no close friends except your gang. He wanted all your attention, and Beth was in the way.'

'Laura's attention, not mine.' I was trembling. Had I understood nothing? Nothing at all, not then, not now?

'Yours, Emma.'

Fifteen

I was fighting my way through cobweb after cobweb, trying to reach something, someone. As soon as I managed to break through one stifling web another enveloped me. Somewhere out there Laura and Beth were patiently waiting for me to reach them. I could see them clearly now. And I couldn't get through that final curtain. Where are you, I was crying out. *Where?* The magic place, of course, I heard one of them cry. The magic place . . .

I tossed and turned and woke up with a start to find Jack sleeping peacefully at my side. I threw my arm around him and must have fallen asleep again just after five, because when I woke again he had gone. There was just a note telling me not to go anywhere on my own – just in case. I had presumed that Tom would be taken in for questioning, but Jack could not be sure of that, I realized, hence the warning.

Were we any nearer the truth about Laura and Beth? Theories that concocted themselves in the early hours vanished when put to the test of daylight, but Tom still stood there, fairly and squarely, in the frame. If – I reminded myself that it was still if – he was guilty of killing Laura, and possibly even Beth, only Jane and I could hold any clues to the truth. Of the two of us, I was the more obvious target because Jane was married to Paul Fritton. Any information she had would have been passed to him long ago.

Tomorrow I would be back in Dulwich, I thought longingly, and yet I knew there was still unfinished business here. In my dream I'd seen the magic place as the end of my search – but what was the search for? Laura, Beth, or the answer to the riddle? Visiting the orchard had produced Beth. The magic place, too, might provide answers.

It had once been a place of happiness, although an eerie one, even then. A place where elves and goblins could prance around all they liked but we children had felt that we were safe. Many episodes there had come back to me now, and I could not understand why it had lain slumbering so long in memory, not only mine, but in Laura's and Jane's. Even Tom had difficulty remembering it clearly. With Tom surely tied up one way or another with Tolling Bells, I reasoned that this was the perfect time to return there. Mindful of Jack's strictures, however, I rang Jane, asking her to come with me. She'd had the same reaction to the place as I had, however, and I could hear her hesitation over the phone.

'I'm not sure, Emma. It's so creepy.'

'Are you scared?' I asked bluntly. 'Now we've remembered Beth, I wouldn't blame you—'

'It's not that,' she interrupted. 'But yes, I am scared. Please don't go, Emma.'

'I have to. I understand how you feel though, so no problem. I'll ask Kate to come or go alone.'

'No, don't do that. I'll come,' Jane said bravely, sounding more her usual self. 'Perhaps it will help us both to concentrate on what happened to Laura. One condition though. Kate said you were leaving tomorrow instead of today.'

'For the time being, yes, but—'

She laughed. 'No arguments. I'll bring a picnic.'

'Good. I'll bring a bottle.' We'd argue later about where we'd eat it. I didn't fancy trying to enjoy Jane's food in what had used to be a magic place but was now so desolate. The sunny hillside for me.

Kate was out so I left a brief note for her and one for Jack, did my packing in advance for tomorrow and set out to meet Jane. I walked again, as befitted a last pilgrimage, and was relieved that I was making this final stab at the truth. Some little thing might make Jane and me dispel all our wild theories and come face to face with our past. What I hoped to find, I didn't know. Certainly not a buried diary with a day-to-day record of long ago. The clue, if any, would come from my mind, not be buried in the ground.

I was early but, as I walked across the fields, I was not surprised to see Jane already there waiting for me, backpack on her back as before. The weather had not been good but, as with Saturday, the sun had decided to shine, albeit weakly. I was relieved as the magic place, with its shade and gloomy remains of a stagnant pool, needed as much light as possible to make it bearable.

'Hi, Jane.' I kissed her affectionately. 'Thanks for coming. Billy and Alice all right?'

'Staying on at school for lunch and then someone's looking after them for me. Bribed by promise of more TV than I usually allow them. How did the big day go on Saturday?'

'Fine,' I said cheerily, not knowing how much, if anything, Jane knew about the troubled Tolling Bells. Absolutely splendid, I thought to myself, what with me doing my volunteer's best, and Jack planning to nick half the guests on fraud charges. I couldn't speak before Jane did, though.

'Judging by Paul's tightly closed lips when I mentioned Holt Capel, my guess is that there was more going on than tea and cakes.'

'Sure. Bubbly and dancing,' I said confidently, and we both laughed. Silly situation, really, with both of us sworn to silence and not even able to talk to each other about it.

All Jane said was, 'I hope Tom's all right.' She glanced at me. 'In the work sense anyway. What do you hope to get out of this trip, Emma?'

'Some clue as to why we blotted the magic place out of our lives. Something that might shed light on Laura's murder.'

'*Laura's* murder?' That shook her, but then she understood. 'Ah. Tom and Jack. I see.'

I wondered whether it was fair to burden Jane with my wilder fantasies, especially as she was married to Paul, but Jane was a sensible lady. She'd sort the wheat from the chaff. 'Kate said you were upset when you rang yesterday.'

Jane flushed and pulled a face. 'You know what nightmares I have. That's why I wasn't sure about coming here. Then I realized I should.'

'You mean that the nightmares centred on the magic place?' *Like mine.* I tried to subdue the instant flutter in my stomach.

'I think so, but it's always so hard to tell in dreams. You were *there*, Emma. That's why I told Kate I was scared for you. Very scared.'

'Well, I'm here, and no hobgoblins yet around,' I comforted her, though she'd reawakened my unease. I remembered the orchard and the way I'd previously blotted Beth out until being in the place again reminded me. What else might lie in my brain cells so deeply that it hadn't been summoned for over twenty years? Earlier, I'd hoped for precisely that, but now I began to dread it.

The birds were chirruping, the crops were rapidly growing to maturity and, on the waste ground we passed on the access road, rosebay willowherb was in flower. The edges of the fields were lined with poppies, and butterflies were hard at work. I should have been calmed by this bright scene, but I wasn't, and yet I was reluctant to leave the sunny meadow where we'd eaten our last picnic. I comforted myself that we could return for this picnic too. Even so, it was hard to turn towards Mereden Wood.

'Here,' I said, as we reached the wall.

Jane was over first, and then turned to give me her hand as I jumped down. 'Funny, isn't it? Coming back here together, all these years later.'

'In a way.' I'd have enjoyed it a lot more if I hadn't had the sense that I'd a job to do.

As we pushed our way through the bracken, I began to regret even more having come, as the wood began to feel claustrophobic. I thought of the old estate and the couple who had created this magic place and then been separated forever. What had happened to them? Was this place holding more secrets than just ours? The ditch was muddier this time, but when we finally stumbled past the high wall of the magic place and out on to the bank, the sun came out fully, almost as if a fairy godmother had waved her wand for the transformation scene to begin.

The pond had regained a little water, which I glimpsed here and there amongst the lush water ferns and reeds. The banks overlooking it were high with overgrown grass where the sun had reached them, but mossy and dank elsewhere. Despite the light, it remained a dismal scene, and I began to think that whatever whim had brought me there had stemmed from pure nostalgia.

Jane obviously agreed with me, for she immediately began to spread her picnic out on the best patch of bank she could find, and I quickly produced my waterproof blanket. Her briskness suggested she was planning a quick getaway – *after* lunch, unfortunately, and I hadn't the heart to insist on our moving back to the hillside.

She had a Thermos with her, which I presumed held tea, but it didn't. 'I had some vichyssoise soup in the freezer,' Jane said happily, 'and I remembered you liked it. The rest of the food's rather thrown together, I'm afraid, but then maybe that's the best sort of picnic.'

'Especially with wine.' I produced my bottle of Chardonnay from my backpack together with the plastic glasses. We indulged ourselves for a while, sitting side by side on the blanket, and dangling our legs over the side of the bank above what had been a pond.

At last Jane sat back contentedly. 'I'm glad we did this.' She was smiling.

'Even though nothing seems to have stirred in our memories?' I felt pleasantly lazy after the wine.

'Perhaps because of that.'

'Good. I think Laura and Beth would have approved.'

'You mean seeing their best friends together and talking of them?'

'Yes,' I agreed. But was that true? If Laura wasn't Laura . . . I put that thought away because somehow I couldn't finish it.

'This place doesn't bring back any nasty memories for me.' Jane was looking puzzled. 'It all looks quite normal. Not magic – not bad magic at least. How about you, Emma?'

'I've had no revelations.' Nothing threatening. Nothing came back but wisps of faces, silently talking at me, but I couldn't hear properly. Or could I?

'Emma, look, there's a newt. I'm sure it is. They're special, aren't they?' Laura was standing by the pond and smiling at me. And Beth too. She was sitting on the bank watching us, and hugging her knees. 'It's nice of you to invite me here,' Beth said. 'I like it. Can I tell my brother about it? He'd like it too. I'd like to be here always.'

Jack. *Did* she tell her brother and did he ever come here? I wondered. I'd talked about this place, but he hadn't said anything to indicate he'd been there himself.

'All that's coming back is a happy memory.' I must have spoken out loud, because I heard Jane reply:

'I can't believe anything bad happened to any of us here. Not to Tom, Jack, Beth, Laura, me – or you, Emma.'

'That's good. Nor can I.'

'Emma, I feel drowsy. Do you?'

'Yes. That wine was stronger than I thought.'

'Shall we sleep, Emma?'

There was an odd note in her voice, and I laughed uncertainly. 'We can have a quick doze, if you like. We've earned it. But aren't you afraid to sleep here, as you've had nightmares about it?'

'Not here, not with you. You're my best friend. We've *always* been best friends, really, haven't we, you and I?'

'Yes,' I agreed, because it was simpler to do so. I seemed to have no energy. It must be the sun draining me, the wine . . . I lay back on the ground and watched the sky above me until my eyelids closed.

'That's good, Emma,' I heard Jane say. 'Let's sleep here. Let's fall asleep forever.' I opened my eyes as she curled up close to me. 'We're best friends at last.'

Forever?

That word. I met the truth head on. I fought drowsiness. I fought it with all my strength. The darkness was there at my side, not inside me. The darkness had always been there, and it had human form.

I hardly recognized my own voice; it was little more than a whisper. 'It was you, wasn't it, Jane? *You.*' I sat up and looked with dazed eyes on a stranger. Someone who had always been there, but whom I had never recognized.

'I had to do it.' She was smiling anxiously now, trying to curl up even closer to me, but I inched away. Not too fast or she'd strike and I would be dead.

'I couldn't get you to realize that I was your best friend, Emma. First of all you thought that was Beth, and then instead of me you chose Laura. I was always on the outside, the third person outside the two of you. But not now. We're best friends at last.'

Best friends? I tried hard to make sense of this, but my mind seemed foggy. 'But you were always our friend.'

'You treated Laura and Beth as *best* though. That's different. I was always left out. Don't you see? But now we're together, just you and me. Why did you go away for so long, after I'd got rid of Laura? I never understood that. I was your friend, and you didn't even telephone me.'

'You're married; you have a family. Lovely children,' I croaked.

'Yes. I do and you don't. I was pleased about that, because it made us equal again. I could do something you couldn't, and I forgot you for a while. Then you came back and I remembered it all. That was lovely though, because you could see what I'd done for myself and we were best friends at last. But then Jack and you both said you wanted children, so I had to warn Jack off. I thought if I took his laptop he'd go back to London and leave you with me. But he wouldn't, and I got tired of watching for another opportunity to make him go away for good. He wouldn't go, and so, Emma, you do see that I've got to make sure it will be us forever this time?'

I didn't register her words or her meaning. I was still concentrating on whether I had understood her correctly. 'You killed Laura? *You* did?'

Jane held up her hands contemplatively. 'I've always had strong hands. I had to be strong at home. I was always second best there too.' She stopped. 'Do you really want to hear all this, Emma? It's boring. I'd rather be together.' She lay down and nestled up to me, her arm clamped over me so that I couldn't move even if I'd had the energy. 'Let me rest my head on you; I'd like that.'

'Laura,' I whispered. 'Why?'

'I didn't want to kill her. I tried everything else first to split you up. I got her to believe Tom was having an affair with you, and Tom to believe that Laura was unfaithful, and all sorts of things like that. Just hints – it's so easy to do and they spread so quickly. I enjoyed that. And with you and Mark it was even true. I thought it was going to work when Laura cancelled that opera trip with you. But it didn't. You still went on being best friends, and then she remembered something.'

'What?' Dear God, what had Laura remembered?

'I don't think she suffered much,' Jane said doubtfully.

I forced my mind to concentrate. 'But her diary. Jack's initials.' Then I realized. '*You* put them there.'

'Of course,' Jane agreed. 'Tom came back from Africa and told me who you were living with. Well, I couldn't have that. I didn't want him telling you things that might upset you. Besides, if you settled down with someone in London, you might forget about me forever, and I would have lost. I knew where Tom kept those diaries, and I put in the J.S. I'm good at copying handwriting. Jack's address was in the book already, which was nice. I thought it would be so easy to split you up from Jack. But it wasn't. You still preferred being with him to being with me.'

'We're grown up now, Jane. Not children.' Her words seemed to be floating over my head, hardly worth bothering with. What things might Jack have told me though? 'We can have partners and lovers and still have best friends too.'

'Oh yes, and I did try to save you. I told you I didn't want to come today, but you insisted. It's your own fault.'

I stared at her without understanding a thing. I wanted to sleep and sleep. But then I thought of Mrs Grenier, heard her saying, 'I should have seen the signs.' What signs? I saw Beth then, sitting peacefully on the bank smiling at me. She was getting to her feet and I knew I had to fight. I had to know what had happened to her.

'Why Beth?' I asked, but sleep was beginning to win.

Beth seemed to be shouting at me though; she wasn't smiling any more. 'My brother,' she was yelling.

Jack. I must think of Jack *and* Beth. Forget everything else. 'Beth,' I cried out. 'What happened to you?'

Jane frowned. 'I didn't like her. You let her win that treasure hunt, and not me. I wanted the prize, but I saw you hang back and break your own thread. So did Laura but she didn't mind. I did.'

'What happened to Beth, Jane? *What happened?*'

She raised her head for a moment and looked puzzled. 'I don't know. Does it matter? Something did happen, I think. I can't remember what. I had nightmares about her too, after you reminded me about her. I'd forgotten it all. You killed her, didn't you, Emma?'

The last nightmare. The last hurdle. Did I? Had I? I wanted to cry, I wanted to sleep and I wanted to die because I must have killed Beth. Jane was saying so . . .

I summoned up my last reserve of willpower. 'No,' I yelled at her. 'That's not true. Tell me, Jane, what happened. Tell me. Then we can sleep.'

Her face crumpled up and she began to cry. 'I don't remember. You're being horrid to me. Please, let's sleep now.' Then her eyes went to the pond lying at the foot of the bank on which we sat. 'There,' she cried out in triumph, pointing. 'I hated her. I made her dead and pushed her in so that you and I could be friends.' She looked at me fearfully. 'Can we sleep now, please?'

She was a child again, but her arm held me in a vice-like grip. I struggled in vain to escape, wondering hazily if she wanted to push me into the water. But she didn't. Instead, she kissed me gently on the cheek. 'There now,' she said, stroking my hair with her other hand, 'we can go sleepy-byes now. We're best friends again. I put them in the vichyssoise because it was your favourite soup and we'll both die happily. Stay with me, Emma. Be with me. I'm so tired and frightened.' Her eyes closed and her head fell on my breast; her grip slackened but I could not move. I had no strength at all and I wanted only to sleep.

'Put what in the soup?' I whispered. But my own eyes closed and this time did not open.

'Laura, have you seen Beth?' I asked anxiously. 'I said we'd meet her outside school, but she's not here.'

'No, I haven't. Why?'

'We were going to the magic place. Remember?'

'Oh yes. I do. Maybe she's gone with Jane.'

'She wouldn't. She doesn't like Jane.'

Laura frowned. 'She might go with her if Jane told her you wanted her to. It's funny though. Let's go up there and see.'

The sun was bright that day, and we giggled our way up to Mereden Wood, putting the small mystery of Beth on one side. The bees were humming, and I stung my leg on nettles as we climbed over the wall, so Laura found me a dock leaf to soothe it. Then we walked through the woodland to the stream, and paddled our way up to the magic place.

Laura was in front of me, and she stopped so suddenly as she climbed up to the bank that I cannoned into her. 'Ow!' I cried, but then I saw what she was looking at it. Jane was standing on the far side of the pool staring down at it. Then she looked across at us.

'Where's Beth?' I called.

'She isn't here. She's gone home. Her brother fetched her.'

It wasn't the words that scared us. It was the look on Jane's face. A sort of smile, a sort of triumph. It was terrifying, but we didn't know why. Laura seized my hand and we splashed back through the stream, with Jane calling after us, something about home and the brother again, but we left her behind. We didn't understand – and there lay the terror. We never spoke of it again. We climbed over the gate, out into the field, and began to run, not along the Ducks Green path, but the quickest path to Cobshaw, to get as far away as possible. It was normal out there. The sun was shining. I stepped in a cow pat and Laura stopped as I halted for a moment.

'Beth must have gone home, Emma. I wonder why she didn't wait for us.'

'Jane said that her brother came. Or maybe it was Tom . . .'

But as we began to run again we saw Tom hurrying towards us. He stopped when he saw us running. 'I thought you were going to the Place,' he said accusingly.

'No,' Laura told him. 'We don't like it any more. It's horrible. Jane's there if you want to go.'

'Where are you going?' His eyes were fixed on Laura.

'To Cobshaw, silly. Down this hill.'

'I'll come with you. Jane's spooky.'

So we went on running, and Tom ran beside us. Running and running, but we none of us knew why.

The next day when the policewomen came they asked Laura and me about Beth, and told us to answer carefully, so we told them the truth. We hadn't seen her and she must have gone home. She should have been waiting for us at the school gate, but she wasn't. So that was what had happened. We never mentioned the magic place because they never asked us about it, and, in any case, Beth had already left. We never went there again; we agreed it was too spooky and Jane never mentioned it either.

Someone was slapping my face, but I didn't want to know. Much more peaceful where I was. But the slapping went on and on, and voices were shouting at me, forcing me to get to my feet, pushing, pulling. I wanted to tell them to stop but I couldn't. My feet were like lead and I had to be half dragged away. I felt cold water sting my cheeks, or was that another slap? And then at last I decided to open my eyes, and Jack was there.

Of course he was, I told myself. He was a man who came back.

Next time I came to, I was being horribly and inelegantly sick.

I was in the field – how had I got there? Kate was at my side, and Jack. Tom seemed to appear from time to time, so did paramedics who alternated between me and the wood. So did the policemen. I watched all this with a disinterested eye as though it were a film taking place before me. I didn't seem to be involved, even when the crime scene tape was put up.

'You're OK,' Jack assured me, holding me while I was retching. 'They're popping you into hospital to keep an eye on you, but—'

'No. I want to go to Dulwich.' I blanked out again.

I woke up in hospital with Kate and Jack right there and no idea of time. I found out later it was the following day. I felt as weak as a baby, although my head, thank heavens, was clear. But then I remembered.

'Jane—?' I asked.

'Dead,' Kate said.

I gripped both their hands in case I cried. There would be time for that later. 'What happened? Her children, Paul . . .' All the terrible consequences paraded themselves before me. It had been Jane all the time, even at the treasure hunt when her desperate need had transformed itself into the dark cloud of jealousy that had frightened Laura and me.

Kate took charge. 'There's nothing you can do, Emma. Jane seems to have blotted out what she'd done. Her conscious memories only kicked in once you mentioned Beth. After that she was in and out of reality all the time. She was worried about her children – that's why she decided to kill herself and take you with her. That's what Jack and I think, and that checks out with the letter she left for poor Paul.'

'But how did you get up to the magic place? You didn't even know just where it was. Talk about the cavalry.' I managed to grin.

'Kate alerted me,' Jack told me lovingly, holding my hand tightly in case, presumably, I tried to escape. No way. I was there to stay. 'I was at police HQ. Kate read your note, and remembering Jane's weird phone call decided to ring Paul. He rushed home, as she'd been behaving so oddly, and when he read her letter he was on to me in a flash, not to mention summoning the cavalry. I was with Tom when Kate rang – thank heavens. He was the only one who knew exactly where this place was. We were out of that interview room so quickly that the staff thought we were fleeing justice.'

I tried to smile, but I hadn't the strength. 'Jack,' I whispered.

'I'm here, sweetheart.'

'Beth. I know what happened to Beth.'

'Dear heart, we know. That was the nightmare Jane had, according to the letter she left for Paul. In the phone call she made to Kate she was genuinely scared for you, Emma. Scared of what she might do to you. It was her last stretch of rational time.'

'And then I rang up and asked her to come with me. Good move,' I said. Then I had to ask, 'But Beth . . .?'

Jack squeezed my hand. 'They're digging in what's left of that pond, darling.' He was trying to sound matter of fact, but I knew he wasn't. I thought of Kate's soft voice once reciting Ophelia's epitaph: 'There is a willow grows aslant a brook . . .' Or was she murmuring it now? I could not tell, but I rolled over and stretched out my other arm to Jack so that I could embrace him. Then I sank back into sleep.

Epilogue

One more duty. One more, a month later.

Jack, Tom, Kate and I went together to Tenterden cemetery. We had made our peace with one another, and now was the time to make it with Laura. Her parents, Jack's and mine were all gathered at her grave as well, and Jamie too, with another posy. Laura had been the sweet, kind person I had always believed her to be, my best friend. The time that Tom and I had spent doubting her had been a black hole that had now passed for good.

Tom had had no charges brought against him for fraud, and was busy with the formalities of winding up the charity, and dealing with solicitors, police and the Charity Commission, who were all pursuing Lee and the trustees. I had felt sorry for Petra, but she'd taken it in her stride, so Tom told me. She'd waited so often for Lee's return that his stretch in prison would be little different. As for Tom, he already had a job lined up for when he had finished his work for Tolling Bells, and the Wests, Tom and Jamie himself were sorting out an amicable arrangement for custody and access. I suspected that Tom's new job would be in the Tenterden area.

There would be another funeral to attend shortly, for the bones of a child had been found deep down in the mud of the pond and identified as Beth's. There was another skeleton too, buried even deeper, that of the former owner's wife who had disappeared. The magic of that garden had long been destroyed by its terrible secrets, and the current owner was planning to bulldoze the lot and plant a garden in memory of two lives cut tragically short.

I lingered behind as the party left the cemetery, just for a moment. 'I'm sorry, Laura,' I whispered. 'I'm sorry I deserted you, but I'm back now.'

Laura smiled at me as I watched Beth take her prize. 'Let's all be friends forever and ever,' she said.

I hurried to catch Jack up, and put my hand in his. His parents glanced round, and I grinned at them. They didn't know yet, but Jack and I were going to give them a whole new family in eight months' time.